BEHIND the Juniper

T.J. DEAL

ISBN-13: 979-8-9907007-1-0

Cover design by: Sarah Hansen © Okay Creations

Proofreading: Katie Engelmann

Editing: Paige Lawson & Sam Moon

To the audacious and badass women who have summoned the confidence to acknowledge their worth and demand the respect they truly deserve.

Contents

Prologue

Olivia

Two and ½ years prior—

Rain pours down around me as I stare at the open grave site that now houses my husband. My black heels have sunk at least an inch deep into the damp grass, and the designer wool pea coat that I'm wearing does nothing to stop the chill from the rain. I'm faintly aware of people milling around me, trying to hover with umbrellas. As if I actually care that I'm drenched in water right now?

A good man was murdered because he was wearing a badge. I just lost my husband. My children just lost their father. I don't care that I look like a drowned rat or that I can't feel my toes.

The only thing keeping me from losing my mind right now is the smell from the Juniper trees around. The woodsy, fresh fragrance mixes with the earthly scent of freshly dug soil, keeping me grounded. Grounded to a place that I don't even want to be. A place where my husband will lay for the rest of time, yet I can't even feel him. At least at our home, he's still everywhere.

The top of Dan's coffin is now bare, showing the beautiful, chestnut color I chose. During the sermon, the Cascadia County Sheriff Department flag was splayed across it, per Dan's request. If I had let the intrusive thoughts win, I would have ripped it off and stomped on it. Dan wouldn't have wanted that, though. He loved his job and this town more than anything else. Hell, he even died serving it.

Two weeks ago, my biggest concern was my husband being home on time. I had no idea he would be shot. I had no idea he would lay on the side of the road fighting for his life. I had no idea my life was about to be flipped upside down.

I close my eyes and lift my face heavenward, feeling the raindrops mix with my tears. The pain and anger in my heart feel unbearable as I try to make sense of this senseless tragedy.

At least my kids aren't witnessing this right now. My best friend Charlie and her boyfriend Hayes swept them out of here as soon as the last prayer was said. They don't need to be photographed to appease the media circus that has descended upon this "family-only" graveside service. The vultures hide from a short distance, snapping photos of a grieving widow, father, and brother. *It makes me sick.*

I look toward Dan's dad, Zeke, known lovingly around our home as 'Pop.' He hasn't left his chair since the sermon was over. Levi, Dan's twin brother, sits next to him, staring into the same hole in the ground as I just was. The three of us undoubtedly prayed the same silent prayer: that this isn't our reality. Only it is. We all have to go on without the man who brought us all together.

"Come on, Pops." I reach for his elbow and help him up, even though he doesn't need it. The man is in better shape than I am for being nearly sixty. For someone who mainly sits behind a desk and delegates as sheriff, you wouldn't be able to tell. He's a single silver fox and has been since he lost Dan's mother, Anne.

Levi doesn't even look at us as we stand, so I kick his shoe gently. "You too." He glances up at me with red-rimmed eyes. His chest makes heavy jerks as he holds in his heartbreak. "Time to go. This isn't where Dan would want us to remember him, anyway."

Chapter One

Andrew

Thump. Thump. Thump. My thumbs drum a slow, steady beat on the steering wheel, helping me calm my nerves. My girlfriend, Heather, and I have a thirty-minute drive from the airport to the small town of Three Sisters, Oregon. After seven years, my little sister Charlie is finally marrying my best friend, Hayes. I should be ecstatic, and I am, but my mind has been stuck in conflict mode since my last deployment.

It doesn't help that this rental car makes me feel like I'm driving a golf cart. It sways with every large gust of wind on the highway. My 6'3" frame is crammed into the driver seat, causing my knees to hit the steering wheel. I glance at Heather; her small frame fits perfectly in the passenger seat.

I try to focus back on the scenery before me as I drive. Sagebrush and juniper trees line the highway. The Cascade Mountains only grow larger, the closer we get to the town. My only hope is that the beautiful landscape Central Oregon has to offer can pull me out of my funk.

When the wind blows the powdery snow across the fields and the highway, I clench my teeth and grip the steering wheel harder. My eyes involuntarily begin scanning the road. Watching for the next possible threat, both in front of me and behind me. It feels like I've been on high alert for months now—if I'm being honest, years. In my career, if you're not vigilant, you're dead. That doesn't just turn off when you go on vacation, especially after the shit I just dealt with.

I've only been stateside for the last three weeks, after a grueling six months overseas. It's safe to say that I still haven't adjusted back to civilian life. At this point, I'm not sure if I will. I can't help but wonder how much more I have left to give. The training, the deployments, missing my family, losing good people—it's all starting to weigh on me.

Heather sits blissfully unaware of my unease as she chatters on about whatever mindless topic she thinks of—trying to "catch me up" on all the things I missed the last few months I was gone. Her gossip is usually mind-numbing enough to distract me, but today it only feels trivial.

I let out a heavy sigh while trying to readjust in my seat. Heather and I have felt off for a while now. We started dating in high school, nearly twelve years ago. Since then, our relationship has been a rollercoaster ride, filled with ups and downs, breakups, and fights. By the grace of God, we've managed to hold on to each other through it all and make it through to the good times. Recently, though, the good times are fewer and farther between.

Heather's hand reaches out and touches my arm, catching me off guard. I instinctively jerk away from her touch, and she recoils from my reaction.

"You good?" She asks with concern dripping from her voice, but when I glance over at her, the narrowing of her eyes feels more accusatory than sympathetic.

"Just uncomfortable; I'm not built for small cars."

"No, you definitely aren't," she giggles and winks one of those baby blues.

There it is. Our safe place—the place in our relationship where we've never struggled. Flirting and sex.

I take a second to admire her; her long platinum hair is curled to perfection, and her make-up is still flawless. She looks like she's heading to a photoshoot, not just getting off a three-hour flight that required us to be at the airport at 04:30.

I grab her hand, pulling it to my lap, and let our hands rest on my thigh while I focus back on driving.

"We should be there soon. Are you excited to see Charlie and Hayes?"

"Hell yeah," I say with a natural smile forming. It's been nearly a year since they came to visit me in San Diego.

Charlie and Hayes have been put through every test in the book and still managed to stay together. I wasn't thrilled when I originally found out Charlie left South Carolina, but as we drive through the little town she settled in, I can see the appeal. I feel like I'm finally starting to understand why Hayes didn't drag her back home to Heartsville.

Everything appears to be on Main Street, and traffic slows down as we drive by storefronts that look like they were built in the late 1800s. The street is lined with busy shops and restaurants that show off the same unique Western style. The temperature gauge reads twenty degrees on the dash and snow falls lightly, yet everyone in this town seems happy. Kids run ahead and play as their parents walk behind them, holding hands and laughing. It looks like something from a Hallmark movie, and I surprisingly don't hate it.

"Can you believe Charlie found this place?" I glanced at Heather, expecting her to have the same reaction. She's from Heartsville as well and used to talk about moving back home and starting a family. Once her career as a social media influencer took off, though, she started referring to Los Angeles as home and stopped talking about marriage and kids.

"Yeah, it's just so... Oregon Trail," she let out a small laugh.

I feel my eyebrows knit together for a second, and then it dawns on me, "The computer game we played in Mr. Smith's 7th grade class?"

"Yes! I hated that game; I always lost all my supplies in the river and then died of, like, dysentery."

Chuckling, I reassure her she has nothing to worry about: "Just leave the food and the river fording to me, and I think we will be okay."

"I will, ya big bad 'frogman.' You could probably just swim all of our stuff across those rivers, anyway."

I flexed my arm a bit and wiggled my brows at her as we turned down the winding road that leads to the resort. I've been a Navy SEAL for the last ten years and have quite the reputation going for me.

Tall pine trees line the driveway, getting thicker as they lead deeper into the forest. The trees open to reveal the resort, which looks like it was plucked out of Aspen and set down in the middle of Oregon. The Cascade Mountain Range is covered in snow and practically glows behind the three-story brick building, which resembles more of a palace than the "typical ski lodge" Charlie described.

The Cascadia Ranch Resort exudes an air of luxury and elegance with its grand entrance and meticulously maintained surroundings. This place is breathtaking, from the architecture to the groomed landscaping that still looks natural. Not a piece of litter on the ground, overgrown shrub, or single leaf out of place.

I glanced up just in time to see the valet jump out of his seat and start rushing toward our car from his booth. He isn't very far, yet my eyes track him the entire time, unease building in my stomach at his erratic movements. By the time he reaches for my door, he has a massive grin plastered on his face. It's only then that I realize I've been subconsciously feeling for my rifle the entire time, ready to neutralize the threat. Except he isn't a threat. He's practically a kid, doing his job

The guilt eats at me as I realize my fuckup. I quickly lower my hand, hoping he didn't notice my instinctive reaction, and force a smile as I exit the tiny car.

"Hello, Sir! Will you be staying with us?"

I nod, forcing myself to smile back. "Our check in isn't until later, though."

"No problem, I can take your bags and then get them to your room when it's available."

The unease from my overreaction was still with me for the rest of our conversation as I helped unload our luggage and handed over the keys. So much so that I end up giving him a more than generous, mostly guilt fueled, tip.

I take a deep breath and close my eyes, taking a second to let the woody Juniper smell that is lingering in the cold air ground me for a moment. Then I let it go and made my way over to Heather, who appeared to be having a flirty conversation with the other valet attendant.

Between my sudden approach and expressionless face, the chump starts scrambling over his feet. He's quick to apologize for any inconvenience caused, while also trying to welcome us to the resort.

I can't help but smirk as Heather steps in front of me and smacks me in the chest while rolling her eyes. She's obviously annoyed that the poor guy felt threatened merely by my presence.

Chuckling, I whisper in her ear as we enter the lobby, "I'm either inspiring or intimidating. If he chooses to be intimidated, that's on him for being weak."

She turns around and wraps her arms around my waist. "Well, maybe next time try that million-dollar smile instead of your normal 'resting bitch face,' and he may act differently."

I mock being offended with a little gasp, "'Resting bitch face?' How dare you?"

She slips out of my grasp and gently pushes me away. "Come on, you big ogre, let's go check out this bougie place."

We walk hand in hand through the lobby. The front desk is discreetly located off to one side, providing guests with a panoramic view of the mountains. The floor to ceiling windows somehow magnify the snow peaks, making it look as if you could step out into them. It's surprisingly even more spectacular inside than it was outside.

I take a second to look around before checking my phone to see where everyone is meeting. The lobby features a coffee shop, a local gift store, three fire places with couches, and an enormous bar. I could spend the entire trip right here. Just get me a blanket and a beer, and I'd be happy to pass out on one of the couches.

Scanning the group chat that Charlie set up with me and seven other people, I found the itinerary she set up. "They're meeting in the ballroom in twenty minutes. Do you mind if we just go there now and wait?"

Heather lifts one shoulder, indifferent. "Sure, I guess I can scout out some shots for my Instagram story on the way. You know, keep the 'Heathies' updated on my adventures."

I internally groan at her calling her 1.4 million followers "Heathies." Considering that 70% of them are men who want in her pants, I doubt they care where she is—only that she's half naked. Even though I'm aware that she is making an incredible amount of money, the fact that it is all based on her appearance is a bit concerning. She's one step behind OnlyFans at this point.

"Hey, this isn't a work trip, remember?" I nudge her with my elbow as I try to make light of the fact that she seems to only care about photo opportunities.

"Excuse me, but I have to work. That's how I make my living! I can't just jet off to some small, unknown town on a whim and not take advantage of the opportunity to create content for my followers. Plus, you never know, this place might have some hidden gems that could boost my engagement even more." Her dedication to her career has always been undeniable, and I used to admire her for it. Somewhere along the line, though, her content changed and now it all feels superficial.

"A whim? It's Charlie and Hayes' wedding; you've known them for over *twelve* years."

She abruptly stops walking, her overpriced white sneakers squeaking on the exceptionally clean floor as she throws her hands in the air.

I brace myself; I should have known better. She has always been one to throw an epic tantrum when someone challenges her.

"Are you *kidding* me? Charlie never even asked me to be one of her bridesmaids!" She crosses her arms, glaring at me, waiting to shoot down any rebuttal I have before she continues. I don't; I have no control over what Charlie does or doesn't do, so I just stay silent. "And Hayes? He barely even acknowledges my existence! I was only invited because I'm your date." *Here we go again.*

It's unbelievable that even after all this time, she's still fixated on his lack of interest in her. She throws it in my face whenever I bring up Hayes, who has only ever been polite toward her. I've tried to talk to him about it, but he just shrugs it off, saying she's not his girl or his problem. I get it; he's always been naturally reserved toward people he isn't close with. I can acknowledge that it may be partly my fault. Hayes has been my confidante since before we even knew what that word meant. He's always the one I go to when I need to vent during fights and inevitable break-ups. I have no doubt he's built some resentment toward her over the years, but I don't know how to fix it at this point.

She is who she is, and he is who he is.

"Look, I'm sorry you're feeling that way. I know..." I scramble for words that won't undercut her feelings or talk badly about Charlie and Hayes. "I know things have always been strained, but I really appreciate you coming with me and spending time with my family."

She uncrosses her arms and looks slightly more appeased, so I pull her into a hug. "Maybe we can get a workout in tomorrow before they need me. I can record you for some content and give you some tips you can share." That has her brightening up immediately as she begins chatting excitedly about how much Ian, her social media manager, will love that.

I try not to roll my eyes at the mention of Ian; the guy has been a pain in my ass for the last two years. Trying to convince me to be in all her stuff and promote that I'm a SEAL, ignoring the fact that it could put my career in jeopardy being that public. It's been an argument popping up more often than not, so I tend to just ignore his name.

We followed the signs down the wide corridor, toward the ballroom. The dark wood floors contrast against the warm cream walls, making each step seem more luxurious than the last. We passed at least three small alcoves that feature stone fireplaces, lounge chairs, and impeccable views. The secluded-ness they offer has me yearning to sit down and get lost in a good book.

It's not long before we see large double doors that are already open, an elegant sign that says "ballroom" is overhead.

Even I feel impressed with how incredible this room is. The front of the room features an imperial staircase that leads to an upstairs balcony. Beyond the staircase, the ballroom appears to be fully set up for the reception tomorrow.

Tucked between the dance floor and expansive floor-to-ceiling windows are opulent couches that overlook a meadow right below the mountains. A full bar and tall tables sit off to the right, and to the left is a long table set up for the reception dinner. The decorations appear to only be floral arrangements of all different colors, sizes, and heights. The atmosphere is fun and elegant, just like Charlie.

My admiration grinds to a halt when I spot a woman behind the long table, teetering atop a ladder, rifling through the bouquets.

She's wearing a long-sleeve fleece button-up flannel, short black running shorts, and dusty cowboy boots. Her brown hair is thrown into a tight pony that swishes behind her as she moves.

My jaw drops when she yanks another flower out of the bouquet, muttering something under her breath, and tosses it carelessly down below her. It feels like my brain is struggling to comprehend who this lady is and why she's dismantling Charlie's centerpieces at a five-star resort.

Heather notices where my gaze has landed and immediately stalks over to the woman.

"Excuse me," she says, starting to scold the woman.

When it's clear she still hasn't noticed us yet, Heather glances over her shoulder at me like, "What the fuck is happening?"

I shrug and motion for her to continue.

"Hello! What are you doing?" she yells, placing both hands on her hips.

The woman startles and quickly turns to look at us, nearly

falling off the ladder. "Oh, shit!" She grabs onto the ladder, catching herself. "Sorry." She holds on this time and looks up at us, her smile getting brighter when she seems to recognize us. "Oh, hey! You must be Drew and Heather! I knew your flight was early, but you guys made great time!"

I bristle at her familiarity. Who the hell is this woman? Hardly anyone calls me Drew; it's either Andrew or Reynolds, mainly depending on whether I'm in uniform or not.

"It's Andrew," I corrected her, my tone clipped. "Who are you?"

Her smile falters for a moment, taking in my hostility. "Oh, I'm Olivia, Charlie's friend and... boss?" She scans my face while talking, noticing the lack of interest, and then adds the last part like it's a question. Her left hand reaches over to twirl her wedding ring, the tell-tale sign of her nervousness.

I recognize her name immediately, and my mood only grows more sour.

Hayes briefly mentioned her when he was looking for Charlie in Three Sisters, a few years ago. All that I really know about her is that she's married with kids, Charlie started working for her, and then she lied to Hayes when he called to talk to Charlie. Since then, I tend to tune out any mention of her.

"Great." My voice drips with sarcasm. "What the fuck are you doing?"

When she notices my temperament toward her hasn't changed, her expression morphs from apprehension into defiance. She plucks another flower—a white rose—and narrows her eyes at me.

"Your sister despises roses—well, white roses," she twirls the flower pointedly, "but especially white ones." She looks at me, one eyebrow raised and lips slightly pursed. "The whole stalker, harassing her situation." She drops the flower like it's a mic drop, effectively putting me in my place. I flinch as remorse and anger surge through my body; it happens every time I think about Charlie's stalker.

Charlie left South Carolina because of a neighbor who fell in love with her and began stalking her. The man went from friendly to obsessive when Charlie didn't return his interest, doing everything he could to get Charlie's attention. Feeling backed into a corner, she just left. She wouldn't tell anyone where she was or where she was going. Charlie was practically a ghost; aside from the occasional contact she had with Hayes' mother, Connie, she was nearly untraceable.

It took Hayes close to a month to track her down and discover what was going on. He even gave up his career as a Navy SEAL to be with her. He found her here, put an end to the stalker situation, and won her back in the process. I respect the hell out of him for giving it all up and protecting her like that.

Olivia continues on her rant. "The florist must have forgotten, even though Charlie *repeatedly* told her she didn't want them," she adds, emphasizing her annoyance with the florist. Her tone becomes somber as she sighs, "I'm just trying to fix the mistake before she gets here." Her brown eyes almost look a little misty-eyed, but she quickly blinks them away and gets back to work on the bouquet.

I may have my issues with Olivia for playing a role in hiding Charlie from us, but I can at least acknowledge her loyalty to my sister. I pinch the bridge of my nose, nodding my sentiments.

Heather, on the other hand, decides to ignore the good deed Olivia is doing and hits her with a jab instead. Distain drips from her voice as she motions toward Olivia's boots and shorts, "And the outfit? To a 5-star resort?"

I almost chuckle; she isn't wrong. Olivia looks like she couldn't decide between going to the gym or a rodeo.

When Olivia looks down at her outfit, her eyes widen slightly, and then she lets out a loud, vibrant laugh. "Isla, Charlie's assistant, called me in a panic when she saw the florist bringing the flowers. I guess when I raced out the door, I instinctively just put on the closest shoes I could find."

Who instinctively puts on shit kickers that look like they truly only kick shit?

Charlie and Hayes chose that moment to walk through the door. Hayes noticed me first, giving me a chin tip as a broad grin crossed his obnoxious face. "'Bout damn time your ugly mug showed up," he bellows through the room.

Charlie looks over, her expression making all the drama this morning worth it. "DREW!" she beams as she sprints to me.

I lift her up and spin her around before setting her down. "Hello, Mrs-soon-to-be-Carrington!"

The scoff in the background comes straight from Olivia.

Hayes nods and says hello to Heather, but bypasses her as he walks over to Olivia. Indirectly proving Heather's point that he doesn't care for her. I watch him whisper to Olivia, but I can't make out what they're saying.

I glance back to Charlie, who is chatting animatedly with Heather, giving me the opportunity to step a little closer to Olivia and Hayes.

In a hushed voice, he lets out a string of curse words, followed by, "I owe you, Liv. Thanks."

She smiles and gestures with her head toward Charlie, "All good. Just get her out of here before she decides to call the florist and raise hell."

He rubs the back of his neck and nods. "Maybe she deserves a good ass chewing, though."

"Don't worry, I already handled it. The florist is giving you a small refund and waving the delivery fee."

"You're the best. I'll distract her; we were planning on showing the new arrivals around town anyway."

Her smile dims a bit at the mention of Heather and me. She glances at us, but quickly looks back to Hayes when she catches me staring. The sugary smile is back as she tries to hide her mixed feelings toward us. "Great, have fun!"

With that, Hayes starts hustling us out of the room, ignoring Charlie's protests that she didn't get to talk to Olivia. Putting my arm around her, I poked at her rib. "Let's go, little Sis! Show me this town you can't bear to leave."

Chapter Two

Andrew

The scent of roasted garlic and fresh bread filled the air as we gathered around the kitchen for Charlie and Hayes' rehearsal dinner. They insisted on hosting us all and showing off their new home. I can't say I wouldn't do the same; the rustic, two-story log home is a sight to behold. Everything is airy and open, with dark trim reflecting off the light-colored wood walls. The open concept expands the great room, kitchen, and dining area, creating one giant space for entertaining.

Charlie flitters around her kitchen, barking orders to Isla, whom I've now officially met. She looks young, but her professional outfit and calming demeanor are a good contrast to Charlie's normal chaos. Her light-brown hair looks mostly natural, and she has it braided to one side. She takes whatever Charlie throws at her without complaint, usually starting the task before Charlie has even asked. Rather than the traditional boss-employee dynamic, they seem more like friends.

Heather sits in the great room, sipping her cocktail while scrolling through her phone. I know she's tired from traveling this morning, but I'm more than a little disappointed that she isn't even trying to be involved in the conversation. I contemplate sitting with her, but, to be honest, I just want to catch up with my family.

I meander toward the dining room, where Hayes is. He's setting the expansive dining room table like the good housewife he is.

"What's with the sixteen-foot table? Planning on starting a basketball team?" I razzed.

"Hell yeah, we are," he grinned. Then, like the little shithead he is, he added, "Already started practicing."

"Fuck off," I grumbled sarcastically, making him laugh even harder.

A loud knock sounds from the front entrance, and I holler that I'll get it, leaving Hayes to finish his duties.

I open the door, happy to see that it is two of my favorite people on the other side.

Everett and his sister, Odessa. The resemblance is uncanny between them; they are both blonde, tall, and lean. Hayes and I met Everett in sixth grade, when his family moved to our small town. We brought him into the fold immediately, and he brought Odessa everywhere he went. It helped that she's only a year older than Charlie as well. From the beginning, those two hit it off like they were long-lost sisters. Or we forced them to. Either way, it worked out for us.

"Well, well, well, if it isn't my best friend and her brother, Everett."

Everett's loud mocking gasp sounds next to her. "How dare you?!"

Odessa rolls her eyes and laughs as she extends her arms for a hug. "Missed your stupid face, Drew Reynolds."

I wrap my arms around her upper body and squeeze tightly while I lift her off the ground. "Missed you too, Dess!

She squirms, so I let her go midair. She drops but lands

solidly. Within a second, she throws her closed left fist into my arm, causing me to wince. I always forget she's a leftie who packs a hell of a punch. She mutters something like "asshole" and steps around me to get in the house.

Everett sees me grinning like the Cheshire cat; messing with Odessa has consistently ranked among my favorite pastimes. She gives as good as she gets, though. Never backing down, always ready to throw a punch, literally.

"How's that dead arm?" Everett walks by, punching me in the same spot his sister just hit me.

"Fuckers. All of you!" I accuse, without any real sentiment behind it. I love these people; I always have. This house is starting to feel like home now that everyone is reunited for the first time in years.

I follow them back into the house, pausing before I get to the kitchen when I notice a few shelves full of framed photos.

The majority of them are Charlie and Hayes together at different stages of their lives. It's nice to see that I'm in most of them too-me holding a baby Charlie, Charlie and me as kids at the beach, and the last family picture we ever took before we lost our parents in a car accident. Hayes, Everett, and me before our senior prom and our high school graduation. The one of Hayes and I during our pinning ceremony after finishing BUD/S is set next to one of our dads when they got their tridents as well. They met on the first day of Basic Conditioning and were best-friends—that is, until Hayes' dad died from cancer. A few years later, Charlie and I lost our parents in a car accident.

Surprisingly, it's the last picture I see that hurts the most: Charlie, Olivia, and what appears to be Olivia's husband and their children at Christmas. I've been trying all day to let go of my resentment toward Olivia, but these little reminders nag at me. Charlie effortlessly moved on and essentially joined a new family without even telling me she had a problem, let alone a psychotic stalker.

I would have dropped everything to be there for her, but instead, she chose to just let me go. The worst part? I was so wrapped up in my career that I didn't even notice. It wasn't until Connie brought it to my attention that I even knew something was wrong. A guilt I'm not sure if I'll ever be able to let go of. Just add it to the list, I guess.

The evening flew by with everyone catching up during dinner; the conversations never lagged, and it wasn't until after everyone had eaten that I noticed Connie wasn't here yet.

Connie is Hayes' mother, who also took in Charlie and me after our parents died. I was nearly 18 years old, but Charlie was only 14; barely starting high school and trying to find herself. I owe a lot to Connie for taking us on, especially Charlie.

Hayes is sitting to my left, so I nudge him with my elbow and ask, "Where's mom?"

"Her flight wouldn't take off because of some malfunction, and they wanted to put her up in a hotel," Hayes responded. "Olivia offered to drive up to Portland and pick her up."

"What the fuck?" I'm instantly pissed off. Olivia is driving nearly three hours away to pick up Mom, and no one even mentioned it to me.

Hayes leans back in his seat, one eyebrow raised at my little outburst.

"Why didn't anyone tell me? I would have made the drive." This isn't just anyone stranded at the airport. It's Connie. His own damn mother. I for one, owe her a lot more than a few hours of driving. I can't believe he would let some bored housewife with a martyr complex be responsible for getting his own mother to his wedding.

I huffed and took a sip of my bourbon, trying to swallow my

unease. There's just something about Olivia that sets me off immediately—seeing her this morning in that crazy outfit, the happy family picture, and how she is always swooping in to save the day.

"Calm down, Reynolds," Hayes admonished me, lowering his voice so the conversation stayed between the two of us. "Olivia didn't want anyone to miss anything, so she volunteered. Said the kids love impromptu road trips, and they'd be stoked to grab burgers. The pass over the mountain was dry, and she's driven it more than you ever have. What's your problem anyway?"

"Don't have one."

Hayes's jaw clenches so hard it ticks—the only sign he's irritated with me. One blink and I would have missed it, but I've been friends with him long enough to know his tells. "Fine, then lose the ego. They should be back after dinner."

Odessa sits across from both of us, clearly noticing the shift in conversation as she glances back and forth between the two of us. I subtly shake my head, hoping she will know to drop it. Her lips purse, but thankfully she redirects the conversation: "So, lovebird's, are you staying in this beautiful town forever?"

Charlie, who is sitting next to Odessa, takes a large sip of her wine while looking at Hayes for his answer. Her wide eyes relax, and I can see her grin through her glass when she sees his enthusiastic nod toward us. Confirming what I already knew, she's genuinely happy here.

"Charlie stumbled upon a place that just feels right," he responded. "All the seasons, outdoor recreation, small-town vibe—we love it. I'm not sure that we could ever find anywhere that fits our lifestyle better."

Without realizing it, I found myself nodding in agreement. I love this little town, too. The stores are small but all local, the people are friendly, and the views alone are enough to make my breathing easier. Even despite the cold weather, the town still manages to thrive. Children were building snowmen in the park, friends sat outside by outdoor fire pits talking and drinking local beers, and the few restaurants were bustling with locals and tourists.

Odessa arches a brow, getting that evil glint in her eye that she always gets before prying where she knows she shouldn't. "How about you, Drew? You seem to be nodding your head in agreement over there."

I chuckle and admit, "Hayes makes some good points; I could see myself settling here."

I take a sip of my bourbon and clear my throat. "Been, uh… Been thinkin' 'bout getting out."

Six heads snap in my direction as the grenade I just threw lands on the table. I skillfully avoided the eyes of everyone now looking at me, waiting for the explosion.

Heather let out a tiny gasp, obviously taken aback by my disclosure. It had always been my plan to retire from the Navy, and I had been set on doing so until a few weeks ago. I probably should have told her first, but it wasn't until I got here that I realized how suffocated I was feeling.

"What?" she shrieked. "Get out! Since when?" Her voice raised so many octaves that I cringed. She catches herself and adds softer, "Hasn't this always been your dream? It's just getting started; why stop now?"

My "dream" wasn't just starting- I've been in the military for eleven years now, and I'm tired of the unknown. It feels like every week is different; every day is different—training, deployments, working out, more training, a different mission. I was lucky to be able to make it to my sister's wedding.

I understand—the concern she is feeling. I felt the same when Hayes first told me he was getting out. The plan was always for us to become SEALs and retire in the Navy with cushy lives and beautiful wives. We were also thirteen when we decided this, young and naive, trying to live up to our father's legacies. Then he ended up falling in love with my sister and changing his dream.

I glance around the group to see everyone is staring at us, waiting for my response.

Trying to lighten the mood, I smirk at her. "Don't worry, I'll still be the badass you fell in love with."

Everett took that moment to throw in his own cocky attitude. "If you want to see a true badass, I'm the one who comes in to save these assholes when shit hits the fan," he scoffed, pointing at himself.

I roll my eyes dramatically at him. We've always given each other grief over going into different military branches right after high school; he went into the Army, while Hayes and I went into the Navy.

"Nah, she ain't into guys that need to compensate with flashy helicopters," I say, my Southern drawl coming out a little thicker than normal. I've almost lost my accent over the past twelve years, but thanks to the Bourbon and the fact that the majority of the people around me are from back home, it's returning just as thick as it did when I left home at the age of 18.

Since that shithead takes offense to nothing, his smirk is now wider than ever. "Me? Compensating? We all know that's a damn lie."

Charlie and Odessa both groan loudly from the other side of the table. "Please stop comparing dick sizes. We just ate."

Not long after dinner, Charlie, Heather, and I piled into Hayes' truck to head back to the lodge. As we drove, I noticed a brand-new, blacked-out Jeep Grand Wagoneer Series III following us. My instincts immediately kicked in again, and I felt on edge as I stared it down. The miles ticked on, but with every turn we took, so did it. The SUV stayed right on our tail, never wavering or falling behind.

Sensing my tension, Hayes quietly said, "It's Olivia with Mom." He knows me well enough to know exactly where my mind went.

My shoulders sagged, and I silently nodded, annoyed at my overactive alertness. While it served me well on missions, I wished there was an off switch for civilian life.

By the time we pulled into the parking lot of the resort, I had already shaken off my frustration with myself and was just excited to see Mom. Hayes hadn't even put the truck in park when I was hurrying out of it. As he threw open his door, he let out a string of curse words, but I was already moving too fast to hear. We had always lovingly competed for Connie's attention, and this would be no different.

Determined to be the first to welcome her, I shot forward like a rocket as I spotted the SUV parking two rows away. Though Hayes is still quick, he's more rusty than he used to be, and I can't help but taunt him as I sprint through the small parking lot.

"Really let yourself go, Carrington!" I'm also fresh off a deployment that has me at peak endurance and skill.

I ripped open Connie's door and threw my body into the passenger seat, wrapping my arms around her. I heard the collective gasps from the others in the car; everyone shocked, I just tore open the door.

"Heavens to Betsy! Andrew, you're going to be the death of me yet!" Connie scolds me, her southern drawl dripping with affection as she shakes her head.

"Hello, Mom!" My grin widens with victory until I glance over. Olivia sits in the driver's seat, the warm interior lights of the car drawing my attention to her honey-colored eyes. Everything about her is warm, from her smile to the light laugh she gives upon hearing Hayes grumbling behind me, trying to yank me out of the car.

I swallow hard and step back away from the car.

Everett appears from behind the SUV and yanks Hayes back while putting him in a headlock. "Back off, Hayes; she loves me more."

Connie tuts at our foolishness, but her laughter betrays her true feelings as she slides out of the car to give them both a hug.

"Helloooo, she's our mom too, and she's here for Charlie's wedding!" Odessa interjects loudly, shoving Everett out of the way so that she and Charlie can stake their claim on Connie's affections. It's true; Connie has been a constant presence in all our lives, stepping in for Everett and Odessa when their parents were less than stellar examples. Through every game, graduation, and holiday, Connie made sure the five of us knew we were loved and cared for. How one person can fill the shoes of six is beyond me, but I'll be forever grateful.

Hayes throws his hands up in the air, pretending to be frustrated and mumbling to himself that it's his wedding too.

I look over his shoulder to see Olivia and her children—a boy who appears to be a few years older than his younger sister — laughing behind him. They both look nothing like their mother; they have blonde hair and blue eyes, whereas she's a brunette with brown eyes.

The little girl lets go of Olivia's hand and walks over to Hayes, reaching her little arms up for him.

He picks her up, and she pats his cheek lovingly, saying, "Uncle Haysy, don't worry, you're just as 'portant as Aunt Char."

He grins from ear to ear and points at Odessa, saying, "You hear that? Just. As. Important." The little girl belly laughs when he throws his hand on his hip and punctuates each word.

I glance at Olivia; she's grinning from ear to ear at the two of them. A tightness in my chest hits out of nowhere, watching them all interact like one big family, while I feel like an outsider.

A flicker of movement catches my eye, and I spot Heather near the front doors of the lodge, chatting on her cellphone. Her smile and wave toward us seem genuine enough, but she doesn't make any moves to approach us. Instead, she mouths and motions that she'll meet me in our room, and then disappears into the lobby.

The disappointment feels overwhelming as I realize she isn't going to try to greet Connie. It seems like such a small thing, but I've always gone above and beyond when we are around her family. They welcomed me into their family a long time ago, and I know that Connie has always tried to do the same with Heather. To see her just walk away, without even saying hello, makes me question everything about our relationship.

I stare at the spot she just vacated and rub at my sternum, hoping to loosen the vice-like grip of disappointment that threatens to suffocate me.

"Everything okay?" Charlie's voice cuts through my thoughts, her eyes searching mine for any sign of distress. Concern radiates off her, and I feel like I'm drowning in pity.

"Fine," I insist, nodding my head to dismiss her worries. "Just going to help with the bags."

I walk to the trunk and can see through the back that Hayes is buckling the little girl back into her car seat. The boy is buckling himself into his own booster seat and chatting to Hayes about a fishing trip he wants to go on with his uncle and him. I don't hear much of the conversation, but it does stand out that he doesn't mention his dad at all.

I tune out the rest of the conversation when Olivia walks up after hugging Connie goodbye.

"Thanks for everything, Boots," I say sincerely, nodding in her direction as I pick up one of Connie's bags. The nickname just sort of slipped out, but I've seen her twice now, both times wearing a different pair of cowboy boots. These boots are only ankle height, though, and she has them paired with a baby blue shirtdress that shows off tan legs.

She shrugs and says, "No big deal." The faintest blush colors her cheeks, though, barely noticeable in the dim light of the parking lot, and I find myself unable to tear my eyes away from her for a split second. This morning, I was too on edge to notice how pretty she was. Her dark chocolate-colored hair is long and full of movement, with one side thrown over her shoulder. Big brown eyes lined with thick lashes, minimal makeup, and plump lips.

She unconsciously begins to spin her wedding ring again, locked into the same trance as I am, sizing each other up.

Thankfully, Charlie snaps us out of it when she comes over and wraps her in a tight hug. Her eyes are filled with tears as she thanks her for taking on so much.

Olivia flashes one of those radiant smiles, and I force myself to pick up the luggage and start moving away.

"Come on, ma," I urged Connie, guiding her towards the lodge. I resist the urge to glance back at Olivia; my mind is at war with the nice things she's done versus the shitty things she did in the past. I don't know if I'll ever be able to understand how Hayes was able to forgive her so quickly. To be honest, I'm not sure if I'd like to. Things are complicated enough in my life already. I don't have the energy to try to understand someone who has proven untrustworthy already.

Chapter Three

Olivia

Ellie and I hurry down the hallway, running nearly twenty minutes late, to get ready for Charlie's wedding. My sweet, loving, little girl turned into a tiny demon this morning and had the tantrums of all tantrums. Now that she's five, they seem to be fewer and farther apart, but occasionally, she can still raise some hell.

This morning, Pop brought donuts over. He'll be hanging with Ben until it's time for the groomsmen to start getting ready. I simply ask Ellie to have a protein-rich breakfast alongside the donut, and she loses it. It took me fifteen minutes to calm her down, convince her to eat a Greek yogurt pouch, and grab a donut for the road.

The beat of loud music and women laughing fills the space outside of Charlie's bridal suite. I couldn't help but chuckle as we got closer, and I caught the tune to 'Thunder' by Imagine Dragons. Charlie's vivacious flair clashes with the sheer elegance of the hallway. Only Charlie could pull something like that off without upsetting the staff.

I glance down at Ellie before I open the door; her eyes are

already wide with excitement. My girl loves to party, and there is definitely a party there.

"Alright, Ellie Bug, remember, this is Charlie's special day, and we need to be on our best behavior."

Her little head nods enthusiastically, "I will, promise mommy!"

I nod back and give her a wink, opening the door.

I guarantee she's going to try to be the center of attention in there, but thankfully Charlie is her biggest fan.

My jaw drops as I take in the bridal suite. "Oh my god!"

It seems as if every room at the Cascadia Ranch Resort is perfectly angled to highlight the mountains beyond it, and this suite isn't any different. The windows along the far wall have delicate white curtains framing them, but they still allow the reflection off the snowy mountains to create a bright natural glow in the room.

Colorful floral arrangements are placed around the room to add to the elegance without being overwhelming.

The suite even has a large table full of gourmet food and a full bar stocked with all the essentials for mimosas.

Ellie was too busy running into Charlie's arms to take notice of the stunning suite. "Auntie Char, I'm so happy for your special day," she practically shouts. She's rocking her lime green leotard and matching tutu from last year's Tinkerbell recital, looking like a tiny fairy.

Charlie swoops her up and smiles, "EllieBellie! I'm so happy you're my flower girl!" Charlie is already practically glowing in her matching white pajama shorts and button-up set.

"I gonna be on my best 'havior, pinky promise!" She assures Charlie, holding up her little pinky.

A light laugh escapes Charlie as she holds up hers too. "Sounds good, sweet girl!"

Ellie scrambles out of Charlie's arm the second she sees Connie and runs over to her.

"Good morning, little Miss Ellie! Want to get some snacks with me, and then maybe your mom will let us wander around this big ole resort?"

Ellie nods enthusiastically and then looks at me with pleading eyes.

"Absolutely, as long as you listen to Ms. Connie the whole time."

"I will! I will! Promise, mommy!"

I'm so freakin' thankful for Charlie and her family's unconditional love for me and the kids. Connie has visited a few times a year since Hayes moved out here, and she's always treated us like family. The kids latched on to her warm and nurturing personality instantly. It's honestly remarkable how quickly they formed a bond with her. Considering the only biological grandparent they have around is Pops, I'm eternally grateful Connie treats them like they're her grandkids.

I look at Charlie, still feeling guilty for being late. "I'm so sorry we're late! We had a... morning."

Charlie just waves it off: "Don't even worry, Liv. Peyton and her team aren't here yet; grab a mimosa and relax." Peyton is the best hairstylist in Three Sisters, and she's bringing a makeup artist and an assistant that will help get us prepped so they can start working their magic.

"Thank goodness, I'm so excited to see what they have planned for me," I say as I make my way toward the mimosa table. It feels like ages since I've been dressed up for anything. Being a mom has consumed my life, and except for the occasional girls' night, I wear pretty minimal makeup and haven't updated my wardrobe in ages.

Odessa grabs the champagne and pours it into a glass for

me. "Right? Last night, Charlie raved to Heather and me about her trial run with Peyton. I'm so eager to meet them!"

"Where is Heather?" Isla asked with an undertone hinting at loathing. She called me last night to vent about Heather referring to her as "the help" in private and how she just generally ignored her presence the rest of the time. Then I told her about my little showdown with Andrew and Heather yesterday morning and my embarrassing outfit.

"Spa," Charlie replied with an eye roll. "She doesn't trust anyone to do her makeup."

"Oh," Isla muttered. "She does seem... particular."

"Particular? Try snotty," Charlie retorted.

Isla and I glance at each other, surprised by her candor. She hasn't spoken much about Heather before this weekend, but the things she said never seemed too negative. Now, I have a feeling she was trying to be nice for Andrew's sake.

Odessa chimes in from her seat at the table, mumbling over a mouth full of pastries, "God, right?!" She quickly chews and swallows and then adds, "Remember Vegas? Her bimbo friends were all over Hayes and she didn't say anything."

I love that they've all been friends for so long. Odessa and Charlie are more like sisters than friends, and it seems like Hayes, Everett, and Andrew have the same familial bond.

Odessa has also visited a few times and even stayed at my house while Charlie and Hayes were still living in their one-bedroom apartment. Every time she comes to town, I love her more. Seriously, I'm obsessed with her life. She travels all over the world as a high-fashion model and is friends with the coolest celebrities. Plus, she is gorgeous in the most natural way—feminine heart-shaped face, flawless skin, and over six feet tall.

"Yep. I just worry about Drew. It feels like everyone but her can see that he's struggling."

Even I could sense it, and I had only just met him. His ridged back with tense shoulders, the tousled hair from running his hands through it repeatedly, and the dark shadows under the eyes that seem to be alert at all times. All classic signs of someone who's seen a little too much and isn't able to let their guard down.

"At least Hayes is there for him," I say, raising my shoulders, trying to be optimistic. "That man is not only loyal to a fault, but has an uncanny ability to be the glue holding someone together." I've been on the receiving end of Hayes being that glue, and I can honestly say that if it weren't for him, I'd still be in pieces on the floor. Charlie as well, she was a constant support for me and the kids.

Charlie gives me a sympathetic smile and nods. "I just hope he can convince him to stay."

"Stay? He's trying to get Andrew to move up here?"

Odessa laughs and looks at me like I'm crazy. "Andrew? You're the first person I've heard call him that in years. Everyone calls him Drew."

I search out Isla's gaze and roll my lips together, hoping she ignores the comment like I intend to do. When she smirks and gets that mischievous glint in her eye, I know I'm about to be thrown under the bus before she even starts talking. "Oh no, he insisted that she call him Andrew."

That little brat. I narrowed my eyes at her, looking at her through slits.

Both of their heads snapped toward me with questioning gazes.

"Whatever, at least they don't call me 'the help!'" I fire back.

Isla chuckles, "True! But it was only Heather calling me that. *Andrew* never said a word about *me* calling him Drew."

Charlie looks downright murderous as she looks between the two of us. "What are you talking about?"

"Helllloooo, beautiful ladies!" Peyton peeks her head through the door before walking in. She's rocking long silver hair that cascades down in waves, a cute black fedora, and a matching black jumpsuit. Thank the good Lord for this woman's impeccable timing. Her "glam squad," as Isla lovingly refers to them, follows in rolling large, hard-boxed cases full of every beauty tool imaginable.

Charlie beams at Peyton, forgetting all about the little slip up we just had.

Odessa doesn't miss a beat, though. With one eyebrow raised and lips pursed, she sharply whispers, "We will be talking about this later."

I nod back in agreement. Odessa is a no-nonsense type of person. Especially when it comes to her friends, and even though we've only been friends for a short while, I have no doubt she would go to bat for me. I'm also kind of excited to hear her stance on why I'm enemy number one.

With the appearance of our new guests, the conversation shifted to hair and makeup, and we prepared for the day ahead.

Peyton's team was just as amazing as she is, working together like a well-oiled machine. By the time they were done with my hair and makeup, I barely even recognized myself. My hair is half-up and half down, with elegant pins holding it in place. Michelle, the make-up artist, did my makeup more dramatic than I normally would, but I love it.

"Alright ladies, time to get dressed!" Charlie clapped her hands together, snapping me out of my thoughts. With a wobbly smile on her face, Connie brings Charlie her wedding dress.

As Connie carefully lifts the delicate gown from its hanger, tears fill her eyes. "I swore I wouldn't cry, but I've been prayin' for this moment since your momma told me she was having a girl."

Charlie sniffles in response and fans her face to keep herself from crying. "Love you. Thank you for..." She huffs and dabs her eyes. "Thank you for stepping into her place so seamlessly."

Connie shakes her head quickly, and blinks away her tears. "Let's get you all gussied up."

We all watch with our own misty eyes as Connie helps Charlie into her dress, carefully looping each dainty pearly button at the back. Charlie's red hair cascades down her back in loose waves, and her makeup is simple yet glamorous.

The A-line silhouette of the dress stuns on Charlie. Enlaced flowers adorn the sheer sleeves, covering her arms and chest. Her tulle skirt shimmers with every movement, reflecting the sunlight streaming in through the windows.

"Auntie CHAR, you look like a real fairy princess!" Ellie gasped loudly, her eyes wide with wonder. We all laughed through our teary eyes, nodding in agreement. Charlie is always beautiful, but today she is radiant.

With her dress now on, Charlie left with the photographer, leaving the rest of us to finish getting ready.

She graciously allowed us to pick out our gowns, the only requirement being that they be a shade of dark blue. Somehow, we had all managed to find the same shade of midnight blue, and our dresses complemented each other perfectly.

Isla's high-neckline gown features crisscrossing swaths of organza that release into a flowing A-line skirt. Her hair is pinned up and braided, creating the prettiest updo I've ever seen. Everything she wears looks like vintage couture, made modern.

Odessa's mermaid-style gown molded perfectly to her curves, accentuating her assets and making her look like a knock-out. She threw on heels, owning her already tall height, and looked like she was ready to hit the runway.

As for myself, I chose a satin gown with a straight neckline and thin straps. Delicate tucks and gatherings at my side waist and bodice create a false skirt and a modest side slit. I can't believe how confident and even a bit sexy I feel. It's been ages since I've shown this much skin, and I'm feeling grateful for Charlie convincing me to spend a week in Mexico last month so that I'm not as white as the snow outside.

"Look at you, little miss dancing queen!" I said as Ellie twirled up beside me, beaming from ear to ear. Connie helps her into a one-shouldered cupcake dress made of layers upon layers of tulle to create the puffiest skirt I'd ever seen. If there's one thing I know for certain, it's that we won't be able to get this girl off the dance floor tonight.

The next hour went by in a blur of pictures with the bride, and before we knew it, it was time to take our positions in the hallway outside the loft where the ceremony would take place.

Isla and Odessa each gracefully made their way down the aisle, taking their spots on the opposite side of a dashing-looking Hayes and his groomsmen—Andrew, Everett, and a very grown-up-looking Ben.

Then it was my turn. Nerves bubbled around in my stomach as I took my first step around the corner.

The beauty and intimacy of the space is breathtaking. Twinkly lights and candles illuminate the small loft. Small bouquets of white flowers, sans roses, line the few rows of chairs. Every guest is dressed up and smiling, waiting to celebrate the union of Charlie and Hayes.

I did my best to ignore the brooding man next to Hayes, but every time he caught my eye, he looked less than pleased to see me. I have no idea what I did to receive the hot and cold attitude from him, but it's starting to grate on my nerves. Even with that scowl, he was undeniably the most handsome man in the room. He's not much taller than Hayes but considerably broader, filling out his suit in the best way. His dark hair and green eyes complement his lightly tanned skin tone, and the barely there scruff on his face does nothing to hide his killer jawline.

Realizing I've been staring at Andrew, I quickly turned my attention back to the guests. Levi and Pops are sitting in the middle row on Charlie's side, both looking like increasingly older versions of Ben. Those Turner family genetics are insanely strong. I didn't stand a prayer for either of the kids to look like me. It was the same for Annie, Dan's late mother. Her brown hair and green eyes didn't transfer to Dan and Levi.

I take my place opposite the groomsmen and turn to face back down the aisle where I just came from. Ellie is dancing and twirling her way toward us, tossing flowers with abandon and giggling. Always being a star without even realizing it.

As she reached the end of the aisle, Ellie ran up to the groomsmen, giving each a fist bump before wrapping her arms around Hayes in a tight hug. She whispered something in his ear, causing him to break into a full grin and laugh wholeheartedly. Having successfully charmed her audience, Ellie flitted over to stand in front of me, and as I looked up, I noticed even Andrew was still smiling at her.

Am I really the only problem?

The music started as the ceremony was about to begin. I couldn't help but feel emotional that this moment is finally here. When Charlie first came to me, broken and scared, I had no idea she would become like a sister to me.

I glance at Hayes; he's smiling while trying to blink the tears away. He's been waiting for this moment for a long time, and there isn't a couple more deserving of the perfect wedding.

"Here comes the bride," Isla whispered through a grin, her

eyes fixed on the entrance. And there she was, a vision in white, looking every bit like the radiant fairy princess Ellie had called her earlier.

I hear Hayes curse under his breath lovingly as he takes in his gorgeous bride. Each step she took down the aisle was filled with grace and elegance, her smile lighting up the room.

As Charlie reached Hayes, her hand trembling slightly, he took her hand in his, and the officiant began the ceremony. His words were heartfelt and sincere, speaking to the love between Hayes and Charlie that had blossomed over time and the life they were now committing to building together. It was a simple yet sentimental ceremony that had most of the guests dabbing their eyes with tissues.

I'm sure my nose will be bright red from trying to keep from being a blubbering mess up here, but I can barely contain the tears threatening to spill.

"By the power vested in me," the officiant announced, "I now pronounce you husband and wife. Mr. and Mrs. Carrington! You may kiss the bride." Hayes wasted no time pulling Charlie in for a passionate, loving kiss, causing a chorus of cheers to erupt from the crowd.

"Finally!" Everett shouted dramatically. Hayes throws his fist in the air in victory, cheering as he continues to kiss his now-wife.

The crowd chuckles and cheers, relieving some built-up emotional tension.

Hayes and Charlie made their way back up the aisle, hand in hand, positively glowing with happiness and love radiating from them. Even Andrew appeared to have softened; in place of his earlier scowl towards me, he now smiled, genuinely happy for his sister and best friend.

We both took steps toward the middle to link arms and follow the happy couple. The second we made eye contact, the brooding was back, and he immediately looked away. I couldn't help but notice the tension in his jaw that he tried to hide behind the smile he gave the other guests.

Yep. I'm the problem.

Letting go of that thought, I prepared myself for the rest of the festivities. I'm determined to enjoy every moment of the reception, despite any lingering tension with Andrew. After all, love was in the air, and for the first time in a long time, I felt genuinely happy.

Chapter Four

Andrew

I feel at ease sitting at a table by myself in the large ballroom with our closest friends, family, and even some unfamiliar faces. Most of the people here I've known my entire life or served alongside in the Navy. Surprisingly, the new faces don't bother me.

Charlie is shining like she deserves to, and Hayes hasn't taken his eyes off her or stopped smiling since he saw her walk down the aisle.

An overwhelming feeling that I belong here overcomes me, and not just at the wedding. I belong in this little town, starting a new chapter near my family.

The next step is to talk to Hayes about moving up here and becoming a partner in his new business. He started a private security and consulting team, taking some of the guys we've worked with in the past and helping them find contracts outside the military. I've been helping him as best I can while deployed, but I know I could do more if I were full-time.

I glance over the empty dance floor at Heather, talking

animatedly to Isla, who looks as if she wishes she were anywhere else. I can't help but chuckle at the juxtaposition of the two of them. Isla looks nearly Amish in her flowy, long dress. Meanwhile, Heather looks like she's ready for a night out in Vegas. Her dress is velvety and dark red, with a nearly see-through corset that barely contains her fake tits. The dress has the highest slit I've ever seen, showing off her hip bones, and she's paired it with matching velvet gloves. She's a bombshell, leaving nothing to the imagination. I should be over there making sure every guy in the room knows she's mine, but I can't muster the energy to care. It's not like they can't see it on her Instagram any time they want anyway.

Everett walks over and slaps me on the shoulder before taking a seat next to me on the couch. He juts his chin toward Heather and says, "Damn, she was out of your league back in high school, but now you don't stand a chance."

I smirk, "Fuck off. Jealousy doesn't suit you."

He cackles at my insinuation because we both know it isn't true. He may hide his attitude toward Heather better than Hayes, but I can tell he doesn't care for her. Isla, though—I've seen the glint in his eye as he's watched Isla all weekend. If Hayes hadn't mentioned she has a douchey boyfriend, I'm sure he would have made his move already.

Rather than respond, he glances out at the crowd, his head bobbing to the beat of the music. We sit in comfortable silence for a bit, just watching the crowd mingle.

Out of the corner of my eye, I see him start rubbing his thumb and index finger together, the same anxious tell that he's had since he was twelve. The tone of his voice is somber when he finally asks, "You good?"

I cleared my throat and looked away, letting out a heavy sigh. "Just tired, man. I see them," my chin tips toward Hayes and Charlie, "and crave it. I tried to talk to Heather after dinner about moving up here, settling down. She said she's not ready. But I'm just tired of this lifestyle."

The talk with Heather had been less than ideal. I tried to talk to Heather about a future up here, but she lost it in our hotel room. She accused me of not caring about her career, of being selfish, and of only thinking about my desires. It only goes to show that our visions for the future aren't aligning and, at this point, may not ever

Everett just nods, still not looking at me, and then adds quietly, "Been thinking the same." He rubs his hand down his face, "transitioning out to civilian life, that is." He gives me a smirk and adds, "definitely not ready to settle down." Coming from the biggest playboy I know, I'm not surprised. He likes his ladies to be different every time.

The conversation hits a pause when we hear a high-pitched shrill, and both jump to our feet, looking for trouble. We both relax when we spot Ellie, grinning from ear to ear while running from the DJ booth to the middle of the dance floor. Her enormous dress bounces as she goes. She plants herself center stage and then shouts for her mom. When she gets her attention, she motions with her little pointer finger from her mom to the spot where she is standing—a move she must have learned from her mom.

The DJ starts his dedication. "Ellie, our favorite dancer, has contributed this one; she wants you to give it your all on the dance floor!"

I turn to see Olivia's shocked expression as the tune of Copperhead Road starts playing. Her husband, whom I recognized from the photograph at Charlie's, bumps her shoulder with hers and beckons her onto the dance floor too. With a shake of her head, she throws her hands up, and they both head out to catch up to Ellie.

The dance floor began to fill with people, but I quickly made my way to the bar before someone could try to pull me out there. I'm not really in the mood for dancing some country jig.

***

With more drinks, a bit of dancing, and even more drinks, the evening passed quickly. Heather went to our room a few hours ago, saying she needed a good night of sleep before we leave tomorrow. I should have felt tired, too, but the adrenaline from the party keeps me wide awake.

The music is still blaring, and people are laughing and having a great time. I glance over at Hayes, who seems to be enjoying himself as well. "You know," he says, leaning closer to me, "I don't think I've ever seen Charlie this happy before." I nod in agreement, a smile tugging at the corners of my lips. It's been a long journey for all of us, but seeing all of Charlie's dreams come true makes it all worth it.

I'm well on my way past buzzed when I notice Olivia dancing with someone who isn't her husband. I look around the room, trying to see why the husband isn't out there ripping that guy's arms off, but there is no sign of him. Now that I think about it, I haven't seen him or their kids in a while. Checking my phone, it's well after midnight, and I realize he's probably already taken them home.

I look back to the guy all over Olivia. He's close to my build, about my height, maybe even a little taller. I hadn't seen him at the ceremony or reception dinner. Curiosity piqued, and I finally asked Hayes, "Who's the guy dancing with Olivia?"

"Luke? He's the sheriff of Cascadia County. He was..." Charlie swoops in before he can finish his sentence, begging Hayes to dance with her. He follows behind her without hesitation, leaving me standing there with my unanswered curiosity about Olivia and the mysterious sheriff.

For a brief few moments, I watch as they dance. His hands are roaming dangerously close to her ass as they slowly sway to the music. They look lost in conversation, too consumed with each other to care how wrong this looks. I wish I could say I was surprised, but I've always had an uneasy feeling about her the entire time.

Annoyed at the sight of them, I walk towards Everett who is sitting at the bar. He's chatting up the blonde bartender, who looks like she's about to drool over every word he says. I have no doubt he's going to be taking her up to his room later.

I set my empty glass on the bar and interrupted him, telling her about South Carolina. "Can I get another, please?" My southern drawl sounds thick and a little slurred, a sign I should probably call it a night soon.

The bartender smiles and blushes a bit before sliding down the bar to grab the Bourbon.

I smirk at him as he rolls his eyes.

Olivia appears on the other side of Everett and sets her hand on his shoulder, giving him that million-dollar smile. I can't help the involuntary curl of my lip as she does it.

Wasn't she just all over some dude on the dance floor?

The smile dims the second she glances at me. She clears her throat and faces the bar again.

Everett turns toward her and says, "Hey, Liv. You having a good time?" *Since when are they buddy-buddy?*

She nods, and a smaller, shy smile plays on her lips. "It's been a *really* good night."

I involuntarily let out a scoff; of course it has. She's kid-free and living it up, dancing and flirting with every guy in here.

Everett only encourages her, though. "Hell yeah, it has! I love it here."

The bartender sets my drink down in front of me and looks at Olivia with a friendly smile and her eyebrows raised.

"Hey Callie! Can I get some water, please?"

"Probably needed, huh?" I throw it out sarcastically while glaring at my drink on the bar.

If it weren't for the sharp intake of breath, I would have thought she hadn't heard me.

Everett's head snaps to look at me, probably wondering where all the hostility is coming from. Not my fault that he's blinded by the pretty face and do-good attitude. I may be the only damn one in this room to truly see her. But I see her.

I glance over him to see her chewing on her bottom lip while she watches the bartender, who I've now learned is named Callie, get her drink.

"Here you go, Livy." She smiles chipperly as she gives her the drink. *God, everyone in this goddamn place loves her.* "Ellie looked like she was having the time of her life tonight! She kept convincing me to give her double maraschino cherries with her Shirley Temples."

Olivia lets out a small chuckle. "I know that girl could charm the birds out of the trees."

Callie nods and smiles. "Just like her dad." Then she pats her hand almost sympathetically and walks to the other end of the bar to help a different guest.

I see Olivia swallow harshly, probably from the guilt of being the town flirt the second her husband is gone.

"Speaking of her dad," I swivel in my chair so that I'm now fully facing her. "How do you think he would feel about you flirting with every guy at this party?"

"Drew!" Everett scolds and looks at me like I've grown two heads, but I cut him off before he can defend her.

"I'm just saying it isn't a good look. I think we both know she should be ashamed of herself."

Her eyes are wide as saucers at this point, shame rolling off her in big, thick waves. Her mouth gapes open like a fish, trying to find an excuse, but nothing comes out.

She startles when Everett slams his beer on the bartop, the amber liquid spilling out. He stands up, cutting off my eye contact with Olivia. "Let's go, now."

I leisurely stand from the stool, and he shoves me toward the door, even though I'm going willingly. It takes a lot to piss off Ev, so I know I'm probably too liquored up to be here anymore.

He doesn't say anything else as we walk out into the hallway.

I look back at him, ready to go toe-to-toe with my best friend. Something flashes in his eyes when he looks at me, and then he's moving around me to hit the button for the elevator.

He steps back. Sadness mixed with a little disappointment is written all over his face, but instead of questioning me, he just asks, "Do you have your key?"

When I nod in return, he scrubs his hand down his face. "Go sleep it off. I'll explain tomorrow how big of a dumbass you are."

Except he won't have the chance. Heather and I have an early flight and will probably be half way back to California before they even wake up.

I step onto the elevator and hit the number seven for my floor. I don't even look at him as the doors close; I just stare down at the luxury carpet of the elevator.

I feel so messed up in my own head right now that I can't even see straight. Choosing to talk shit to a woman I barely know rather than facing my own problems.

I see Heather flirt with guys all the time. Not once have I felt the rage that I felt toward Olivia tonight. I don't know if it's because she's married and has kids or if it's just the expensive liquor working its way through an angry mind. Either way, my blood was boiling by the end of the night and Olivia was my target.

Chapter Five

Olivia

Six months later—

My hair is ripping through the wind as I leisurely drive down the back roads toward town in my old Jeep. The familiar comfort of the worn-out seats and the sound of the engine purring beneath me bring a smile to my face. Sunny spring weather shines down on my face, country music blares through the outdated stereo, and the smell of the Juniper Trees surround me. It's a good day.

I dig around in the center console until I find a pair of old Rayban Aviators. As I slip them on, I instantly feel a sense of nostalgia as I reminisce about the countless drives I've taken in this Jeep.

I rarely get to drive "Mildred," named lovingly by my grand-aunt Lovey because of its slight Mildewy smell when I first bought it. It isn't modernized enough to safely have two car seats in the back. However, seeing as Levi offered to take the kids for the day, I couldn't resist bringing her out of the garage for a little drive.

I love this old piece of junk. It reminds me of my younger, carefree days. Before kids and marriage, my biggest concern was making the curfew that Lovey set and graduating from high school.

The nostalgia of it all hits me harder than normal today. Lovey died about a year after Ben was born, leaving her entire company to me. I inherited millions, but I lost the only real motherly figure I ever had. My biological mother was arrested on a slew of drug charges when I was only five. She cut a deal with the prosecution, giving my grand-aunt full custody of me. My maternal grandmother's sister, Louise Lynne Ellison, flew to Texas and picked up a terrified little girl. She brought me back to Oregon, legally adopted me, and changed my last name to her married name, Ellison. She saved my life. Blessed me with things I never thought possible.

I pull into the empty office parking lot and reach into the passenger's seat to grab my purse. Only to find it isn't there.

In all my excitement to break Mildred out of her winter prison, I forgot my purse in my SUV.

My shoulders fall as I try to think of what to do.

I have a few things I want to check on inside, but I would rather not drive all the way back to my house. It's only about eight miles outside of town, but if the kids see me, I won't make it back out again.

I do have a spare key hidden, but it's not exactly easy to get to.

I contemplate calling Charlie or Isla, but I'd feel bad interrupting their weekend.

Isla's boyfriend always gets upset with her when she has to do anything work-related on the weekend, and I'd hate to be the cause of more grief in her already tumultuous relationship.

Charlie and Hayes are surely wrapped up in their own little love bubble right now.

Groaning, I roll my forehead on the cracked leather steering wheel.

Guess it's going to be the spare key.

I glance at our beautifully restored office building, pulling in ultramodern elements with classic touches. It's a two-story brick building that still shows the original brick inlay. The windows are all adorned with colorful flower boxes that boast an arrangement of overflowing flowers, thanks to our landscaping crew.

It won't be impossible to get the spare key. I placed it there for a reason, but that was back when we had a ladder hanging out in the toolshed. However, we had a few random break-ins, and the landscapers ended up taking the toolshed back to their house.

I decided that using the Jeep is my best option. The window that has the spare key is closest to the front of the building. If I'm careful, I can use the roll bar to give me a little extra height and reach the flower box.

I cautiously pull Mildred forward so that I am parallel with the side of the office building. I have to give her a little extra gas so that the left side can hop up onto the sidewalk. The Jeep jolts me a bit, as it gives, but in the next second, I'm on the sidewalk.

I keep pulling forward, careful not to take out my side mirror.

A smile lights up my face when I jump out to check my work and see that it's perfect.

I'm about a foot and a half away, the perfect distance to use the building as a support as I shimmy my way up.

I crawl back through the driver side and use the passenger seat and door frame to help me climb to the top of the roll bar. I widen my legs as I grip the brick wall with my fingertips to help steady me while I reach for the spare.

A breeze brushes across my bare legs, a reminder that I need to hurry before someone driving by spots my exposed butt cheeks from my too-short shorts. I reach over the flower box and try to feel around, but as I glide my hand over the window seal, I can't find it.

Right as I begin to feel the plastic of the ziplock bag, Mildred starts to roll forward. Instinctively, I grip onto the bricks, trying to figure out my next move. Right when the panic really starts to hit, the driver door is yanked open, and someone throws it into gear.

A gruff voice behind me bellows, "What the *fuck* are you doing?"

Shit.

I haven't heard that angry growl in months, but I know who it is before I even turn around. Andrew Reynolds. Enemy #1. Although he's not really my enemy, it's him who has had problems with me since the beginning.

I turn on my sunniest smile and turn to face the devil himself.

"Forgot my key," I say, with a little shoulder shrug. "What are *you* doing here?" I attempt to sound light and airy, but my voice hits a higher octave than normal, and I definitely sound like my five-year-old when she gets caught with her hand in the cookie jar.

A soft chuckle escapes at how pissed off he is at me already. It's reminiscent of the first time he spotted me balancing in a precarious spot. If he wasn't so irritable-looking, I'd be blushing with his stare. Seriously, how does this man always look so good?

"Get down."

I point up at the flower box, "I still need my key."

"I swear to God, Boots. Get down right fucking now."

Boots. It gave me butterflies the first time he called me that, and unfortunately, it still does. I should loathe this man based on how he talks to me. Yet, I turn into a sixteen-year-old hormonal girl in his presence.

I bend so that my knees are kneeling on the roll bar, and then step down into the passenger seat. Crawling back out of the driver's side door and around Mildred until I'm only a few feet away.

The tension in his shoulders seemed to have eased, but he's still looking at me like I'm a gnat that won't go away.

I ogled him for probably a second too long, but how could I not? His white shirt is stretched tight over his broad chest, and his black shorts hit above the knee, showing off his muscular thighs. I'm practically panting at a man who is shooting laser beams out of his eyes at me.

I clear my throat. "So, uh, I take it you're officially moved in. Charlie mentioned you'd be working with Hayes."

Is my voice seriously shaking right now?

I need to get myself in check. This man has a girlfriend—an incredibly hot, supermodel girlfriend—whose entire career is based on her looks. I'm a mom, rocking barely any makeup, with my hair looking like a tornado.

"Why don't you have your keycard?"

"It's in my purse, which is in my SUV. I brought Mildred."

His face scrunches as he quietly asks, "Mildred?"

I gesture behind me toward my Jeep. "Yep. Must have forgotten it."

His features darken at my impassiveness. "You forgot? Are you that unreliable? What about standing on the Jeep?! Are you really that reckless?"

Jesus Christ, this man knows how to make me feel about two feet tall.

"Yeah, I forgot; people forget things sometimes!" I shout back, defending myself for the first time. I have a full-time career while also trying to raise two kids without a husband. I'm allowed to forget a fucking bag.

He sneers. "At my work, people forget things, and good people die."

Damn, talk about a big dose of reality.

It feels like he just threw a bucket of cold water on my hot temper.

His life has depended on everyone around him being the best. If one of them slips, it could mean life or death. Forgetting a bag isn't so simple when you have lives relying on you.

I look him in the eyes and nod. I don't even have a response to give him, and with the disappointment radiating from him, I doubt he even wants one.

He holds up his keycard and says, "Next time, you call." There is no room for discussion as he turns to walk back to the front of the building.

The last time he saw me, he told me I should be ashamed of my flirting; this time he's calling me unreliable and careless. My ego is feels pretty bruised anytime he's around.

Andrew

I couldn't help but notice the shell Olivia crawled back into after I lashed out at her for forgetting her key. To be honest, the sheer panic I felt when I saw her standing ten feet in the air on top of a literal rolling death trap was a surprise to me. I'm trained to handle situations with calm and ease, and I almost ripped her down from there myself. Then, I was so angry at myself for caring that I scolded her like I would have a new guy on the team, forgetting something minor. Only this isn't the Navy, and she's not my responsibility.

When I unlocked the door for her and held it open, she didn't even make eye contact. I could swear her eyes were shimmering with unshed tears, but she quickly swept by and took the stairs two at a time to the top floor.

I slowed my pace, checking out the first floor of the building for the first time. Two offices sit in the front, a few small storage rooms, and a decent-sized gym in the back. From the state-of-the-art equipment to the cold plunge tub in the men's locker room, it has Hayes design written all over it.

By the time I start to make my way up the stairs, my path crosses Olivia's again.

She puts on that big fake smile when she sees me. "Thanks for the save! I appreciate the advice as well."

My brows instantly furrowed. What advice? Before I get a chance to ask, she's hustling those boots down the stairs.

I hear the door close behind her, but I still haven't moved from my spot on the stairs.

I'm having a hard time figuring out why I have such a gnawing feeling in my gut every time she is around. It's either trying to warn me that Olivia is the best actress in the entire world, or that I'm missing something big.

I try to shake off our encounter as I finish walking up the stairs to my new office.

The upstairs is incredible; large steel partitions and glass windows divide up the space into four unique offices, with the stairs and a landing in the middle of them.

Olivia and Charlie's office run parallel to Hayes and mine. The girls have large plants in every corner and different awards hanging on the walls. Their individual desks face each other near the front of the building, and the other side has a few lounge chairs that surround a large circular coffee table.

Our office is nearly identical in shape and size but is considerably more sterile; two small desks sit near each other, and there is a large conference table. Hayes has spent a considerable amount of time here, yet he still hasn't put much into the decor. I don't mind, though; it's better than most of the shoebox offices we had on deployment.

In between our offices is a full-game room with a ping-pong table, large TV, bean bag chairs, and cozy couches. I'm assuming that's where Olivia's kids hang out when they aren't in school.

Running parallel to the game room, on the other side of the stairs, is a fully equipped kitchen. The center has an island with bar stools, and a dining room table is off to the side. I'm not sure how often it's used, but it's cool to have the option. It's better and bigger than most people's apartments in California.

Whoever designed this building did an incredible job. Everything is sleek and modern, but it still has a rustic feel that balances out the new pieces and the history of the building.

I have a feeling I'm going to like this place and enjoy working up here. It's been too long since I've worked with Hayes and been near Charlie. This is an opportunity I won't pass up just because Olivia may not be my favorite person. I'll avoid her like the plague if I have to.

Chapter Six

Andrew

My phone lights up with a security notification that someone just pulled into the driveway and is waiting at the gate. I opened the app to see a smiling Olivia and let out a loud groan. I'm not in the mood for entertaining unwanted house guests. Even though I'm pretty sure I'm staying for free at one of her rental properties, it's not like she doesn't own half of Central Oregon anyway.

Charlie's the one who set me up in this place. No questions were asked; she simply gave me the keys and said rent was free for the first year. My pride wanted me to argue, but I need to save as much money as I can until Hayes and I's business takes off.

As for free places, this one isn't too shabby either. It's an older ranch-style house with three bedrooms and two bathrooms. Everything in it has been updated with different shades of gray, white, and dark wood to look like something from one of those TLC shows. It's also only about a mile from Charlie and Hayes' house.

A small knock at the door brings me back from my

thoughts, and I open the door. Olivia is standing there, her hair curly and windblown, wearing a jean jacket over her flowy white dress and a pair of brown and turquoise western boots. An older wicker basket rests on her hip.

Her smile falters when she sees my expressionless face. I don't know why she would expect a warm welcome; it's only been a few weeks since the forgotten key incident, and we've been avoiding each other since.

"Hey, sorry to just drop by. The kids are camping with Levi for the long weekend. I didn't know what to do with my time. So, I baked." I keep my face as neutral as possible while she continues to babble on.

She pulls the basket from her hip and gestures at it: "Fresh bread, brownies, chocolate chip cookies, and a peach cobbler." She blushes bashfully. It would almost be cute if I wasn't feeling so jaded toward her.

"I also need to apologize. I think you got the wrong impression of me at the wedding. I'm..."

I put my hand up and stopped her mid-sentence. "I don't want an apology. We aren't friends, and we don't need to be friends."

Her eyebrows pinch together. "What about Charlie?"

"What about her?" Charlie is not reason enough for us to be friends. We can coexist for her sake, but that doesn't mean we have to be close.

"I just don't want it to be awkward whenever we are all together."

"I don't really care if it is." I replied bluntly, not bothering to hide my indifference.

"But..." she starts to protest, but I interrupt her again.

"No! I don't want to hear it. I don't trust you. Plain and simple. You lied to Hayes about Charlie being here. You had no respect for your family at Charlie and Hayes' wedding. Your decision-making skills seem questionable at best. So, that's it. As long as we can be civil, I don't see a problem."

Her mouth is stuck, hanging open, and her eyes are impossibly wide. She blinks it away quickly, sets the basket down on the front porch, and walks away. I almost think the conversation is over, but halfway to her Jeep, she stops and looks over her shoulder at me.

"Peonies. For when you're ready to apologize." I raise an eyebrow at her audacity but remain silent. She climbs into the Jeep and doesn't give me another look as she turns around in the wide driveway and leaves.

Standing on the porch, guilt starts to gnaw at my gut. My temper flares the second she is around. Like oil in water. I can't even hear her voice without my lip involuntarily curling. My body naturally just has a negative visceral reaction when she's near me.

I don't have time to dwell on that because I hear Heather's ringtone going off from back in the house. We've set aside a few hours on Sunday afternoons for FaceTime, and it's gone surprisingly well the last few weeks. For some reason, we've always done better long distance.

"Hey, Heath. It's good to see that smilin' face of yours." She's positively beaming on the other side. Her hair is thrown up in a messy bun, and she has a fresh face, clear of makeup. She looks like the Heather I remember from before she moved to L.A.

"Drew! You'll never believe which energy drink wants to sponsor me! Redbull! Can you believe it? I'm not even a famous athlete or actress, and they still chose me!"

I grin back at her. "That's an incredible deal!" She's been working her ass off for years to get where she's at in her career. I may not always agree with her posts and what she does, but I'm proud of her for chasing her dreams.

We spend the next thirty minutes talking about the sponsorship, a new diet she is trying, and her upcoming visit in a few weeks. It's not until the end of the call that I realize she didn't even ask about me.

A few hours later, I'm heading to the Carrington's for Sunday night dinner. They started it the weekend I moved up here, and we've continued it every week since then.

I knock once to be polite, even though I know the security alarm has already notified them I'm here, and I open the door. A laugh too loud to be Hayes is coming from the kitchen, but I'd recognize that hyena cackle anywhere: Everett.

I stomp into the house, making sure my presence is known. "Well, well, well. Did the Army finally kick your lame ass out?"

Chuckling back, Everett says, "Nah, Hayes just begged me to come save the company you two are floundering in."

Hayes rolls his eyes at the two of us. "Offered him the same job I offered you; it just took him a bit longer to get here."

I nod and rub my chin. "Well, you were always a bit slower."

Everett walks over and pats my shoulder. "Whatever, Roomie!"

I glance at Charlie, who holds her hand up. "We have NO other rentals! You're lucky Olivia offered up her house."

I freeze. "What do you mean Olivia offered up her house?"

Her face grows somber, and her eyes close for a brief moment. "It was her first house. She's never rented it before. It's just been sitting empty." She lets out a big sigh and looks at me. "She has the maintenance staff check on it, and lawn care goes every few weeks, but I don't think she's been near it since she moved into the new house."

That's weird. Why would someone whose entire career is based on renting the houses they own not rent out a house? I'm about to ask when the oven timer goes off, and she's back to hustling around the kitchen, finishing up dinner.

Everett slaps me on the shoulder. "What's the room situation? I didn't bring much. Not that I had much to begin with. Never exactly set down any roots." I understand what he means. I've only been here a few weeks and already feel more at home than I ever did in the Navy.

"The house is mostly furnished. Charlie and I went on a shopping spree a few weeks ago, but if you don't like anything, we can change it."

"Nah, man. I don't need much, just a TV and a bed."

"Let's go, boys. Dinner is ready!" Charlie announces this as she walks toward the dining room while carrying an enormous casserole dish. I had no idea she could cook, but she's impressed me every week with different dishes. My baby sister is officially domesticated, and I feel like I missed the entire transformation.

"So, no more birds? You ready for a desk job? I asked Everett. He's been flying helicopters since before he even went into the Army. I'm surprised he's here, giving that up.

He chews and swallows his bite of chicken tortilla casserole. "For a bit. I did a 16-week academy, so Luke can hire me on with the sheriff's department. Search and rescue-type flights, but he isn't sure if they have the money for that yet. I was thinking I might check with the hospital in Bend, too. See if they are hiring pilots."

"You should talk to Levi, Olivia's brother-in-law. He's a medic. I'm pretty sure he knows everyone who works at that hospital. Hell, it seems like he knows everyone within a forty-five-mile radius."

I take another bite of my dinner, trying not to roll my eyes at Hayes' mention of Olivia.

Everett nodded in agreement. "Good idea. I talked to him a bit at the reception before they left. Seems like a good dude."

It took me a bit too long to make the connection between "brother-in-law" and the name Levi. I swear I overheard someone call Olivia's husband Levi at the reception.

"What do you mean, brother-in-law? Levi, the blonde guy from the wedding? I thought that was her husband. I saw the picture in your entryway." I say, pointing toward the front of the house, even though they can't see it from here.

Everett's head snaps toward mine. "Shit, I had a feeling you didn't know that night. I was planning on telling you the next morning, but you left early."

I look between Hayes, Charlie, and him warily. "Tell me what?"

Hayes sighs and drops his fork on the plate. "Olivia's husband's name was Dan; he worked for the sheriff's office. He died a few years ago while on duty. Levi is his identical twin. He helps her a lot with the kids. The older guy who was there and dropped Ben off with us is their dad, Ezekiel, but we all call him Pops. He was the sheriff when it happened but retired a little after."

My heart does a little stutter as nausea swirls in my stomach. The puzzle pieces began slamming together. Olivia's lack of physical affection toward Levi, his ringless finger, yet the close relationship with the kids. Damn it, what a mindfuck that must be to see your dead husband's face all the time.

I had no idea she was a widow; I would have never been able to tell, not that it is something you can tell by looking at someone. But fuck, she's so young. The kids—they're so young. I know firsthand how hard it is to lose a parent, but at least I had my parents through most of my teenage years.

I'm lost in thought for a second, and then a chill runs down my spine: "The house. My rental? It was theirs." I try to choke out. Charlie mentioned she hadn't been back to the house and wasn't renting it out to anyone. It must be too hard to think about anyone else making any memories there.

Charlie nods. "Yeah, she stayed there for a while with the kids but built the new house. She said it became too hard walking around with all the memories."

I pinch between my eyebrows as hard as I can, trying to ease the tension in my head.

"Fuck!" I slam my palm on the flat surface of the dining table, causing the dinnerware to vibrate against the wood. "She stopped by today with a basket, trying to clear the air. I all but slammed the door in her face."

My own ignorant stupidity has me cringing as the memories come flying back. "I think I also called her self-absorbed and a cheater."

Charlie's eyes widen to comical size, while red splotches begin to appear on her face. She hasn't looked this pissed at me in years. Not since she was six, and I popped the head off her favorite Barbie.

She definitely didn't sound this enraged back then, though. "Are you fucking kidding me, Drew?!"

I hang my head in surrender, waiting for the storm that is Charlotte Reynolds, now Carrington, to hit me. I deserve an ass chewing that would make any training officer at BUD/S seem like a preschool teacher. There's nothing I can say to make this better; I messed up.

Instead of the berating I deserve, though, Charlie storms out of the house. The large front door slams behind her, rattling the entire house. A few seconds later, an engine starts.

I glance at Hayes with my eyebrows raised with confusion.

"Olivia's property borders ours; I'm sure she's going over to check on her." I'm starting to realize I don't know a thing about her. I've tuned out damn near everything they've ever said about her.

Everett offers me a sympathetic pat on the back as he carries his plate into the kitchen.

Hayes studied me, a mixture of anger and sadness molding his features. He knows me better than anyone. He knows I'm not a malicious person. He knows my head isn't where it should be right now, and I haven't been thinking clearly lately.

He runs his thumb down the condensation of his beer glass while staring at it. Clearing his throat and then letting out a deep breath, he said, "Dan became a friend of mine pretty quickly. A damn good friend, actually. I was in the office when the patrol car showed up to tell her. I hadn't met the deputies before that day, but I knew the second they got out of the car what they were going to say. Reminded me of the day your parents died, when we were just sitting in my living room wondering why there was a cop outside."

He shakes his head, clearing that memory to go back to his original story. "I froze. I physically felt like I couldn't move. I kept telling myself to stop them, to get to Olivia, and to just get up. But it felt like..." I hear the rhythmic thump of his toe tapping the ground while he pauses to gather his thoughts. "Fuck, man. It felt like I couldn't even breathe; my muscles were tense, and my vision had just tunneled. I sat there and watched them walk up the stairs. Watched Olivia's face light up, like they were her best friends just visiting to shoot the shit. Watched her heart break as she collapsed to the floor in sobs. We've seen a lot of shit... A lot of dark fucking days. That day, though, that was right there with the worst."

I don't take anything he is saying lightly; Hayes is no stranger to the tragedies of the world.

My throat feels thick with emotion, but as much as I swallow it won't go away, so I just nod.

"You know I love you; you've always been a brother to me.

But. You messed up. Let whatever bullshit you're still holding on to cloud your judgment. You know it, and I know it."

I'm bobbing my head like a damn bobble-head caught in a windstorm.

"Olivia... She's a good person. She saved Charlie. I know you hit another deployment right when everything really blew up, so you only got the cliff notes. However, she did her best to keep our girl safe, and she barely even knew her. She'll forgive you. But I'm letting you know right now that Olivia is family. Her kids are family. Apologize to her." He doesn't have to add that he will kick my ass if I hurt her anymore. I know he would, and I'd let him.

I stare at the food on my half-eaten plate, mentally chastising myself for being such an idiot. I should be better than this. I'm trained to be better than this. I shouldn't be making assumptions and then sticking to my guns out of pride.

Olivia didn't deserve any of the shit I threw at her.

I need to apologize.

I need to rebuild the bridge I set on fire.

I need peonies.

Chapter Seven

Olivia

I sit at my desk in the office, scrolling through Google, and plotting out places to visit this summer with the kids. I should be working, but I can't seem to focus on the mile-long to-do list. I normally love being at work, the routine, and the camaraderie that Isla, Charlie, and I have. The office is always buzzing with people, but this morning, it's been unusually quiet.

Isla and Charlie are dropping my SUV off at the dealership to be serviced, and Hayes is picking them up so that they can run errands while they wait. Andrew hasn't shown up yet, either. So, except for the occasional clatter of gym equipment downstairs, it's eerily silent up here.

I drum my fingers on the desk and contemplate filing some paperwork downstairs. Hayes and Andrew have some recruits who are waiting on contracts and spend most of their time shirtless in the gym. I'm not interested in dating any of them, but I do love to occasionally admire them as I walk by, and with bodies like Greek gods, they deserve to be admired.

Dan was always in incredible shape, but he had the slim

body of a runner. He was always running, training for the next marathon, and before kids, I was right there with him. After kids, though, I barely had time to wash my hair, let alone train for a marathon. I lost a lot of the baby weight, but my body just changed, and I always felt a little self-conscious standing next to his tall, thin frame.

These guys, though. Just their presence alone looks like it takes up most of the room. It's hard to feel self-conscious when you see them bench press double your weight. Andrew, especially, has broad shoulders and drool-worthy arms that look like they were made to throw you around on the bed. Not that I've taken much notice. He's just down there a lot, and I happened to notice him while checking out the group collectively. At least that's what I tell myself, but in reality, I've got a school-grade crush on the one guy who hasn't liked me from the beginning.

To be honest, that's probably my draw to him. He doesn't like me, so I don't have to worry about it going any further than lustful attraction. It doesn't help that the last time I walked by, he had his shirt off while he was doing tricep dips, and the mixture of defined abs, protruding veins, and glistening sweat had me panting.

I'm so lost in my fantasy of tan skin and rippling muscles that I don't hear the chime on the front door or the footsteps of someone walking up the stairs. It's not until said fantasized man is rounding the corner of the landing that I notice him and nearly fall off my chair.

Real fucking smooth, Olivia.

Andrew is carrying the biggest bouquet of pink and white peonies I have ever seen. The gruffness and sheer muscle, in juxtaposition with the most delicate flowers, have my mouth gaping open.

The loud shrill of my cell phone's ringing snaps me out of

whatever spell I was under. I snatch it off my desk as if it were the cause of my anxiety and press the answer button.

"Hello?" I answered a little too high-pitched.

He approaches the door frame cautiously, a regretful smile pulling at his lips. I give him the one-minute gesture as the caller starts talking.

"Is this Olivia Turner?" A woman's voice, which I don't recognize, asks.

"Yes, this is her." My brows draw together; something about this call is already sitting heavy in my gut.

"This is Karen; I work in the front office at TSE." Three Sisters Elementary, where Ben goes. My heart stutters as my mind races to try to put the puzzle pieces together that I don't have. "Principal Grum asked me to inform you that he has Ben in his office and needs you to come down."

"Is he okay? What happened?"

"I'm not at liberty to discuss the matter, but he's okay. When will you be here?" She sounds detached—just another call to another parent. Yet, here I am, on the verge of a panic attack.

"I'm on my way, five minutes away." I hit the red button and tried to suck in air, forcing myself to breathe. He's okay; she said he's okay. I need to calm down and move, but instead I just stare at the screensaver on my phone of Ellie and Ben.

I'm faintly aware of the flower bouquet being placed on my desk and then Andrew placing his hands on my shoulders, turning me to face him.

I blink up at him, taking in his masculine features. He looks strong and battle-ready when he asks me, "What's wrong?"

Under different circumstances, I would have laughed; it's the same look Charlie gets. Emerald eyes full of confidence, lips slightly pursed, and a small worry line between their eyebrows. The look screams, "No matter what the problem is, I'll have your back." Only coming from Andrew; I know it's from guilt and not friendship.

That thought alone sours my stomach, and I shake myself out of the trance. I step away from him, yank my desk drawer open, and grab my purse. I start walking while frantically searching for my keys at the bottom of the bag. I nearly trip over my own feet, but a strong hand catches my elbow and straightens me.

Tears fill my eyes when I look up at him, and that sets him over the edge. "Boots! What happened?"

"I don't know! Ben is in the Principal's office, and *Karen* wouldn't tell me why! And... And I can't find my keys!" I exploded at him. My breathing is coming out in ragged puffs as I try to get my thoughts together.

"Okay, calm down for a second. Isla and Charlie dropped off your SUV this morning, right?"

"FUCK!" I hit my hand on the metal bar that wraps around the staircase ledge, causing shooting pain to go through my hand up to my elbow. I clench my teeth and my hand gingerly, wishing my brain was working at full capacity to come up with a plan.

"Let's go. I'll drive." I look up at him, trying to determine whether he's joking or not, but he's already walking down the steps toward the front door.

I follow behind like a duckling, clambering into his passenger seat and buckling up. Without a word, he drives me to the school. I don't even ask how he knows where the school is; it's a small enough town, and Andrew seems like he doesn't miss a thing.

I take a deep, steady breath, trying to ground myself before I face whatever is going on in there. I know that I need to go in there with a clear head and a calm demeanor, despite the fact that it feels like the weight of the world rests solely on my shoulders. Just another paper cut that reminds me I no longer have Dan to stand by me.

The second Andrew pulls in front of the school and parks, I open the door and march my way into battle, prepared to handle this by myself, like the single-widowed mom I am.

Ben's head snaps up as I open the door to the school office. My steps falter when I see him sitting in a chair outside the principal's office, curled into himself, tears streaking down his face. His little eight-year-old body looks so damn small in that chair by himself. I cover the office in two large steps the second I hear his sad little voice say, "Mom!"

Crouching down in front of his chair, I wrap my arms around his shaking frame. I can hear a female voice ranting from inside the principal's office, and then I hear Principal Grum's monotone voice reassuring her he will handle it. How long have they been in there talking with him out here alone, having to listen? The rage inside begins to grow like a small ember, about to catch dry sagebrush on a dry summer day, threatening to burn everything in sight down.

I pull back a little, so I can look at him. "What happened, bud?"

His sniffles rock his frame as he says, "I did what Coach said to do." The "coach" he is referring to is the Jiu Jitsu instructor at the martial arts school that he's been going to since he was four.

I nod, encouraging him to continue. "He stomped on Theo's new glasses, so I—"

I'm vaguely aware of the presence now lingering in the doorframe of the principal's office, but I don't look away from Ben.

"Miss Turner, you two can come into my office now," Principal Grum drones in that terribly boring voice of his. The familiar stab in my gut is there when he refers to me as "Ms."

instead of "Mrs." but I let it go. My concern is my barely eight-year-old, who was just sitting by himself listening to some hag rant about him.

I let out a heavy sigh and turned to Principal Grum. "Give us a few minutes, and we will be in."

"No. We will *all* speak in my office. Now." *The gall.*

My molars grind together, and I inhale a breath, ready to snap.

"They just need a minute," Andrew says from behind me, his deep voice calm but assertive. I didn't even know he had followed me in; the stealth of this man is incredible. I swoon slightly when I look over my shoulder and catch a glimpse of him directing a "don't fuck with them" look at Principal Grum. He could have just waited in his truck or come back to get us, but instead, he followed me in here to make sure we were okay. *Hot.*

Principal Grum narrows his eyes. "And you are?"

I respond before he even finishes asking, "Family." This asshole doesn't need to know anything. If I want our fucking UPS driver here, they can be here.

"Two minutes," he demands, and then turns on his heel to walk back into his office.

Yeah, sure, asshat.

I gave Ben another reassuring smile; his eyes hadn't stopped bouncing between the three of us. Clearly, he was aware of the pissing match going on without even realizing what it meant.

I lightly touch the outside of his arm. "Take a breath through your nose and let it out."

He does a small "huff," and I let out a quiet laugh. "A little bigger; really breathe all that good oxygen in." I mimic what he should do, and he copies.

"Okay, buddy, I've got your back in that room no matter

what. Whatever happened, we will fix it. You and me." I squeeze his hand, making sure he's with me, and he nods.

"Tell me what happened."

His shoulders sag, as everything is catching up to him. "Mrs. Sheldon noticed that Theo hadn't come back from the library yet; she asked me to go check if he needed help. I got to the big hallway, and this older kid was holding his glasses up high. Theo was crying and saying please over and over again. So I ran over there and told him to give them back! And then he threw the glasses down! I tried to pick them up, and he grabbed me!" He looks down at his hands, seemingly ashamed of what happened next, but keeps going. "I told him to let go! But he didn't, so I took him down and told Theo to go get Mrs. Sheldon."

I wait for him to look up at me and say, "Okay, so you took him down?"

He nods, his voice trembling from frustration and anger. "Yeah, I let go when Mrs. Sheldon got there! But she said we were fighting and sent us here. That.. That.. BULLY told Principal Grum I started it and I didn't!"

Hugging him tightly to my chest, I try to reassure him, "I know, buddy, I know. You've got a good heart, Benjamin Turner."

I pull away and look at him, putting on a false bravado. "We've gotta go in there now. You know that poker face Uncle Levi taught you during guys' night? I need you to put it on and don't let it go. No matter what they say or what I say, you keep that poker face on. I promise you, I have *your* back in there."

I stand up and reach for his hand, pulling him to stand as well.

I glance back at Andrew; his exterior looks calm and collected, but I can see the same fire reflected in his eyes that I have in mine. With a head tilt, I gesture for him to come with us, and then walk into the lion's den.

Guiding Ben to the seat furthest from the rabid mom and her son, I place myself between them. The tension in the small room is thick. Principal Grum sits behind his desk, reading through a large binder. I look at the mom sitting to my right. I've briefly seen her in passing, but our paths haven't crossed much. She's perfectly blonde with blue eyes that look like they're trying to incinerate me. I give her my sweetest smile, refusing to let her intimidate me.

She rolls her eyes in return and looks back at Principal Grum. "Well, have you called the police? This is assault! That little..."

Oh *hell, no. We are not name-calling 1st graders.*

I cut her off with a growl. "WOAH, woah, woah! Don't even think about calling my son anything besides his name." *So much for being calm, cool, and collected.*

She tries to level me with a look, and I glare back just as hard. She looks like she just left the country club, with her tennis skirt and sweater delicately placed over her shoulder. Makeup to the nines, and not a hair out of place.

Principal Grum sighs, like it pains him to agree with me. "I'm going to have to agree with Ms. Turner. Mrs. Bushnell, please refrain from using any derogatory language."

Yeah! Or at least keep it to yourself like a respectable adult, you bimbo.

Then the bastard zones in on me: "We have zero tolerance for bullying at this school. Your son was found on top of another student, disabling him from moving." *Disabling him from moving? Kind of the point, dipshit.*

I raise my eyebrow at him, not revealing any of my cards just yet.

"Yes, my son!" screeches Miss Real Housewife of Small Town. Her nasally voice has me cringing away from her.

I scan over her one more time and then take a second to look at the kid who put us in this situation. He looks like he's at least a grade or two above Ben. He has short, dark hair, and his eyes are the same shade of blue as his mother's, though they are framed by dark, bushy eyebrows.

Crossing my legs, I look back at Principal Grum. "So zero tolerance for bullying? Who determines what is classified as bullying?"

I hear a loud scoff from the chair next to mine. "Are you serious? This is ridiculous! Archie was attacked!" She throws her hands in the air and then scowls at me. "My husband is a respected attorney, and we will be pressing charges!"

"Can we see the footage from the security cameras?" Andrew asks from behind. Mrs. Bushnell does a double take, now noticing the Greek god standing behind us. A faint blush spreads across her cheeks, and she crosses her legs daintily while tucking her hair behind her ear.

Yeah, get in line, Blondie; he's taken. Well, not by me, but taken nonetheless.

Principal Grum narrows his eyes. "The school district is in charge of all the security footage."

"Okay, call whoever you need to call," he responds.

"Yes, preferably the police department!" says blonde Barbie Bushnell.

I let out a humorous laugh. "I think you mean the sheriff's department."

Principal Grum gives me a stern look, clearly unamused by my comment. "Regardless, we will handle this situation appropriately and follow the protocol," he says firmly while tapping his binder.

Mrs. Bushnell shoots me a disapproving glare, but I can't help but smirk at her reaction.

I hear footsteps and turn to see the tired, adult version of Archie, wearing a sophisticated-looking suit, walk in. The man in it is trying to emulate wealth and social standing, but the 5 o'clock shadow and dark circles under his eyes reveal a different story, especially because it's not even noon.

"Sorry, I'm late, Principal Grum. I was in a meeting with a client." He offers a smarmy smile while reaching across the desk to shake his hand. "Cameron Bushnell, Archibald's father."

Principal Grum nods his approval. "Glad you could make it."

I almost gag at whatever toxic masculinity is transferring across the desk between the two of them.

I look back at Andrew, silently trying to say, "What the fuck?" And receive a very small smirk in return. *Was that almost a smile? Is this how Olympic gold medalists feel after their first big win? Because I could get addicted to that real fast.*

The mood quickly turned back to sour when Principal Grum said, "Mr. Bushnell, these two were caught fighting in the hallway."

"Please call me Cameron. So, where do we go from here? I believe you mentioned a protocol before I interrupted." I'll give it to him; he's at least more courteous than his wife.

"Yes. We have zero tolerance for bullying. An automatic suspension of three days will be enacted. The school will do an investigation and determine if more days are necessary, with a maximum of seven, or consider expulsion."

Cameron nods, contemplating the seriousness of the situation. Something tells me this isn't the first time they've been in a principal's office like this. "Who does this investigation? Is there security camera footage we can see?"

Principal Grum rubs his forehead. "That, uh, well, it takes a lot of paperwork. I have to talk to the superintendent."

A ghost of a smile tugs at my lips. "Oh, Calvin Anderson? Let me give him a call." Cameron's gaze snapped in my direction for the first time, finally acknowledging my presence. With one eyebrow raised, he clearly tries to size up his competition. I give him my sweetest smile and whip out my phone.

Calvin was not only a teacher of mine, but also very close with Lovey and a big part of the "pseudo family," as she called it. She didn't have any family in Oregon, but she created her own, and they all loved each other thoroughly. Calvin's wife, Elise, was the one who taught me how to swim and gave me lessons from kindergarten to 5th grade. They've been there for me through the best moments of my life to the worst—from birthdays to my first breakup, from my high school graduation to Lovey getting sick, from my wedding to Dan to his funeral. They've held me up. So I shouldn't be surprised that when I need help, the universe sends them my way.

I put the phone on speaker, and thankfully, he answered after the second ring. "Well, to what do I owe this pleasure, Liv?"

"Hey Cal, I have you on speakerphone here. I'm actually at TSE, sitting in Principal Grum's office right now. It seems Ben and another student had a misunderstanding. I'm just calling to see if you could figure out a way to expedite the footage from the hall camera."

I hear a small intake of breath from Calvin, and then he says, "I'm just down the road; I'll be there in two minutes."

The line ends, and I smile at my audience. I give a small coy shrug and say, "He's a family friend."

Cameron's eyes narrow at me, but he looks back to Principal Grum and asks, "How does this affect their personal records?"

"It will go on both of their records, unless one is proved to have instigated the bullying."

He nods, and the room falls silent while we all wait for Calvin to arrive. The office fills with the same thick tension it had before, but I feel comfortable in it now. Even Ben seems more relaxed now that he knows "Grandpa Cal" is on the way.

Not even a minute later, Calvin breezes in. He introduces himself to the Bushnell's and then turns and does a double take when he sees Andrew behind me. He glances between the two of us, nods his head, and turns his attention to Principal Grum.

"How can I help? You should have access to all cameras inside and out of this building through the school portal."

Principal Grum winces, "Well, I don't know how to access that."

Calvin walks behind the desk and leans over, scrolling and pressing a few buttons until he finds what he's looking for. He has to be at least fifteen years older than Principal Grum, but he's still as sharp as a tack.

"Which hallway?" Calvin looks at me, and I look to Ben, encouraging him to talk. He quietly says, "C, near the library."

He scrolls again until he finds the right camera, glancing at Principal Grum this time.

"It was about an hour ago," he sighs and rubs his forehead. They both lean in, assessing the footage.

I involuntarily hold my breath, watching Calvin's face for any sign of concern, but he doesn't give away anything.

When Calvin touches the keyboard again, Principal Grum tosses his glasses onto his desk and lets out a heavy sigh.

Calvin turns the laptop around and hits play. I swear everybody on our side of the desk leans in at the exact same time to watch the grainy footage.

Archie passes Theo, who is carrying a handful of books, and then sits on a set of steps, waiting for Theo to come back from the library. He jumps out and scares Theo from the stairwell; the glasses fly out of Theo's hand, and Archie snatches them up before Theo can. Then he begins taunting him, holding the glasses just out of reach, and shoving him whenever he tries to reach them. Ben enters the frame and places himself between Archie and Theo, clearly trying to be a peacemaker. Archie drops the glasses, and Ben leans down to grab them. Archie throws his arm around Ben and puts him in a half-ass choke hold. In a matter of seconds, Ben has this much bigger kid on the ground, locking him in a side control.

I can't stop the grin spreading across my face. I'm so proud of this kid! Standing up for his friend. Four years, nearly five thousand dollars later, and my son is (respectfully) kicking ass and taking names.

"See! Right there! He needs to be expelled!" Mrs. Bushnell starts to stand, but her husband grabs her shoulders from behind and forcefully sits her back down. The look on his face screams, 'Please shut the hell up,' but he quickly clears it.

"Now, now, honey, let's just calm down. They're only kids." *Ah, smart man.* He sees what everyone else in the room sees. Archie is the bully who instigated the entire thing.

I smash my lips together to keep my smile contained, and I try to prevent the celebratory shoulder dance I want to do. "Well, you see, I believe your wife mentioned a few times calling local law enforcement. Is that now off the table?" I hold my phone up and say, "I can call Sheriff Haynes; I'm sure he wouldn't mind swinging by as well." I couldn't help the jab, knowing damn well I wouldn't call Luke. If I had, I guarantee he would have been here faster than even Calvin was. Lights, sirens, and all. I know that this kid needs some serious intervention, but I don't think scared straight is called for just yet.

Her face visibly pales, but Cameron remains his easy-going self. "Not necessary on our part; I say we chalk this up to kids being kids; let them do the punishment that is required, apologize, and move on."

Principal Grum nods. He looks exhausted, like we've taken years off his life in the last twenty minutes. "My suggestion is the minimum three-day suspension for Benjamin, with nothing on his permanent record. As for Archibald, for instigating the altercation, a seven-day suspension with a mark on his permanent record.

Cameron visibly winces but nods nonetheless. "That sounds fine. Thank you, Principal Grum."

My chin involuntarily tips to the side, and a small huff comes out. *Are they kidding?*

Calvin looks at me and asks, "Olivia, how do you feel about that?"

"A seven-day suspension? You think missing out on seven days at the end of the year is going to teach him anything?" I ask incredulously. That's just an early start to summer vacation at this point.

"Well.. I..." Principal Grum stutters.

I put my hand up to stop him. "three-day suspension. For both. Neither kid gets any marks on their record." It's elementary school, for fuck' sake. A mark on their record means practically nothing at this age.

My gaze hardens when I look at Mr. and Mrs. Bushnell and point my finger. "But. You sign Archie up for at least three months at Gracie Martial Arts."

Ben's poker face slips for the first time, and his head whips toward mine.

"It's where Ben goes; they have a good program and *emphasize* doing the right thing."

I glance back at Ben to make sure he's okay with this, but his poker face is back, and he stares straight ahead.Cameron lights up at my suggestion: "Absolutely, that seems like a great, very fair idea!"

Calvin nods his agreement and then looks to Principal Grum and pats his shoulder. "I agree with Olivia as well. Let's write this up and get on with our afternoon. The boys can return to school on Thursday. Sound good, everyone?"

We all agree, and Principal Grum excuses us from his office. Cameron exits first, leaving his wife and son to scramble behind him.

I stand up and reach for Ben's hand again. He willingly takes it, and then Andrew motions for us to walk out in front of him. He lightly places his hand on the small of my back, guiding us out while offering a small amount of comfort I didn't know I needed. I might be a single-widowed mother, but at least I have people in my corner. Shockingly enough, I think one of those people might be Andrew.

Chapter Eight

Andrew

The engine humming and the tires thumping as they rotate on the pavement are the only sounds in the truck as we drive back toward the office. I can't help but glance at Olivia and Ben in the rearview mirror, the same look of shock, confusion, and a little anger clouding their features. It was almost hypnotic watching her defend Ben—unleashing a fiery side of Olivia that I haven't seen before. Not that I blame her; it's been a while since I felt as enraged as I did when I saw Ben sitting by himself in that chair.

I spot the little diner I eat dinner at a few nights a week, the SnowPeak, an idea already forming as I whip my truck into a parking spot. I turn around to see them both looking questioningly between me and the restaurant.

With an exaggerated shrug of my shoulders, I explain: "My dad used to say, 'There isn't a problem in the world that a good cheeseburger and milkshake can't fix, and if it doesn't fix it, at least you had a cheeseburger and milkshake.'"

Ben nods his head at me, like that's the best advice he's ever heard. Olivia looks at me with slightly parted lips, as if she were stunned that I am offering this to them.

She quickly shakes it off and then chuckles while helping Ben unbuckle. "Sounds like a wise man. Also explains Charlie's infatuation with this place the first year she moved here." I don't let my smile falter, even though that feels like a stab to my heart. Knowing how scared and alone Charlie must have felt almost kills me.

We settle into a small booth near the window; the red upholstery looks well-worn, with cracks and a few tears—a testament to countless late-night conversations and shared meals, I'm sure. These types of diners are my favorites. A place for locals and tourists to support a small business that special-izes in greasy food and good conversations.

As we waited for our waitress, I watch Ben and Olivia. She's the picture of patience, waiting for him to gather his thoughts; his youthful brain is no doubt wrestling with the day's events.

The waitress appears at our table—an older woman who looks like she's been working here for decades, her silver hair pulled tight into a neat bun with a giant smile. She's been my server almost every time I've come in, which has surprisingly been a lot these last few weeks. Maybe Charlie and I have that in common.

"Hey, sweetheart." She squeezes my shoulder and then glances at Olivia. "What do we have here? My two favorite customers, dining with my most frequent customer." She winks at me, and then a frown appears when she looks back at Olivia and Ben. "Where's my girl, Ellie, though?"

Olivia gives her a small smile and says, "Still in school."

Before she can ask any further questions, I give her my most charming smile and begin placing our order: "Three cheeseburgers, please." Then I glance at Olivia to see if we need more directions. "Ketchup only on Bens, please," she says as she points to him.

"Banana cream pie milkshake for me and..." I look at Ben, raising my eyebrows.

He peeks over at his mom, and when she nods, encouraging him to say what he wants, he blurts out, "Chocolate fudge brownie!" Then, calmer, he adds, "Please."

Olivia hands over the menus and says, "I'll have the banana cream pie as well. Thanks, Sandra."

When she glances back at me, she raises one perfect eyebrow. "Seriously? Banana cream pie?"

"What's wrong with that? You ordered the same!"

Olivia shakes her head, amusement dancing in her eyes. "I just hadn't pegged you as the sweet-tooth type." She rakes her gaze down my body, and I puff up a bit without realizing what I'm doing.

"Everyone's got their guilty pleasures," I shoot back, smirking.

I wiggle my eyebrows. "Mine just happens to come in greasy diner food and desserts."

She laughs in response, "Mhm, and what's this about 'most frequent customer?'"

"Everett and I eat her a few nights a week. We're not the best cooks."

Her smile doesn't quite reach her eyes this time as she worriedly glances at Ben. Noticing that the funk he was in before we ordered is back.

Sandra returns with our drinks and lets us know our burgers will be right out.

Ben takes a drink and then fiddles with the straw in the cup. Finally, he sighs, "Do you think Dad would be disappointed in me for getting suspended?"

I hold my breath, suddenly feeling like an intruder in the booth.

The only sign that this is affecting Olivia is the slight whimper she lets out. She clears her throat quickly, though. "Well, buddy, are you disappointed in yourself?" she asks casually, picking up her shake to take a drink.

"Not really; I did everything Coach told me to do. I told him to stop. Then, when he grabbed me, I reached around his waist, grabbed the opposite wrist, and then fell to my side. Once I felt in control, I told Theo to go find a teacher."

"I agree, so what makes you think dad would be disappointed?"

He looks at her, sadness written all over his face. "I still got in trouble."

Olivia lets out a small sigh. "Sometimes, even doing the right thing has consequences. But it's important to remember that standing up for yourself and others is always worth it, regardless of the outcome. It shows you have strength and integrity."

Ben doesn't say anything; he just continues fiddling with his milkshake straw.

"I'm proud of you. You've been in martial arts for four years. Four years of commitment, working hard, and practicing. Today was the first day you got to show everyone how much you've learned, and you helped someone in the process. That's something to celebrate, if you ask me.

"I almost clapped when I saw your takedown." I pipe up and then cringe.

I probably shouldn't have interrupted that moment, but Olivia looked at me with a massive grin on her face."Me too. I wanted to ask if he could rewind it and play it in slow motion."

Ben grins up at both of us, his shoulders finally relaxing from the tension.

Sandra brings our burgers over and lingers a little too long, making sure we have everything we need.

Ben takes a french fry and dips it in his milkshake. "So, do you think we can get a copy of that video? I want to show Coach! And Hayes!"

"Already on it, I texted Cal, and he agreed to email me the clip. I'll check when we get back to the office; maybe we can put it on the big screen in the game room."

Ben takes a big bite of his cheeseburger and smiles for the rest of lunch.

Guess my dad was right—not much a cheeseburger and milkshake can't fix.

We get back in the truck, and this time Olivia sits in the passenger seat next to me. She looked a million times more relaxed than she did when we left the office.

I can't help the uncontrollable laughter that starts when I think about Olivia in that principal's office. Ben looks at me through the rearview mirror. "What's so funny up there?"

"Just thinking how badass it was watching your mom go toe-to-toe with Principal Grum-py Pants back there.

"Ha! Ha! Very punny." Olivia rolls her eyes, but her lips are twitching from trying not to smile.

Ben snorts a laugh. "He's right, mom! You definitely lost your poker face a few times."

Olivia turns around in her seat, sticks her tongue out at Ben, and then laughs.

We head to the office, and everyone is back in. Most of the guys were upstairs chatting, so I motioned for them to meet us in the game room.

"Have a seat, gentleman! We've got a little clip to show y'all." My southern accent is coming out a little too much. I used to think it was only when I drank, but I haven't had anything today. I'm just happy, a feeling I haven't felt fully in a long time.

Hayes walks in first, a look of concern on his face when he sees Ben. "No school today, Benster?"

Ben stands in the front of the room, shuffling his feet. He looks like a deer caught in the headlights as all the guys file in, unintentionally ignoring Hayes's question.

"We'll get to that." I tell Hayes, as I walk by him, to stand next to Ben and wait for everyone to find a spot.

Hayes narrows his eyes at me, confusion covering his face as he tries to figure out the situation. It doesn't help that the last time we talked, I had majorly messed up with Olivia.

"Ben, here, became quite the hero today. He got suspended for it and everything, but he stepped up and put the welfare and security of others before himself. Think we got the makes of one of us..." I grip his shoulder and smile down at him.

He rewards me with a face-splitting grin.

I glance at Olivia sitting in the back; she's smiling, but her eyes are glistening with unshed proud tears.

"Olivia, could you do the honors and play the clip?" She nods and hits play on her phone. The screen behind us starts playing, and all the guys lean in to watch.

The murmurs of "Who's that kid" and "What the fuck" start to fill the space until Hayes begins shushing them, like if they stop talking, he will be able to hear the soundless video.

The room goes deadly silent when Ben enters the frame. The tension is palpable when Archie puts Ben in the headlock, and then the next second, Ben has the kid on the ground and everyone is on their feet cheering. A chorus of "rewind it" starts so that they can see the actual takedown.

Ben looks like a kid on Christmas morning, all smiles. Such a contrast to the tear-streaked face I saw just a few hours ago.

I'm thankful for these guys every day, but today especially.

A group of misfit, military-trained killers who have seen more terrible things than any human should ever see are cheering this little boy on like it's the coolest thing they've ever seen.

"Let's go, Ben! Do it to me! Show me exactly what you did." Lincoln, demands. The man looks like a hipster lumberjack—covered in tattoos, big burly beard, and always wearing a beanie. We served together for a few years, but he got out about a year before Hayes did because of a trauma wound. His exit was a little rougher than ours, but we're glad to have him here. He also played a vital role in finding Charlie, so I'm forever indebted to him.

As the guys all start taking turns doing takedowns and laughing with Ben, I go stand next to Olivia.

"Can we go talk for a second?" I motion toward her office.

She looks at Hayes. "Mind keeping an eye on Ben for a few minutes?"

Bypassing her office, she opens the door that leads to a balcony off the back of the building. An outdoor loveseat is the only furniture, so we sit next to each other. I've only been out here a few times, but the view is incredible. You can see the bustle of the little town with the mountains in the background.

"This was always my favorite place to hang out during the summer when Lovey was in charge. I even thought about picking up smoking, just so I had a reason to come out here."

"Yeah, why didn't you?" I ask, enjoying the easy banter we have now.

"Coughed so hard I threw up the first cigarette I ever had." She smiles her genuine smile and relaxes back onto the couch, putting her feet up on the railing.

I grin back. "Never been one of my vices either."

"Just banana cream pie milkshakes, then?"

"Occasionally. Or a good bourbon. Depending on how bad the day was."

"Ahhh."

I look back out at the town, preparing myself for the hard part. "So I guess it's safe to say you knew I was coming in to apologize earlier."

She nods her head and says, "Saw the peonies. They're beautiful, by the way."

"I fucked up pretty badly. I've got plenty of excuses, but to be honest, they are just excuses. I'm sorry that I didn't take the time to get to know you. I shut you down at every opportunity. You deserved more, especially after what you did for Charlie, and I see that now. I was misplacing a lot of resentment about the Charlie situation onto you. I made a lot of assumptions, and well, it turns out it did, in fact, make an ass out of me."

She laughs, "That's true; I let it happen, though, so I guess that only adage is true."

"Pfft, no, I'm the only ass here.

"Look, I know how hard it is to let people in and trust people you've just met. I was going out of my way to try to win you over, and I think it came off as insincere. We all have our own baggage."

"Yeah." We certainly do. "But I'd still like to make this right with you."

"If the whole Ben's bodyguard thing at the school hadn't made up for it already, pumping up his ego with all the guys would have. I worry about him, ya know? I'm so thankful he has Levi and Pop, even Hayes, but growing up without a dad isn't going to be easy. For Ellie, either, but she was so young when we lost Dan, I don't think she remembers much from before."

I nod, suddenly feeling protective. This family wormed its way into my heart faster than I thought possible. No wonder Charlie met them and then never left. They fill a hole I didn't even know existed.

"They're both good kids." We sit in silence for a few

seconds and then I bump her shoulder with mine. "You're a good mom, too."

She doesn't say anything back, and when I look at her, a small furrow between her eyebrows appears.

"I'm serious. The way you went to bat for Ben. Not once did you question him or degrade him, and then you did the same for that other kid." I let out a little chuckle and shook my head. "The restraint you held not to knock that mom's teeth out."

"Ha! I thought about it; I was mentally ripping her to fucking shreds." She gives me an evil grin and then sighs. "I know Ben, though; he's got a big heart and a good head on his shoulders."

She's describing herself without even realizing it. I can see the similarities between them so clearly—both strong and compassionate souls. "Yeah, just like his mom."

She gives me a bashful smile. "Probably. Ellie's all charm and show, like her dad was. People were just drawn in like magnets."

It seems to me like she's describing herself again, but I'm not ready to admit that to her or myself yet.

"He must have been a good husband." I try to ignore the swirl of jealousy I feel toward a ghost. But this man had everything I had ever envisioned growing up: the perfect wife and kids, the house, the career.

She crosses and then uncrosses her legs, fidgeting while clearly weighing her next words before she says them. "He was. To his career."

Shock ripples through my body. I turn to her, my mouth opening and closing.

She takes pity on my confusion and lack of words and continues on.

"He was married to the job. We barely saw each other

before the kids were born, but I chalked it up to us just starting out in our careers. Lovey was preparing for me to take over this flourishing company, even though I hadn't known it at the time. Dan had been a deputy for about a week when we met. We got married pretty quickly, and then I was pregnant with Ben a little after. It was all a whirlwind. Don't get me wrong, we had a good marriage, but it was a lot of going through the motions. The only real time we spent with him was when he would swoop in and cart us around town, showing us off. His goal was to take over for Pop as sheriff when he retired. I supported that —the long hours, the over-time, the volunteering—I just thought that was a marriage. Being a good support system."

I had no idea that she had felt that way about Dan. Then again, I didn't know he existed until yesterday. It's my own fault that I'm in a constant state of playing catch-up, but with every new piece of information, I crave more.

"Sounds like there's a *but* in there."

"Well, you've seen Charlie and Hayes..." She gives me a playful smile full of mischief and sexual innuendo.

A full-body cringe rolls through me. "Blech, don't remind me!"

She giggles so hard that the little couch shakes. I do my best to ignore how much I love that sound. "Exactly. The passion? It just got lost before it even had a chance to start."

I get that. I've been envious of what Charlie and Hayes have for a long time.

Before either of us gets a chance to say anything else, the door opens, and Charlie pops her head out. "Friends yet?" She asks in that sing-song voice she does.

I shove down the slight frustration I feel toward my sister for breaking up our bonding moment.

Olivia laughs and stands up. "The white flags have been raised. I should get going anyway. Pop picked up Ellie for me, but if he has her for too long, she will surely talk him into shopping and candy."

I can't help but notice she didn't answer Charlie's question. Are we friends? I can't remember the last time I had a friend who was a girl I wasn't related to. Sure, guys on my team had wives I was close to, but I wouldn't spend time with them if their husbands weren't there. Maybe Heather's friends? But honestly, I couldn't remember most of their names half the time.

That's when it hits me. I haven't thought about Heather since I talked to her yesterday before I went to dinner. Did I even text her this morning? I grab my phone to check. Four new texts sit unread from her.

The guilt starts to eat at me as I try to excuse my behavior. Nothing inappropriate happened between Olivia and me. I was genuinely trying to help out her and Ben. Then I needed to apologize for treating her so poorly. No lines were crossed. Yet, I still feel like I betrayed Heather somehow.

I immediately text her back an apology and swear I'll fill her in on Sunday.

Then I spend another twenty minutes staring out at the little town, trying to figure out just what the hell I'm supposed to do next.

Chapter Nine

Andrew

I stood in my bedroom, staring at the new clothes I had been pressured into buying earlier at Buckaroo Bill's Western Wear. Hayes had taken Everett and me, claiming that if we wanted to fit in at the rodeo tonight, we'd have to dress the part. Cowboy boots, pearl snaps, and wranglers were the order of the day—a stark contrast to the South Carolina prep we'd worn at home in our teens and the tactical clothing we'd thrown on in the military. As always, that sneaky bastard is like a chameleon, adapting to any environment with ease. I, on the other hand, feel like a fraud wearing a Halloween costume.

It doesn't help that I'm feeling antsy about going anyway. Crowds aren't really my thing anymore; I feel constantly on edge, waiting for something bad to happen. If Ellie hadn't insisted I come, I probably would have bailed already. It sounds like this is the biggest event the town has, attracting people from all around the state. I'm not sure what's so entertaining to people about grown men fucking up their bodies on bulls, but I understand why they do it—adrenaline junkies don't care how they get their high.

The ding on my phone alerts me to someone pulling into the driveway, and I walk to the front window to look out.

Everett whips in and hangs out the driver-side window of his brand-new Toyota 4Runner, gleaming white in the sunlight. "Get in, loser, we're going shopping!"

I stare at him deadpan—no doubt some chick-flick movie he's quoting again.

"Come on! Mean Girls?!"

I shake my head but still chuckle. "Whatever. Nice ride, asshole. You land yourself that job yet?" He's been trying to get all his information and licenses sent over and approved while he waits to apply for the flight search and rescue job here.

"Nah, just gonna keep cashing the checks you write me," he added with a cocky grin.

I roll my eyes at him dramatically. He acts as if he hasn't been a major asset to our team, but he's already brought three guys in and has contacts all over the world that are bringing in contracts. Between the three of us, our company has started to explode.

I walk around the new ride and admire it while he tells me everything they upgraded. It's lifted higher than normal with a state of the art suspension system, meaty off-road tires, and a sleek black leather interior.

"It's alright," I say sarcastically, admiring the details but still trying to mess with him.

He gave me a lopsided grin from over the top of the windshield. "Don't be a jealous prick."

I hop into the passenger seat, ready to just get this evening over with.

"So a little birdie told me you swooped in to help your frenemy the other day." Everett offhandedly mentions.

I let out a heavy sigh. I have no doubt Hayes is that little birdie; he gossips more than little old ladies at church. "Yep. I was heading into her office to apologize when she got the call from the school."

"You suddenly had the urge to play knight in shining armor?" Everett raises an eyebrow, clearly skeptical.

I chuckle, knowing exactly what he's thinking. Knight and shining armor roles have always been more of his and Hayes' thing, not mine. I keep my nose down and out of other people's business. "Look, she needed a ride; her car was getting serviced."

"I bet she did," he says with a smirk.

For fuck's sake.

"You're looking for something that isn't there." I'm not sure why I'm defending myself so much, but my hackles are raised by all of his comments.

"Cool, so you don't mind if I ask her out on a date?"

I almost gave myself whiplash, turning my head to look at him.

His mouth twitches at my reaction, and I sputter out, "What?"

He shrugs his shoulders, feigning innocence, "just a date. Two people, getting dinner and a drink."

"So you can fuck her and delete her number the next day?" Irrational anger rolls through my body. Everett is a manwhore when it comes to one-night stands and relationships. He gets plenty of women and never agrees to more than one date.

"Nah, man. Just fucking with you; I wanted to make sure my theory was right," he says with a cheshire grin.

"Yeah, what's that theory?" I unclench the fists that I hadn't realized I'd clenched and wipe my sweaty palms on my jeans.

"You have feelings for her. But you won't even admit it. Not even to yourself."

My hands freeze on my thigh as his verbal gut punch sinks in. I slowly turn my head to look at him, trying to keep my composure this time. "You think I have feelings for Olivia? Are you fucking serious? I've been with Heather for twelve years." I said, my voice full of disbelief and frustration.

"Hmm, notice how you didn't deny that you do have feelings. You seem to be getting very defensive about a so-called friend."

"Are you fucking with me right now?!" I roared at him. "You're calling me a cheater? Fuck you, man! I helped her; that's it."

Trembles rake through my body with the insinuation that I would be falling for someone else when I am clearly in a relationship.

He takes both hands off the steering wheel and holds them in a quick surrender. "Easy, brother. I'm not calling you anything." His mood shifts to deadly serious. "I know how loyal you are; I know you wouldn't cross a line. But that doesn't mean you aren't starting to realize that maybe your relationship with Heather isn't enough for you any more."

I shake my head as my molars grind together. I stare out the front windshield at the dry desert climate. My best friend's words hit closer to home than even I realized. The doubt has been creeping in for months now, and being called out on it makes it seem more real.

He takes my silence for what it is, but still gets one last jab in: "You and I both know you're choosing the safest route by being with Heather. You're guarding your heart behind a steel cage and dating someone who doesn't care to break into it." *Ironic, coming from the guy who's pining for a girl in a relationship.*

I'm too frustrated to even engage in this conversation. At

the end of the day, this is my relationship, and the decision is mine to make. He doesn't remember how good things were in the beginning. How much Heather helped me through the loss of my parents. I don't know if we will ever get back to that point, but I don't need anyone else's opinion on my relationship.

The atmosphere in the SUV suddenly became stifling as my thoughts whirled around. I'm not sure why his words are hitting so hard this time. Especially considering that the guys have questioned me about Heather before. Hayes jokes regularly that the only thing I half-ass is my relationship. I usually just let it roll off my back. Just because my relationship with Heather looks different from most doesn't mean I'm not invested in it.

Everett didn't utter another word after his thought-provoking declaration, electing to let me seethe in his brutal honesty. It's even more frustrating, considering he's always been the one to make light of serious matters.

I roll my window down as we approach the event grounds, trying to let the fresh air dissipate the tension in the cab.

Deputies on horses are guiding traffic, and my mind wanders to Olivia again. Does she know these guys? Did her husband do this sort of stuff? Does it hurt her to see them working a job that took her husband away?

Everett speaks first. "That's Luke Haynes, the sheriff," he says, pointing toward the man Olivia danced with at the wedding. I don't ask, but I'm curious what the situation is between the two of them. I don't think they're dating, but based on that dance, they could be more than just friends.

He gestures toward another guy walking toward the entrance, carrying a little boy. "Ethan and Jake Flacco. Ethan owns the Ponderosa Pines Tavern and the former NFL quarterback. The couple behind them are Mr. and Mrs. Mitchell, Isla's parents."

"Cool."

"Oh, come on. Lighten the fuck up. I said what I had to say and dropped it. Now put your big girl panties on and get over it."

"Fine." I reach for the handle on the door and then turn to him. "But you owe me a beer for ruining my perfectly good mood."

We hand over our tickets and head inside to grab beers and find our friends.

I'm still on edge over the shit Everett said on the way here, and it's not helping to have a mass of people clogging up my space.

We find the group sitting at the top of the bleachers. Hayes and three of the guys on our team, Lincoln, Keller, and Delta, all have their backs against the top wall, scanning the crowd. *Apparently, I'm not the only one feeling a little uneasy tonight.* In front of them, Charlie and Isla sit on one side of Olivia, happily chatting away. Ben, Ellie, and Levi sit on the other side of Olivia and laugh at something on Levi's phone.

I feel the familiar squeeze in my chest that I always do when I see Olivia. She has on tall cowboy boots and a short summer dress—her standard summer outfit so far. Her face lights up when she sees us, and she gestures to an open spot in front of her.

I shake my head but keep my facial expression neutral while I point to a very small spot next to Hayes. I don't miss the disappointment and confusion that crosses her face as she glances behind her. That spot would be tight for even Ellie, but I'm hoping everyone will make room when I force my way in. Luckily, they all move a few inches, and I squeeze in. Everett's conversation earlier has me still feeling rattled, and I need the distance to get my head straight with Olivia.

Everett, being the smug asshole that he is, chooses to plant himself right in front of Olivia. I know he's just trying to get a rise out of me, so when he wraps his arms around her in a big hug, I give him a condescending smirk and pretend it doesn't bother me.

The cheers and laughter of the crowd echo off the metal bleachers. We are about halfway through the events, and I hadn't realized how cool half this shit would be. Seeing grown men throw themselves off a horse to wrestle with a steer is a blast to watch.

I've done my best to avoid glancing toward Olivia, but when my gaze lands on her, I can't help but notice how nervous she looks all of a sudden. I watch her bend down and whisper something in Ben's ear, causing him to completely shut down and stare straight ahead. She then turned the other way and whispered something in Ellie's ear, giving her an encouraging smile. Ellie tucked herself into her mother's side, her little arms wrapping around her mother's waist.

I look at Hayes, and he already knows what I'm thinking before I even ask. He gestures with a head nod, his gaze staying fixed on the arena.

The crowd erupts in a cheer as three horses carrying men in uniform galloped into the center of the arena. Sheriff Luke Haynes led the horses, the American flag flying proudly behind him. Two additional horses followed him, one of which was carrying the Oregon State flag and the other the Cascadia Sheriff Department flag.

Luke pulled up to a halt and surveyed the arena, his gaze finally locking on Olivia's face. He hesitated for a moment before continuing to scan the crowd. The three riders' display of strength and patriotism in the arena captivated the audience. Meanwhile, I could only focus on Olivia and the kids.

Ben stood ramrod straight, his baseball cap already over his heart, as he stared into the center arena. Ellie kept one arm around her mom, but the other began fidgeting with the ruffles of her shirt. Seeing Olivia, though, almost broke me. Even though her chin was tipped up and her shoulders were back, I didn't miss the slight tremor in her hand that was around Ellie.

The men sat proudly atop their horses, their flags fluttering in the breeze. Luke sat in the center, showing his dominance while being a symbol of American pride. The crowd rose to their feet, and a hush fell over the arena as a woman belted out the lyrics to the National Anthem.

When the woman finished, the crowd erupted into cheers, but the men still stayed out there. It wasn't until the rodeo announcer began speaking again that I realized why Olivia and the kids looked tense.

"Today we remember and honor the courage and dedication of our men and women in uniform and the ultimate sacrifice some of them make. Daniel Turner, a beloved member of our community, was taken away from us too soon. Dan's family has been an integral part of this community for generations. He's remembered here by his wife, Olivia, and two children, Benjamin and Eleanor, who will continue to carry on his memory."

I barely hear the slight whimper from Olivia, but she stands strong and unmoving throughout the entire speech. Hayes reaches out when he hears it too, putting his hand on her shoulder, giving her the comfort I wish I could.

"Let us take a moment of silence in Dan's memory." The crowd stands in respectful silence, feeling the loss of a great man.

With her head held high and her kids close, she is the

epitome of strength and resilience. All around her, people had tears in their eyes, their hearts heavy with grief for Dan and the family he left behind.

After a few moments, the announcer begins to speak again. "Daniel Turner will never be forgotten, and his legacy will live on in our hearts forever."

Luke breaks away at a quick pace as he spurs his horse on, riding out of the arena to a roar of applause from the crowd.

Chapter Ten

Olivia

I took a deep, raggedy breath and turned toward Ben, trying my best to keep my smile in place. "Good job, buddy!"

He nodded, but still wouldn't make eye contact. "Can we go get a hot dog or something?" His little voice was barely audible over the crowd.

Ellie didn't miss it, though. That girl has the ears of a hawk when it comes to food. "And cotton candy!"

Mercifully, Levi stepped in and offered to take them, allowing me a few minutes of solitude. I always need a few minutes alone to shake off the stares and whispers that come with widowed-mother territory. However, as they started walking down the bleachers, my plans went up in some BDE flames. Ellie's spot suddenly filled with a large form that I recognized without even looking over.

He's always had a strange effect on my body; my mind feels calm, but my heart feels like it's going to beat out of my chest. I tried to breathe and calm the racing of my heart while I contemplated what to say. It's the first Dan spectacle he's been around for, and they always lay it on thick. I shouldn't feel as despondent as I do when they make the effort, but the grief feels multiplied and overwhelming by an entire audience watching us.

The hot summer evening suddenly feels stifling on the bleachers, and I can feel a bead of sweat forming on my forehead. I shift on the hard metal, trying to keep my face trained toward the pie-eating contest. My thigh unintentionally touches the roughness of his jeans, and I freeze while tiny bolts of electricity zap through me. I have to consciously make the effort to resist shifting away or leaning into him more. Being this close to him is both exciting and unsettling, stirring up a mix of conflicting emotions that make me feel insane. I can't even remember the last time I was so aware of any man.

His knee unmistakably bumps into mine, and my traitorous eyes glance down at the contact and up at him. His eyes are already waiting for mine to meet his, and the intensity sends a shiver down my spine.

"You okay?" he asks, his voice soft and hesitant.

I nod, unable to speak. It's almost laughable how nervous I feel around him. Every other man around us is equally attractive, but this one has me tongue-tied.

When he looks at me like that, it's difficult to remember that he's only here to check on me after that very public tribute to my late husband. That thought alone is like a douse of cold water, bringing me back to reality. I don't need to be caught up in my feelings towards someone who is not only in a relationship, but only trying to be a good friend.

"Yeah. They do it every year. This makes the third. It took us by surprise the first time; it had only been a few months since we lost Dan. Ben cried so hard that I had to take him home early. Pops tried to warn me, but even he didn't know what they had planned."

He nods his head in understanding, rubbing his large hand below his chin. "I can't imagine how hard that is for y'all."

I swallow down the lump that has formed in the back of my throat and quickly divert my gaze. "They mean well, but fuck, it takes days of mental preparation before any of these big events. It just feels like a big, monumental moment for the town and everyone here. But for me and the kids, it's like they're picking at a scab that will never heal. Then the next second, the crowd is cheering on a pie-eating contest, and the kids and I are left bleeding all over the bleachers."

Andrew lets out a muffled curse word and then sets his hand on my thigh, giving me a reassuring squeeze. "It's a shitty situation," he grumbles low in my ear. "But you've got plenty of people in your corner that know how to use a tourniquet."

His ability to go from serious to lighthearted catches me off guard, causing me to let out an uncharacteristically loud laugh. When I pull back to look at him, he's blessing me with a full-blown grin.

He winks and stands up, just as an overly excited Ellie comes running up, grinning from ear to ear, with bags of kettle corn and cotton candy. Ben is hot on her tail while juggling four hot dogs.

Levi trails behind, carrying sodas and a beer, with an impish look.

"Levi Turner, where is your backbone?" I pretend to reprimand him for letting the kids get whatever they want.

"They insisted they'd share with the group," he casually says back.

Ellie plants her little butt next to me, grabs a hot dog from Ben, and nearly inhales it.

"Hey, hey, slow down, little bug. You'll choke if you don't chew that properly," I remind her.

She finishes chewing, slowing slightly, and says, "Sorry,

Mommy! But Uncle Levi said, 'No sugar' until we've eaten all our food, and I simply cannot wait to try that cotton candy!"

I shoot a look at Levi, and his eyes are wide at her as he looks back and forth between us. "I didn't mean eat the whole thing in one bite, Ellie!"

"Gotta be very direct with that one." Ben nods his head toward Ellie and smiles. I'm so relieved that the surrounding energy has already lightened tenfold from what it was a few minutes ago. The men in my life are always stepping up to make sure we are okay, and without them, I have no idea how I'd survive.

When I glance over my shoulder, I catch Andrew watching us. His expression is unreadable, but the corner of his mouth is tugging up into a small, almost shy smile before he quickly looks away. He's always been so guarded around me, but those brief glimpses of emotion he can't seem to control feel like I'm winning a race I didn't know I was in.

The evening has flown by, the sun has already set, and the rodeo is finishing up their main event. The smell of dust and sweat is heavy in the air. The crowd in the stands has slimmed a bit, but most people are still actively cheering on the bull riders.

Levi, Lincoln, Delta, and Keller are out on the prowl looking for women. I have no doubt the four of them are going to end up bringing some lucky girls home tonight. Levi never had a problem in that department before, but now that he's hanging out with the "bod squad," he's in an entirely different league.

Ben moved to sit with some friends from martial arts that were a few rows down from us. I only winced a fraction when he asked. It seems like only yesterday that he was Ellie's age, and she was just a tiny tot sitting in my lap. Now he's getting old enough to ditch his mom and hang out with friends.

Charlie and Isla had to move down a row and spread out a touch to put an energetic Ellie bouncing around in the stands between them and Andrew and Hayes. Everett and I flank her sides, keeping her boxed in but still letting her live her best life. Her little eyes are wide with anticipation as she cheers on each rider's attempt.

Andrew and Hayes have been infected by her wild, sugar-induced energy and the few beers they've had. The three of them quickly became nothing but trouble. They're hollering at the Rodeo Clowns, spurring on more antics, and getting down-right rowdy whenever the music blares a 90s country song. Ellie knows every word, and I feel a sense of pride at my little one belting out Garth Brooks with the boys.

Sober Everett is almost as bad as them, constantly egging them on to do more and sing louder. Then again, the entire crowd seems to be having the time of their lives tonight. Our little group is just one of the masses laughing and singing along, cheering on the men surviving eight seconds on a nearly two thousand-pound animal.

The only tension left in the evening comes from Jeff, Isla's boyfriend, who is sitting in "box seating." He occasionally looks over at us, but always with a sneer. I have a feeling he doesn't love that Isla's office is now swarming with elitely trained men. His ego can't handle the fact that anyone might be better than him. He hangs all over his "high-class" friends, pretending like he's better than half the town. The funniest part is that one of those guys is Cameron Bushnell, Archie's dad. I know for a fact that Cameron thinks that Jeff is sleazy, but because Jeff's dad is the mayor, Cameron won't say anything. It's surprising how much Cameron's grown on me, but he seems to be a decent dad and lawyer. He's also brought his son to every class, and he actually seems to enjoy it. His wife, though, is still right there on my shit list with Jeff.

Hayes swoops up Ellie into his arms as they try to get the rodeo clown's attention for the hundredth time. They're shooting t-shirt's out of hand-held launchers, and Ellie has been trying her hardest to get one. I can't help but notice the way Charlie's been starry-eyed all evening over the two of them. They're so in love and drooly over each other most of the time that I almost didn't notice her hand resting lightly on her flat stomach. My eyebrows must hit my hairline as the puzzle pieces start fitting together. She isn't drinking tonight, her subtle hand placement, and I caught her crying yesterday morning because she spilled her tea. That girl is pregnant.

I glare at her until she notices and makes eye contact. I arch my brow in a silent question while taking a glance at her hand. For a split second, her face shows total surprise, but then she winks and quickly puts her finger to her lips to let me know it's still a secret.

I nod my head, letting her know that her secret is safe with me. But despite my best efforts, I can't help the wide grin spread across my face. Andrew, of course, is the only one to notice and call me out on it.

"Hey! What got you smilin' like that, Boots?" He asked, that southern drawl coming out thick, with an amused look on his face.

Something about the way he uses that nickname, like it's just between him and me, has me feeling things I know I shouldn't. It's like he lights a fire in my soul every time he uses it. That's something to worry about tomorrow, though. Tonight, I'm relishing in all my people being in one spot and happy.

"Just a damn good night," I beam at him.

His grin was a perfect mirror of mine as he nodded his head in agreement. His emerald-green eyes never leave mine. "A damn good night, indeed."

Chapter Eleven

Olivia

Andrew has been keeping his distance from me since the Rodeo two weeks ago. I feel like I should be surprised, but I've yet to understand what makes him tick. Occasionally, he's fun and friendly, maybe even flirty, but the next he's cold and distant.

I was trying to let it go and ride the rollercoaster, but Ellie insisted on knocking on his office door to invite him to our upcoming pool party. I'd been avoiding the interaction all week, but since it's tomorrow, I figured she wouldn't let me get away with that anymore. To be honest, it scares me how much I want him to come and how disappointed I'll be if he can't.

I glanced over, and he seemed to only be scrolling on his computer, so I took a deep breath and mustered up the courage to join Ellie as she walked to his office door.

"Remember, this is his work; he's probably very busy, so knock and ask if it's a good time. Let's make it quick so we aren't bugging him."

"Psh, mom, we could never bug him! He's my bestest

friend!" She says it like it's the most obvious thing in the world. After their little rodeo mischief, she's been calling him her "bestest" friend. At first, I thought it was cute, but since the cold shoulder has been activated towards me, it's now making me nervous.

She runs over, knocks on the door frame, and peeks her little head in. "Hey, Mr. Drew. You busy? My mom said I could invite you to our party tomorrow! It's a pool party, so you gotta wear your trunks! Do you have trunks?" I swear she said it all in one breath.

I'm hanging outside the office, examining my boots, and trying to look anywhere but at the man sitting at his desk. I'm trying so hard to seem nonchalant that I almost miss him declining the invitation. "Sorry, Ells! I wish I could make it, but Heather is coming to town. We've got some plans already made."

My head snaps up just in time to see her little face fall. She gives him a weak smile and says, "That's okay, another time."

The man looks downright devastated, seeing her trying to be stoic. He looks up at me, hoping for some type of guidance, but I don't offer any. This girl knows how to throw on the theatrics to get her way. It's nice to have those puppy-dog eyes used against someone other than me.

"I'm really sorry, Ellie. Maybe I can."

Everett interrupts him by stalking past me and swooping Ellie up into his arms.

How are all of these guys so stealthy? I didn't even know he was in the building, let alone the office.

"No worries, Princess! I'll be there, and I'm way more fun than that guy!" He gives Andrew an overly dramatic wink.

I don't miss the tension that sets in Andrew's jaw and the way his eyes narrow at Everett, but before he can say anything, his work phone starts ringing. He glances at it and sighs, "I gotta take this. Billionaire oil tycoon is under threat, and his daughter is becoming a major target. There's already been an attempted kidnapping, and she's trying to refuse security."

Everett nods and offers his advice: "Send Keller. He'll know how to talk her into it, and he won't stick any body parts where they don't belong."

Whatever Andrew was thinking when Everett swooped in is clearly gone because he nods his appreciation and tells him thanks before answering his phone.

Everett carries Ellie out of the office just as she's asking, "What is it, and why doesn't it belong there?"

He stammers, 'Uh, his hand... caught in the cookie jar,' while gesturing with his hand.

She nods, like that's a completely appropriate response.

I bump my shoulder into him as we walk over to my office. "Nice save."

"I always forget how inquisitive this little one is," he says, tickling her belly. "Thank God you don't have a quarter jar or something like that. I'd be broke."

"Nah, the kids understand some words are "adult words" and some words are "kid words."

"Just like drinks, Mommy," Ellie adds.

I reach for her and say, "You're very right, love bug."

I sit at my desk in the office, relieved that the workday is almost over and the kids haven't mentioned my birthday. I've kept them occupied in the game room. Ben has a new Marvel Lego set to play with, and Ellie has a dance mat that connects to the TV.

I'm close to shutting down my computer for the day when I look up and see Charlie and Hayes carrying at least a dozen balloons and what appears to be a huge cake box.

Internally, I groan while trying to hide my grimace behind my computer screen. I was so close to getting out of here without a scene! It's not that I don't like my birthday. It's just that, if I know Charlie, she's already invited everyone in the building up here to celebrate.

Ellie and Ben try to stealthily run to help Charlie set up, but I can hear the giggles and chatter the entire time. I'm not surprised these little traitors are in on the surprise office party.

I shrink a little in my seat, praying I can disappear behind the computer.

Ten minutes later, I hear the puttering of little feet heading my way. I quickly close my computer down and prepare myself to throw on my happiest face.

"SURPRISE, MOMMY!" Ellie comes barreling through the open door. I open my mouth and widen my eyes, pretending to be shocked as I look to the kitchen to see a fully decorated birthday party, banners, and streamers included.

"Oh my goodness, all this for *me?!*"

I pick her up, and she wraps her little arms around my neck in a loose hug. "Yes! Charlie and I planned the whole thing!"

"I planned a little too," Ben grumbles with a bashful look. I pull him into Ellie and me, hugging them both.

"I must be the luckiest mommy in the entire world to be blessed with you two!"

The kids half drag and half guide me towards the seemingly very cramped kitchen. Hayes and his entire team (sans Andrew), Everett, and Isla are now confirming my earlier anxiety. It's a full-office party, and all eyes are on me.

It never fails to surprise me how much space these guys take up, just with their sheer masculinity. Five men, all of different heights and builds, fill up a room that could easily fit twenty.

"Happy Birthday!" A chorus shouts at me as I walk through the doorway.

No need for blush today; I'm sure my cheeks could stop traffic. "Thank you!"

Hayes embraces me first; he must have noticed the terror in my eyes because he is already grinning. "I promise this is all we have planned!"

I make my way through the group, thanking them for the birthday wishes, and finally get to Charlie, who is cutting the cake.

"It's your favorite, so you can't even be mad!"

Truly, it is. Ice cream cake with the little fudge bits. *Chefs kiss.*

"Not mad.. Only slightly flustered being the center of all this manly attention."

Uh oh. That grin she's wearing looks almost evil. I guarantee that was her plan all along.

I take my cake from her outstretched hand and turn to find a place to sit.

One of the guys, Keller, gestures to the open chair next to him. Ben is already seated at the same table, as are Lincoln and a man they jokingly referred to as 'Delta,' all devouring huge cake slices.

I sit by them, easily chatting about the summer activities they have planned—hiking, mountain biking, whitewater rafting, and the places they've been thinking about camping. I throw out a few other must-sees around us and watch their adrenaline-junkie eyes light up. I know these are the most elite-trained men in the country, but right now, they just seem like regular dudes shooting the breeze with a boy and his mom.

Keller is the easiest to talk to; he's not the shortest of them all, but he's clearly a few inches shorter than Hayes and Everett. He practically oozes charm, and has the perfect smile, with thick blonde hair. Honestly, he looks like Paul Walker and Ryan Gosling had a baby. Speaking to him for more than two minutes, and I can clearly see that Everett was right earlier—this man could talk the panties off a nun.

I don't mind sitting with them, but it's growing exponentially harder to avoid looking at the office directly in front of me. A pissed-off Andrew is pacing his office while talking on the phone. I'm guessing it's about the Oil Tycoon still, but I can't help but wonder why the one time we made eye contact, his eyes seemed to bore into mine with regret and guilt.

Andrew

The Oil Tycoon, John Kach, is about to hear me lose my shit on him.

I've been discussing the contract and our non-negotiable protocols with him for over three hours, and he has an argument for everything. I was so engrossed in the call that I missed an entire party being set up and starting in the kitchen. It wasn't until I heard muffled cheering that I looked up to see a pink-cheeked Olivia and the entire crew clustered around the marble island, with a giant cake box in the middle.

I can't even focus on what this guy is bitching about now.

My mind feels slow as it processes the scene unfolding. Charlie is cutting a very large cake, Ellie is fluttering around playing with the balloons, and Olivia smiles brightly as she takes her sweet time hugging each of the guys.

Did Keller just lift her off the ground? Is his hand touching her ass? Why the fuck is she hugging all of them?

I inhale deeply through my nose, and my heartbeat feels

like it's hitting harder than normal. The realization hit me like a Mac truck.

It's her fucking birthday.

I start pacing my little corner office, trying to focus back on John Kach, but I'm in spiral mode. His questions are bullshit, and after another ten minutes, I snap. "Listen, John, you want the best; we have the best. Protect your daughter or not; I don't care. We have protocols for a reason. The client is the one being protected, not the one who is paying us. If she declines security, that's it. Either way, you sign, and you pay. I've got a guy who is well-trained and versed in dealing with difficult people. Take him or leave him."

He pauses a second longer than agrees. "Fine. He better be worth it. Send the paperwork today."

He ends the call, and the small moment of relief I feel evaporates when I see Olivia laughing at something Keller is saying. As much as I like this guy, I can't stand him right now. At least I know he will be spending the next six months playing babysitter to a billionaire heiress who wants nothing to do with her father. I get the added bonus of knowing he will be keeping his grimy hands to himself.

Everett was right, though; Keller has nearly as many sisters as Joey did on Friends. He knows how to handle whatever a woman can throw at him and never crosses any professional lines. He was our top choice to interview women during or after a mission. It was like they took one look at him and couldn't stop the words coming out of their mouths.

I throw my work phone onto the desk and storm into the kitchen. Charlie is still standing by the marble island, and I whisper shouted to her. "Is there a reason no one told me today was Olivia's birthday?"

She looks at me with a mix of surprise and indignation. "Uhm, didn't you see the text?"

"Obviously not," I grind out.

"Not my problem, brother, dearest. What's your deal, anyway?"

I ignore her and walk over to the table most of them are sitting at.

Olivia has her back to me, but Ben sees me and grins. "Hey, Drew! It's my mom's birthday; want some cake?"

I try to pass as easygoing, but the rigidity in my body is probably giving me serial killer vibes. "Thanks, my man! I'm going to get one in a second. Was hoping I could talk to your mom first, though."

I don't miss the way her entire body tenses at first. Then she turns with the sugary fake smile she gives the town and stands to follow me. I ignore all the side glances everyone gives me as we walk by; it isn't any of their business.

I head toward the side door that leads to the same balcony where I made my first apology. The summer heat is already sweltering, but at least the balcony has some shade right now.

I hold the door open for her, and she squeezes by, opting to stand on the far side of the small balcony while I sit on the couch. Her body language is telling me she would rather be anywhere but here right now. She hasn't made eye contact, she's been fidgeting with Dan's wedding ring, and her lip is going to bleed if she chews on it any harder.

"Wanted to apologize; I didn't know the party Ellie was inviting me to was your birthday party."

She nods, still avoiding eye contact. "There's nothing to apologize for. You're busy, and it was a last-minute invite. She understands, but she also knows how to guilt into submission with those pitiful eyes."

"I'm going to talk to Heather and see if we can make it." That finally gets her attention, her eyes snapping down to me, eyebrows furrowing together.

"It's really okay. You don't need to change plans for us." Her defensive tone catches me off guard. The insecure side of me has me wondering if she didn't tell me until the day before because she was hoping I wouldn't come. For some reason, that only makes me want to push harder.

"I want to." Sincerity dripped from my voice.

"I'm sure Heather will be happy to see everyone too." That's not entirely true; she hasn't asked about anyone in a long time, but I'm hopeful it's just an out-of-sight, out-of-mind thing.

She immediately looks away, and her mouth snaps shut into a frown. I'm still trying to process her reaction when she looks back at me with that damn fake smile.

"Whatever works for you both, we'd love to have you, but no worries if you can't make it."

Even though it grates on my nerves, I force a smile to match hers. "Thanks; I hope we can."

I stand up and suddenly feel very close to her on this small balcony. I turn to retreat inside when she reaches out and grabs my arm.

I pause for a moment and then turn to look into those panicked, honey-colored eyes. "Look Andrew..."

"You can call me Drew, if you want." I don't necessarily want her tow. Somehow it's become our thing. But I know that I should at least give her the option. The wedding debacle seems like a lifetime away now, and I don't even remember why I was adamant that she called me Andrew anyway.

A small smile plays on her lips. "I'll consider it."

We stand there in awkward silence for a few breaths, just staring at each other, and then she shakes her head to clear it. "Will you not mention that you might come to Ellie or Ben? They'll take 'maybe' as a yes, and I don't want them to be disappointed. Ben, especially, idolizes you. He'd be really bummed if he got his hopes up and then you didn't come."

I never thought the weight of two kids' opinions could feel so heavy, but I find myself caring more about what Ellie and Ben think than I do most adults.

Nodding my head, I turn and walk back inside. This conversation didn't go at all how I expected it to, but it seems none of ours do most of the time.

Chapter Twelve

Olivia

The morning was frantic getting everything set up for the party, and the kids did their best to help, but I felt lame throwing myself a party. I should be used to it by now, but for some reason, it's hitting a little harder this year. For so long, it felt like I had to prove that I could do everything alone, but now it's just starting to feel lonely.

Charlie dropped off the decorations she used at the office yesterday, per the kid's request. Balloons, random streamers, and a banner I hadn't even realized she had put up. I spread them all out on the patio out back, appreciating that it's a large space. A few balloons are by the corners of the pool, the banner is hanging in the window behind the outdoor dining table, and the streamers are loosely strung from the juniper beams of the ceiling. Seeing the cheesy decorations almost makes me cringe, but I continue to convince myself it's for the kids.

I spent nearly an hour trying to decide what to wear, how to do my hair, and how much makeup to wear. Just standing in my walk-in closet, spinning in circles, as I realized I hadn't gone shopping in years. The thought of having a surplus of hot men parading themselves around my pool made me almost queasy. I still don't even consider myself "on-the-market," but that doesn't mean I don't want to look good.

I settled on loose waves that could easily be thrown up and a little extra makeup, but only waterproof, so I wouldn't end up looking like a drowned raccoon. My favorite black one-piece swimsuit, which gives me a waist and makes my boobs look phenomenal, cutoff denim shorts, and a white button-down coverup that I can leave open. It's almost amusing that I spent so long obsessing over what to wear, only to wear something so casual.

The one thing I don't have to worry about is food. Ethan, my lifelong friend, offered to have his restaurant cater with my favorite foods. He bought the Ponderosa Pine Bar and Grill when he moved back to town a few years ago. It's the best upscale restaurant in town, thanks to him. Despite the circumstances of his moving back, he's been a blessing in our lives. Ethan didn't know the first thing about babies and became the single dad of a newborn overnight. He showed up back in town a few days after that, and since then, Jake and Ellie have been inseparable.

It's supposed to be the hottest day we've had, and it's already hit mid-eighty, before three o'clock. We typically have hot, dry summers, but that doesn't usually start until at least mid-July. I'm not complaining, though; it makes the perfect day for a pool party.

I glance around the backyard; it seems like everyone who can make it is already here. A mixture of disappointment and relief fills me as I take note that Andrew and Heather didn't come.

Pops volunteered to be on kid duty and is watching Ben,

Ellie, and Jake splash around the pool. We are all sticklers for water safety, but the guys are especially. Pops, Dan, and Levi have all been dispatched to accidental drowning incidents, and those experiences have made them all hyper-vigilant around water. Pops and Levi both spent hours testing out the sliding pool deck cover to make sure it was safe before we even moved into the house.

Charlie and Hayes are perched on the loveseat, with him lovingly massaging her feet. He's been doting on her every move since he found out she was pregnant. They decided to tell everyone last weekend that they're expecting and due in February. Even though it's still early, they felt those closest to them should be in the know.

Cooper and Lincoln are playing cornhole against Everett and Delta. I have a feeling competition runs thick with everyone in this room, but especially between these guys. It's Army vs. Navy right now, and the shit-talking has hit an all-time high. Fortunately, the kids are playing too hard to pay them any attention.

Ethan is acting as bartender right now to Levi and Keller while they sit at the outdoor bar.

I bump into Ethan's elbow with my shoulder; he's almost a foot taller than my 5ft 6in, so I have to look up at him any time I talk to him. "You brought the food, and you're playing bartender? This is the best birthday ever!"

He chuckles, but doesn't even look up as he mixes a margarita for Levi. "Even better than in 4th grade when Lovey brought the full Sundae bar into school?"

I let out a small gasp. "I almost forgot about that!"

Keller looks between us confused and asks, "Why would that be the best?"

"The "Sundae bar" had all the regular fixings but also cupcakes and cookies, and she brought it for lunch."

Ethan steps in, finishing my thought. "Every kid in our class was hopped up on so much sugar that Mrs. Burton couldn't get us to do anything the rest of the day."

It was one of the best days of my life. Mrs. Burton threw such a fit that they almost stopped letting parents bring desserts in, but Lovey "apologized," and from then on, they sent out strict guidelines about how much sugar was allowed.

Levi laughs. "Yeah, well, Mrs. Burton was a bitch. She sent me to the principal's office like three times."

I mock him. "Didn't every teacher send you to the principal's office?"

He shrugs, but his smile is unapologetic. "They were all bitches."

I can't help but laugh. Levi has always been charming but a troublemaker. Dan had always acted like his moral compass when they were younger, but he still tried to push the limits as far as he could. Still does.

Ethan startles me out of my laughter when he yells, "You made it!"

I look up to see Luke walk out of the back doors of my house, followed by Andrew and Heather.

I'm shocked to see all three of them, to be honest. However, Luke is the one who has me gasping and shrieking with excitement.

It's been a few years since Luke last made it to a party. From work to checking in with his girlfriend, Madelyn, he never has time for socializing. He not only carries the weight of our little town on his shoulders, but his personal life is just as heavy as the rest. Madelyn was in a car accident the day that Dan was killed. He was already at the hospital when Dan was brought in, waiting for her to get out of surgery. She survived but needs long-term, around-the-clock care after suffering from anterograde amnesia. She can remember everything before the accident but can't create new memories. Luke visits her almost every day in the care-facility she lives at. He doesn't talk about it much, but I know how much it weighs on him that she's been stuck in an endless loop from three years ago.

I ran around the counter and met Luke halfway. I all but jumped on him, giving him a big hug and soaking up the moment. I pull back my head a little to see his face. "I'm so glad you're here. Can you stay a bit? Have a drink?"

He beams back at me. "Yep. Zeke insisted I take the next 24 hours off, and if shit hits the fan, he would cover."

Pop gives him a big dad hug. "Of course I will. I told you I would. Anytime you need me." Luke took over as sheriff about a year after our collective doomsday happened. Pop had already been thinking about retiring, and he knew Luke needed a distraction.

I glance behind them and realize I'm being a terrible host for ignoring the second surprise that walked out the door.

My smile is still natural as I move around Luke and Pop. I'm actually feeling glad they made it; seeing them together is helping me get over my little crush. Plus, I know Ellie will be stoked to see her "bestie."

Charlie and Hayes are standing next to Heather and Andrew, greeting them, so I stand off to the side and wait for a break in conversation.

Heather is the epitome of hot girl energy; her cut-off denim shorts are paired with a beautiful off-the-shoulder white crop top that has a lace red floral design. She looks like she just left the salon with her thick buttercream blonde hair and loose, large curls. *Jessica Simpson, who?*

Andrew glances toward me, so I awkwardly take my opportunity. "Hey! Thank you so much for coming!"

Heather doesn't even so much as look at me, seemingly very engrossed in congratulating Charlie on the baby.

Andrew looks... Almost annoyed? I try to get a read on his facial expression, but in a blink, it's perfectly masked in indifference. "Yep. Happy Birthday."

Gut punch. The disappointment of his reappearing cold shoulder falls over me like a sneaker wave. Yesterday, he acted as if he wanted to be here and felt bad he couldn't make it. Today, he's looking at me like I'm the burden interrupting his big plans.

He hands me a small envelope with my name written on it. The masculine writing makes my stomach do flips, but I shove down the unwarranted feeling.

I glance up at him, hoping to get a sliver of emotion, only to see his carefully blank expression still in place. "Thanks; you didn't have to get me anything."

With a small, single nod, he shifts his body back toward Charlie and Heather.

Feeling dismissed and a little bewildered, I look to Hayes. His eyes seemed to spark the same confusion mine had. I shrug my now sagging shoulders and give a small head shake, hoping he won't press him on it. Hayes furrows his brow in response, but ultimately lets it go.

Everett starts shouting from behind the guys. "I see you for what you truly are! Which is OO-GLAY!"

I looked between Hayes and Andrew. "Did he just quote, 'She's the Man?'"

Hayes chuckles. "Probably. He's always loved chick-flicks. Come on, let's go make sure Everett and Delta don't get their asses kicked."

I try to shake off that weird encounter as they walk away. I'm always a step behind how he's feeling, and today is no different.

Charlie's smile is radiant as she talks about the baby. "I know, we are due at the end of February! Thankfully, Liv saved so much baby gear that we are set on a lot of the big stuff."

A look of horror and shock crosses Heather's face. "Won't it be a little dated, and doesn't that stuff, like, expire?" She shakes her perfectly blonde head in bewilderment. "Her kids are just so much older."

Wow, two minutes in, and the shots are already being fired.

Charlie just shrugs her off. "Meh, I'm not worried about that. Plus, I was with her and picked out most of Ellie's stuff anyway."

I laugh and take the opportunity to speak up. "That's true! And if we didn't go together, I just sent you to pick out whatever you thought would look good."

Heather finally deigns to look in my direction, seemingly just noticing I'm here. Then she places a big fake smile on her face. "In that case, I bet it's all amazing!"

She steps over and gives me a half-hug. "Thanks for inviting Drew and me! Your house is just so... homey." The words coming from her mouth sound positive, yet the intentions behind them screams otherwise.

My gut clenches, and I swallow my sarcastic retort. "Thank you, and thanks for coming! I know you two have plans, so I appreciate you being here."

She gives me a coy smile. "Don't worry, we aren't staying long."

Thank god.

I smile, even though I want to roll my eyes. "All right, Ethan is mixing the best cocktails." I gesture toward the bar. "And if you need a swimsuit, there are some brand-new ones inside." I point to the doors behind the outdoor kitchen.

Heather never missed a beat. Her eyes raked down my entire body and then back up again. "That's okay; I doubt we are the same size anyway."

Charlie's jaw becomes practically unhinged after hearing Heather volley insults at me. I'm sure she wants me to stand up for myself, but I'm not trying to pick a fight with Heather. Especially since Andrew and I are barely on good terms.

I give a fake laugh, like I'm so dumb that I missed the dig. "Of course not! I try to keep an array of sizes in there. All new. Just in case someone doesn't have one."

I shrug nonchalantly and start to back away. "I should go help Ethan with the drinks."

I quickly turn and march back over to the guys at the bar, feeling a little uneasy and a whole lot awkward.

Ethan's still back there, slicing some limes while staying involved in the conversation; he's still a natural, even though he only helps out behind the bar when he's needed.

I start to make myself busy by tidying up the bar, basically just moving things around, and then end up knocking over a bottle of tequila. Ethan catches it before it even hits the counter.

"Are you okay?" he says quietly enough for only me to hear.

My shoulders slump in defeat. "That woman will never like me."

"Who? Drew's girlfriend?"

I roll my eyes. "Yep. Everything she says to me is an insult disguised as a compliment. I'm trying to ignore it, though."

He softly touches my elbow, turning me to look at him. "You don't always have to take the high road. If she crosses a line, stick up for yourself."

I nodded, my eyes suddenly feeling a little misty. "I know that I should, but I want to keep the peace with Andrew and Charlie—not have a cat fight at my birthday party."

"What a way to start out, 29! My bets are on you, though. Don't forget, I saw you break Lynn Hopkins' nose."

My jaw fell slack. I can't believe he would call me out like that. "I was 16, she was sleeping with my boyfriend, AND she bitch slapped me first!" My voice rose to an uncharacteristically high pitch at the last part, causing Levi and Keller to look up.

Lincoln mocks surprise, his brown eyes going wide. "You, Ms. Perfect, did what?!"

Shit.

I put my hand up, trying to end the conversation. "It doesn't matter. Ethan was just being an asshole." I shoot a glare at Ethan, which just causes him to chuckle.

Keller smirks, pretending to rub his nonexistent beard, and then points at me. "You know, Liv. I'd pay good money to watch you in a cat fight."

Cocking my head to the side, I raise my eyebrow at him. "How much we talking, Kell?"

"How much you...?" He doesn't get to finish his question before a large hand is squeezing his shoulder, cutting him off. Keller's head snaps to the side, and when he sees that it's Andrew, his eyes widen a fraction, but he doesn't back down; his cocky grin only gets wider. "What's up, Reynolds?"

"You got your bags packed? You leave tomorrow morning." His gruff voice sends shivers down my spine, and I have to look away. I knew that the contract went through, but I was still a little bummed that it happened so quickly. It's starting to feel like a revolving door of men around here, and the second I become friends with one, they're leaving.

"Yep, all good. Wanted to make sure I got to celebrate Liv's birthday." Andrew glances my way for the first time, and I quickly turn around to keep busy in the kitchen. I have no doubt my face is fifty shades of red right now.

"You want something to drink?" Ethan asks from behind me.

Heather's chirpy voice answers. "Sure, what's back there that isn't bottom shelf?"

I'm glad my back is turned so she can't see my sneer. *"Bottom shelf?"* Every liquor bottle is mid-to-top shelf, but she just can't resist the dig.

Ethan's tone raises no illusion that he's pandering to her. "Literally everything. Liv knows more about expensive liquor than I do, and I own a bar." He's not wrong there; I spent a morning helping him with his first liquor order when he bought the bar. He was completely clueless because he's never been a big drinker and was always too focused on football and getting to the NFL. Even after he got drafted, alcohol wasn't one of his vices. The one time he got a little too drunk, well, Jake happened.

I spent the next hour bopping around the party, trying to make sure everyone was having fun. The kids played happily in the pool, with Pop watching them. Most of the guys rotate between the pool and the bar.

Charlie, Hayes, Everett, Andrew, and Heather have been sitting on the patio couches, laughing and catching up most of the time. I tried to sit with them, but I felt like an outsider listening to most of the stories they reminisced about, so I ended up excusing myself to set up the food.

Ethan brought enough to feed an army. I guess with these guys, you have to, but as I stand back and look at the spread, it looks far too excessive. He brought sandwiches and paninis, six different side dishes, multiple salads, a full charcuterie board, and desserts. It looks like we are having a wedding, not a small birthday party. I look over at him, still playing bartender, and yell his name to get his attention.

He looks up at me, and I gesture at the table, eyebrows raised, like, "What the fuck?"

His laugh is loud, and then he yells "Happy birthday!" back at me.

My returning smile is undeniable. It feels good to have friends who go above and beyond for me.

I walk toward the bar and let everyone know the food is out and they should eat. Then I helped the kids get a plate and set them up at the smaller kids table we have off to the side.

Twenty minutes later, almost everyone, except Heather, had already grabbed a plate and finished eating. The kids are already back in the pool after scarfing down their food as fast as they could.

I settle into the lounge chair next to the one Isla is sitting in. Charlie and Hayes relax in the same loveseat they have claimed as their own, and Heather sits across from Isla and me. I couldn't help but notice Andrew scurrying away as fast as he could when I sat down, but I'm trying to ignore the pang I felt when he did.

Charlie finishes her second plate of food and then looks at Heather and says, "Are you going to grab something to eat? It's all so good! I'm seriously considering getting thirds."

Heather looks at the full spread and then cringes. "I can't eat most of that; I'm on a new diet that is really strict. Only whole foods."

Isla, being our resident health nut, smiles at her and says, "I think I've heard of that! No sugar, no gluten, nothing processed, right?"

Sounds like no fun.

She beams back at Isla, "Yes, I feel incredible too!" Then she looks directly at me when she says, "I've lost like five pounds; you should totally try it, Olivia. I guarantee you'll lose all the baby weight. I'll send you the book!" *This bitch.*

The hits just keep coming. My fake smile is feeling more like a grimace, but I still manage a nod. "Thanks; I'll think about it."

She does look incredible, but at what cost? Not eating at a

birthday party? I'm all for balance; making sure we are an active family that also eats healthy options, but not enjoying desserts at a party? It seems sacrilegious.

"It would be so good for you! And your family. Even Ellie would probably get used to it, and since she has your body type, it's important to get on top of stuff like that.

My jaw hits the floor with that. Is she seriously insulting a five-year-old? My perfect five-year-old?! That is completely within a normal size for height and weight for her age? Is she serious?

This dumb broad doesn't even know the line she just crossed. I sit up straighter in my chair, about to go off, when I hear the unmistakable growl of a pissed-off Hayes.

I look over, and he's now sitting up too, his relaxed position gone. He leans forward, placing his forearms on his knees. His clenched jaw is showing no mercy. This is the first time I've ever seen him look like the true, menacing badass I've heard he can be. "What the fuck did you just say?"

Despite the music being on and the fact that Hayes didn't even raise his voice, his tone has everyone sitting at the bar turning in our direction. It's not often that Hayes sounds like he's ready to rip someone to shreds, and based on their faces, every guy on his team looks at him like they're ready to have his back.

Andrew is already on his feet, stepping in our direction, his eyes bouncing between the three of us.

Heather's shocked face blinks at Hayes as she opens and closes her mouth. Finally, she mumbles out, "I just... I meant, this program is so good, they could benefit from a health adjustment. Everyone here could, really." If she hadn't just insulted my kid, I would have laughed. Every guy here has a body-fat percentage equal to an elite athlete. I think they're doing just fine.

"Are you...?" Hayes starts his voice raising slightly, but this time I cut him off.

"It's time for you to go." I stand up, holding my palm out to stop Hayes. This is my battle, and I need to handle it. I've been avoiding a fight with her all day to keep the peace, and I shouldn't have. I just didn't think she would go so far as to bring my kids into her negative bullshit.

Her eye blinking picks up more rapidly, and her gaping mouth is hanging so far open that I would feel bad for her if she hadn't been downright awful the entire time.

"You are a vile human being to talk about a healthy five-year-old like that." I'm careful not to raise my voice, but I guarantee my tone is lethal.

Andrew quickly steps between the two of us. He's only looking at me, concern etched on his face. "What's going on?"

Heather stands up behind him and nearly screeches. "They're attacking me!"

Charlie starts laughing with a truly maniacal laugh. "Attacking you? You've been a bitch the entire time, and if Liv hadn't muzzled all of us, you would have been cursed out an hour ago!"

I glance at my best friend; she looks as vengeful as Hayes did. I was hoping it never came to them picking sides, but I'd be lying if I said I wasn't relieved. Charlie is just as much family to me as Levi and Pop, I'd hate for anyone to come in between us.

Heather looks stunned at Charlie, like she can't believe she isn't sticking up for her. "Charlie, are you serious?"

Charlie starts arguing, but I interrupt her. "Andrew, please just go." I threw my hand out to the side, gesturing toward the door they came in through. Those beautiful green eyes of his flashed to mine, looking unmistakably hurt and pissed off. I don't know if that anger is toward me, the situation, or Heather, but right now, I don't care. I don't want his friendship if this is the type of woman he loves and brings around.

He gives me a single nod and looks at Heather. "Let's go."

Not caring to listen to whatever she says next, I walk past the two of them and plant myself at the bar in between Keller and Luke. Both men lean their shoulders onto mine, and it feels like an impenetrable wall of support holding me up.

I peered over my shoulder at the kids, praying they didn't hear any of that. Levi is splashing them with the water floaties; they're blissfully unaware of everything that just went down.

Pops sits on the edge of the pool with his sunglasses on, and when he catches me looking, he raises his eyebrow in question. I shrug my shoulders in return and hope he drops it. If I know Pops, though, he's going to have more questions than I have answers to.

It's not long until I hear the door click shut behind them.

It feels like all eyes are on me now, trying to gauge my reaction to how we proceed with the party.

"Shots. We need tequila, limes, and someone to turn the music up."

Ethan grins at me. "There's our party girl. It only took a cat fight to bring her out."

Keller smirks at me, "and I didn't even have to pay."

I roll my eyes dramatically back at both of them.

Today is not the day for me to dwell on Andrew or his awful girlfriend. It's my birthday party. I have my closest friends, some really hot men to ogle at, and my kids are happily playing in the pool. By all accounts, it should be a good day. I'll worry about everything else tomorrow.

Ethan pours a round of shots for everyone drinking, and I hand them out to those around us. "Cheers, friends! Time to start this party."

I take my shot, relish the slight burn, and then set my shot glass back on the counter. Then I surprised everyone by running and jumping in the pool. The cool water envelops me, washing away any lingering tension. Resurfacing, I feel refreshed and ready to embrace the carefree atmosphere the evening brings.

Splashes sound around me as everyone else jumps in too.

Laughter fills the air, and I realize I should have kicked her out long before I did.

Chapter Thirteen

Andrew

As I drove us toward the house, I felt as tense as I did before a big mission. I need to slow down and formulate a plan to get Heather back to California and apologize to Olivia. I don't have all the facts about what just happened, but what I do know is that Heather and I shouldn't be together, and I'm going to be buying the florist out of peonies.

In the midst of my frustration, Heather sits in the passenger seat, trying to plead her case, but to be honest, I'm not even paying attention. I can't focus on anything but the scene that just unfolded at Olivia's house.

When I heard the rigidity in Hayes's voice, I immediately knew something was wrong. Then, when I turned around to see an enraged Olivia, my heart sank. The last time I saw her with that look in her eye, ready to burn down the world, was when Ben was accused of bullying at the school.

It felt like a kick to the ribs when she looked at me like I was the one who hurt her and asked me to leave. I understood that it wasn't anything I did, but I hadn't realized guilt by association could hurt so bad.

I needed to focus on the road. Focus on my breathing. Focus on getting back so that I can grab her luggage and drop her off at a hotel near the airport. However, all I could think about was the anguish in Olivia's eyes.

My silence hung in the air like a poisonous fog, which only spurred on her ranting. The short drive started to make me feel trapped in my own truck.

The second I shut off the truck, I jumped out like it was on fire and slammed the door behind me. Heather barrels out of her side and chases after me, clawing at my arm.

"Please just listen to me!" She begs as I turn toward her.

"Why?" I shouted, my voice laced with frustration. The intensity of my tone seemed to stun her momentarily, leaving us both standing there in silence, our emotions hanging heavy in the air.

I scanned her face, trying to find any remorse hidden behind the "everything's perfect" mask she always keeps on.

"I feel like I don't know you anymore," I say, my voice cracking.

Tears welled up in her eyes as she looked at me, her grip on my arm loosening. "Whose fault is that?! You chose to leave and to move up here!"

"That's not what this is about." We weren't even living in the same city in California. It isn't like I left some beautiful, happy home that we shared. We only saw each other on the occasional weekend when she wasn't busy, or I wasn't deployed.

I unlock the door and stomp inside. She follows me and grips my arm again, forcing me to turn around.

Her baby blues are pleading with me now, tears streaming down her face. "It was a misunderstanding! Please, Drew, let me explain!"

I soften a touch; she looks truly desperate. "Fine, explain.

What did you do to set off Charlie, Hayes, and Olivia? To the point that she kicked us out?"

Her face transforms from sad to angry. "I was jealous."

She takes a deep breath, probably to get enough oxygen to fuel the rest of her tirade. I stare at her with indignation, waiting for her to get her tantrum out. I know it's coming, and she's about to realize it's not going to work anymore.

"I'm jealous. Everyone talks about her like she hung the moon!" She stomps her foot like a petulant toddler. "She has it all—the perfect house, the perfect kids, the perfect career. Do you even realize how much you talk about them?"

Confusion rocks through me. Have I been talking about them? Sure, I mentioned the funny things Ellie did or the things Ben accomplished. But Olivia? I was careful to keep her limited. I don't even think I mentioned the kids any more than I would talk about Everett or Hayes, but maybe I did without realizing it.

"I swear to you, I wasn't trying to call either of them fat." My head rears back, and I try to take a step back, but she grips on harder to my forearm. "I was just talking about my health goals and mentioned how good I feel. I said Ellie has Olivia's body shape. But I didn't mean it badly—just that Ben is naturally tall and lean, while Olivia and Ellie are naturally shorter and have more muscle."

I shake my head at her. Although I can understand how what she said could've been misconstrued, her excuse feels like a cop out. Calling Olivia fat? Not okay. Talking about a five-year-old like that? No wonder Olivia looked enraged.

"Why did Charlie make it seem like that wasn't the first comment you made?" Charlie has always been a no-bullshitter. If she felt Olivia was being slighted, there's a reason.

"I don't even know! I was so insecure being there. You've

started this new life with everyone here, and I don't know where I fit anymore."

Honestly, neither do I. It feels like we used to be ships crossing at night, just trying to stay going in the same direction. For a long time, it worked—the long-distance phone calls, the thrill of seeing each other after a few months—but now it feels like we aren't even in the same ocean.

"I don't either. We've been on different paths for a while now." I try to keep my answer honest without being hurtful.

She sniffled and then shook her head as if to clear it. "That doesn't mean we have to break up. We used to be so good together." Wrapping her arms around my waist and resting her head on my chest. "I don't know where we went wrong; it's not like us being away from each other is new."

Placing my hand on the back of her head, I hold her to me. I've had the same thoughts swirling around for longer than I should have. Neither of us were ready to admit we've grown apart to the point where there may be no coming back.

I pull back and grab her hand, pulling her toward the couch. It seems like the much-needed talk I've been dreading is finally here. I perch on the edge of the middle seat while she relaxes into the corner seat facing me, picking her feet up and curling into herself.

Taking a slow, deep breath, I release it quickly, letting my cheeks puff out, with it. "When I mentioned getting out and settling down up here, you didn't seem interested."

She lets out an exaggerated sigh. "I thought being up here was just a reset you needed to do, and you'd end up back in Southern California in a few months."

I shake my head at her, my eyebrows creasing together. "It's not; I hate living in a big city. Even if I didn't love it here, I couldn't move back there. It felt suffocating."

The more I talk, the more I realize how true those words

are. I felt on edge every moment of every day—the noise, the traffic, the people. Here, in the wide open space, with fresh air rolling off the mountains, it feels like I'm able to relax and let my guard down.

She squeezes her eyes shut. "So that's it for us? You moved up here and forgot the last twelve years."

Placing my hand on her knee, I give it a gentle squeeze. "I'm not forgetting about anything, but I don't see a way for this to keep working long distance."

"What about Kara's wedding? You're in it. My family loves you. They're going to be devastated."

My hand scrubs down my face and neck, while my head tips back. *I forgot about the wedding.* I love her family too; they've always welcomed me with open arms. Even after the few splits we had, they never held it against me or even really mentioned it. Kara, especially, has always been like a little sister to me. I don't want to disappoint any of them, but even more so Kara.

Before I think it through, I offer a solution that may benefit us both. "I'll still go. Maybe the time apart will be good for us. We can clear our heads and get out of this limbo."

She gaped at me, eyes widening in uncertainty. "Like a break? What does that even mean?"

Groaning, I respond, "I don't know, Heather. I just know *this*," I point between her and me, "isn't working anymore. Neither of us knows what we want for ourselves, let alone our relationship. I need to get my head straight. After that last..."

She cuts me off mid-sentence, not even paying attention to the fact that I was trying to open up to her. "So we are breaking up. Dating other people? Screwing random people?"

Frustration and confusion ripple through my body. "I never mentioned other people; you did."

She dramatically rolls her eyes at me. "Well, if that's what you want, fine! Fuck whoever you want; get *her* out of your system. You'll realize how good you have it with me and come back with a 'clear head.'"

I stare at her, flabbergasted that she went there with this. I can't believe that she's being so cavalier about me hooking up with other women. At this point, I don't even know why I'm surprised. Our relationship has grown so monotonous over the years that I can't help but wonder if she's intentionally trying to push me away. Maybe she's hoping that by giving me this freedom, I'll finally realize what we're missing and try to reignite the spark between us.

Instead, it's just giving me the out I've been secretly craving.

"But promise me, you won't get into a relationship before the wedding. You owe me that. We've spent twelve years together, and I deserve a proper breakup if that's what this turns out to be."

Feeling a mix of resignation and sympathy, I nod my head. I'm not planning on dating anyone or even thinking about a rebound. I have enough drama in my life; I don't need to jump into bed with some random woman, let alone start a relationship with someone.

"Yeah, I promise. We give it to the wedding and just see where both of our heads are at."

"Fine. I'm going to bed. Are you coming?" She's already standing and walking toward the bedroom.

"Later," I call out, despite the fact that I have every intention of sleeping on the couch.

The next morning was awkward, to say the least. We mumbled a few words to each other, but she was mainly focused on getting ready and leaving early. Thankfully, she was able to move her flight up a few hours and said she would rather wait at the airport than with me.

Heather scrolled through her phone the entire drive to Bend. I was barely aware she was even in the truck. I spent the drive consumed by what happened at Olivia's house and what I should say to her. I should be pretty damn good at apologizing to her by now, but this time seemed different.

The look in her eyes hadn't just been hurt; there was also rage. I was the one who brought a wolf in sheep's clothing into her bear cave, and she was ready to tear us both apart. I couldn't even blame her; I know how fiercely she loves and protects her kids.

We finally got to the airport, and I was antsy to call Hayes; he'd give me the full story and tell me just how fucked I truly was.

I helped Heather get her luggage out of the truck and said a hasty goodbye. She had animosity written all over her face, but there wasn't anything I could do about that. We agreed to give it six months, and I still thought that was the best. In time, I hope she does too.

The second my door was closed, I hit the call list on my truck dash and started to drive away. He answered on the first ring, and I didn't even greet him; I just started ranting about the fight, the breakup, and the deal we made. I'm pretty sure he called me a "fucking idiot" when I mentioned the promise to Heather, but I was too focused on getting it all out so that I could interrogate him about yesterday.

"So that's that for now. What happened at Olivia's? I didn't even notice Heather talking to her much, and then all of a sudden, claws were out."

His sigh is loud enough to hear through the truck speakers,

and my eyes close for a brief second as I wince. I have a feeling this will be a rough conversation.

"It was bad, man. Liv pulled each of us aside and said that it meant a lot that you made it to the party, and she didn't want to ruin that. She asked if we would just ignore the shitty comments Heather made toward her."

"Ahh, thus Charlie's muzzle comment."

"Yeah, I'm pretty sure I have bruises on my arm from how tightly your sister was gripping it. She looked like she was about to explode a few times from holding it all in."

"What was Heather saying? Calling Ellie fat? I can't believe anyone would say that."

Another loud sigh escapes him. "She didn't, well... Not exactly. Everything was backhanded compliments and insults disguised as helpful tips. She didn't say much to Olivia. However, when she did, it was always a shitty comment—her house, her hair, her body—nothing was safe. She was firing missiles left and right. Liv deflected them with a smile, but I could tell they were eating at her."

"Fuck. How did I miss all that?"

A hint of anger hits his tone. "It didn't seem like you even talked to Olivia the entire time. I was wondering why you even showed up."

Damn, I should've known he'd notice. The sixth sense for us to read a room without anyone knowing, feeling out everyone's motives before they do. All the guys on our team are trained to be more aware and vigilant, and that doesn't just stop, even when you're at a party. No wonder all the guys were on edge around me yesterday.

"Heather and I got into it on the way there; I was already frustrated, and then..." I pause, not wanting to get into that part.

Of course, he won't let me get away with that, though. "And

then you saw Liv give that big warm welcome to Luke and not you." He mocks, and I can almost hear him smirking.

Yeah, that's undoubtedly what set me off. She looked at him like all her prayers had been answered, and he showed up. I knew it was irrational; my girlfriend was standing right next to me, and I wasn't allowed to be jealous. But, if I'm being honest with myself, I was so green with envy that I was practically the Hulk.

I let out a small growl as my back molars gnashed together. "What's with that guy anyway? Why was it such a big deal he was there?"

Hayes chuckles. "Not my story to tell, but I promise you, there's nothing to worry about between him and Olivia."

I'm not sure about that; I saw the way he looked at her and even at me. He knew I was jealous and hadn't even officially met me before. I'm sure being a sheriff gives him that same sixth sense we have, but I've always speculated there's more going on between them.

"Anyway," he continues, "it was all those little digs, and then she brought up this diet she is on. She implied that Olivia needed to lose weight and then mentioned that Ellie could benefit too. I fucking snapped, man. I thought that was the moment you were going to be choosing sides between her and me. It's probably a good thing Liv cut me off when she did. I was about to make every insult we got during BUD/S look like a compliment."

"Yeah, I don't blame you. It's not okay to bring Ellie into her bullshit. I'm going to call Olivia, start groveling now, and hope she forgives me by next winter."

"That's good.." He trails off and pauses. I swallow, knowing he's about to start his lecture on me. "Listen, man. I know you're sorting through your shit right now, but I need you to be careful with Olivia. You and I both know something has been brewing between you two for a while now. I don't want you to jump into anything with her, but I think you'll be disappointed in yourself if you don't explore that. You're officially single now, but you've been out of that relationship longer than you think you have. Take some time to get your head straight, but not so much that you lose a girl like Olivia."

My stomach clenches at his words. He's right, there's something about Olivia that has me drawn to her like a magnet, but I'm nowhere near ready to start anything new. She doesn't seem like she's looking for a relationship anyway.

"I appreciate the advice, but I'm not looking for anything like that. Heather and I agreed to six months—no rebounds, no relationships. I promised."

He lets out a humorless laugh. "Well, you're an even bigger dumbass than I thought you were then."

I nod my head even though he can't see it because he's right. "Yeah, yeah. Talk later, asshole." I hit the red button on the dash to end the call and search for Olivia in my contacts.

I saved her contact information as 'Boots' the day of the wedding, but I don't think I've ever used it. We've been in a few group chats together, though, so hopefully she saved my number.

Trying to ignore the depressing thought that maybe she hadn't cared to save it, I hit call.

With each ring, the sinking feeling in my stomach grows. By the last one, I know she isn't going to answer, and it guts me. I'm still debating leaving a voicemail when her voice comes through the speaker. "You've reached Olivia Turner; leave a little message, and I'll get back as soon as I can. Thanks!"

Her voice sounds so cute that a small smile plays on my lips. I take a deep breath and hear the beep. "Hey, Boots. I wanted to apologize for last night, so can you call me back?" God, I sound like such a pansy, but I continue, "I'll bring the peonies to family dinner tonight, but..." I pause, trying to figure out what to say, but it all feels sappy and disingenuous over the phone. Quietly, I finally say, "I don't know; I guess it just felt wrong waiting until then to reach out. Alright, well, call me. Bye."

During the last five minutes of the drive home, I tortured myself with an endless loop of thoughts about how badly I'd fucked up the last few months. I should've ended things with Heather the day I moved up here. I should've gotten to know Olivia from the beginning; the things I said to her were awful. Putting her on this never-ending rollercoaster of hot and cold just because I couldn't get my feelings in check was inexcusable. But the worst one of all was that I didn't stand up for her last night at the party. I should've pushed to see exactly what had happened and then called Heather out on it there.

Heather crossed so many lines that I don't think I'll ever be able to forgive her. I still stand by the fact that I need to be single for a while, but I'm realizing that making that promise was a bad idea.

Chapter Fourteen

Andrew

MONDAY—

I'm in a rush to get to the office this morning, hoping Olivia will be there early after dropping the kids off at Summer Camp. They didn't show up to family dinner last night, and I almost left early to drag them over there. I'm not going to let her miss out on stuff because of me anymore. Charlie caught me, tugging my cowboy boots back on at the door, and told me to give her space.

I was planning on it until I overheard Everett take a phone call from her as he was walking out the door. The asshole rubbed it in my face by answering "Hellooo, Ohhhlivia" and slamming the door behind him.

Everett wasn't back at the house when I got there, and it took most of my willpower not to text him to see if he was with her.

Instead, I tossed and turned most of the night, trying to come up with a plan to get her forgiveness. The best I could come up with was to pretty much corner her and apologize profusely.

I pull into the parking lot and let out a string of curses; her SUV isn't here yet. I set the bouquet on her desk and trudge back to my office, hoping I'll get some work done but knowing I'll be staring into the parking lot waiting for her car.

Midday, I can't handle wondering where she is anymore. I spot Charlie sitting at her desk and storm in.

I give her a "Well, where is she?" look.

Playing dumb, Charlie gives me a lopsided grin and says, "How can I help you today, brother dearest?"

I narrowed my eyes at her. "Where's your boss?"

"Not in today," she says curtly, and she goes back to typing.

I let out a small growl. "Charlotte Amelia Reynolds, I'm not playing today."

Her evil grin back tells me she's loving every bit of annoying me. "It's Carrington now, and I'm not five. You can't intimidate me."

I sigh and pinch the bridge of my nose. I'm not above begging when it comes to Olivia, so that's just what I do. Sincerity drips from my voice. "Please, Char. I just want to make it right."

Her shoulders fall. "She was already planning most of the week off; the kids don't have camp, so she kept her schedule light. She might be in on Wednesday or Thursday." She stands up and walks around her desk, giving me a hug. "Just give her time. You've already called, and I mentioned the flowers on her desk about an hour ago. She knows you feel bad."

The guilt is eating me alive, like it always does when Olivia is upset at me. I need her in my orbit, even if it's at a distance. "Why won't she call me back?"

"I don't want to kick you while you're down, but I don't know why she would want to." She begins ticking off her fingers, making her points. "You hate her. Then you're her friend. Then back to acquaintance," she says, gesturing up like a light bulb went off. "Or even better, let me spend three hours building a Lego set with your son, but ignore you when you walk in to compliment it."

Everyone in the office is more aware than I'd like them to be.

Her words sting, but I understand what she's saying. I've been a confusing asshole.

"I get it. I'll be patient; she deserves it."

Yet, that doesn't stop me from grilling Everett that evening about his phone call with her. My hackles are immediately up with the way he dodges my questions, though.

Is there something going on between them?

He calls me out the second I think that, knowing me even better than I know myself. "Don't even think like that. She's just a friend, Dickhead. I think of her like Charlie, off-limits since the beginning."

I'm a mess, but I believe him. We've always been loyal to each other to a fault. If I even thought he might be into a girl, I wouldn't go near her.

TUESDAY—

The day mercilessly dragged on with no communication, and I was mindlessly scrolling through social media when I noticed Olivia had posted a new "story." My stomach does a flip just at the circle icon selfie of her. Her hair is long and wavy, and her smile lights up her face. It's nice that I can finally admit how beautiful she is without feeling guilty. Because damn, she is gorgeous.

I click on the icon and see Ellie dancing around the kitchen using a whisk as a microphone while belting out "It

Ain't My Fault" by Brothers Osborne. She slides around in her socks, dramatically dancing as she nails every single lyric. That little girl has more energy and confidence than anyone I know.

I hit reply without even thinking. "She crushed it! Love the mic covered in... frosting?" Before I could second-guess it, I hit send.

The read mark is immediate, and I sit up in bed. Staring at the three dots, praying for anything to come back.

The dots disappear, and my stomach clenches. I almost threw my phone against the wall, but a second later it vibrated when a message came through.

"Cream cheese frosting for the brownies we made to leave at the office tomorrow. Thank you for the flowers! I'll try to catch up with you when I stop by."

A million questions are running through my mind that I was to ask. Does this mean she isn't still mad? What time will she be in the office? Will I ever stop messing everything up around her?

Before I spiral too hard, I type out a quick response. "You're welcome. It's still not enough to make up for the shitshow Saturday was. I'll see you tomorrow. Night, Boots."

I don't expect a response, but I'd be lying if I said I wasn't disappointed that one didn't come back.

WEDNESDAY—

I'm on a call with a Presidential elect, explaining our policy, when I see Olivia come up the stairs carrying the brownies. I waved, and she gave me a half-smile back but didn't stop walking.

She pops into the office kitchen, sets the pan on the island, and then makes her way into her office. I watch her laugh at something Charlie says, and then she goes to her desk, grabs some mail, and chitchats.

Skimming through my notes, I try to remember the answer to whatever this guy asked.

When I glance up again, she's walking out of her office door toward me. She's biting her lip, and I silently beg for her to look at me. Like magnets, she finally does at the last second. Then she gives me another small, empathetic smile, and she turns her back to me to walk down the stairs.

So much for catching up today. My hope is dwindling with each day, and I know I need a Hail Mary at this point.

FRIDAY—

I worked through lunch, busting out contracts and sending two guys still in California out to the field. I pack up my stuff early and start preparing for my Hail Mary.

I picked up three pizzas, a board game, and a bag full of sugary treats. The drive to Olivia's house had me feeling like a ball of nervous energy, praying she didn't kick me out.

My heart pounds in my chest as I knock on Olivia's door. I have to consciously remind myself to take a deep breath and stay calm.

Olivia opens the door, wearing gym shorts, a thin white tank, and a hot pink sports bra. Her hair is in a high ponytail, and she looks like I just interrupted a workout. Cheeks flushed and mouth slightly parted. She looks so cute, all sweaty, and surprised to see me at her door.

She stammers over her words, clearly still reeling. I showed up unannounced. "What are you doing here?"

Ellie comes running past her, right through the door her mom is holding open while yelling my name. She steam rolls into my leg to give me a hug.

Quickly, I move the pizzas to the side so that I can see her smiling face. "Hi, Els! I brought pizza. Think we can convince your mom to have that movie night we talked about?"

Olivia's eyes went even wider than before as she looked between the two of us, trying to figure out how we plotted this.

"Oh. My. Gosh. MOMMY, Please, please, please. Drewy told me at your birthday party he hasn't seen any 'Minions' yet!" I try not to cringe at her use of words. I was hoping all birthday party mentions would be saved until after Olivia agreed to this. "Can we please, please, please watch them?" Ellie goes for gold when she sticks her lip out and puts her hands together like she's praying.

My plan is going perfectly so far. I have one kid on my side. Now, I just need Ben, and we have this sold. He walks around the corner, surely hearing his sister's begging and coming to see what's going on.

His whole face lights up when he sees me and what I'm carrying. "DREW! PIZZA!" He then looks at his mom and asks, "Are we having a pizza night?" His eyes grow impossibly wide with excitement.

I fight the smile of victory as I take in the two of them working their little magic.

Olivia sighs, and her shoulders drop, trying to muster a smile. "Let me just go get changed, and we can set up in the living room." She starts to back away but leaves the door open.

I beam at the kids and say, "I've got another bag in the car." I wiggle my eyebrows at them now. "Lots of really yummy treats for us!"

Olivia throws her hands in the air and huffs as she walks to her bedroom.

Ben runs out to grab the other bag for me, and Ellie drags me into the kitchen to start setting stuff down.

I take a second to look around the open floor plan. Luke let

Heather and me in the last time we were here, and we followed him right out the backdoor to the party. Her house is amazing—all high ceilings, soft colors, and warmth.

The kitchen is a chef's paradise, and I can tell Olivia uses it lovingly based on all the baked goods she brings around. Everything is white or a light-colored wood that somehow looks warm and cozy without feeling sterile. The countertops are a beautiful white marble, and the large island in the center of the kitchen is big enough to seat at least five people comfortably. Stainless-steel appliances with gold accents give the room a modern and sleek feel.

Olivia comes back out, wearing light pink silk pajama shorts that make her legs look a mile long and a matching button top that is tucked in on one side. Her hair is brushed out now, and loose waves frame her face. My mouth goes dry at the sight of her, and the only thing I do is blink at her. She looks sexy as hell, and I'm starting to think this movie night was a bad idea.

"What? What's wrong?" She looks down at herself, self-conscious.

I clear my throat and try to ignore the tightness in my pants. "Nothin'. Like that color on you."

Her brows draw together, but she keeps walking into the kitchen and grabbing things out of the cupboards. She struggles to reach the top of a high cupboard, and her shorts ride up a few inches, giving me a very nice view of the bottom of her ass cheeks. I think I might pass out right here. I know that I should offer to reach it, but I can't deny how much I enjoy the view. Then, just like that, she finds what she's looking for, and my view is over.

She glances at me and says, "Could you grab the movie night plate? It's in the laundry room, by the garage. Tucked in beside the washer."

Raising my eyebrow in question, she laughs, "It's not really a plate, more like a giant charcuterie board, but after hearing Ben and Ellie try to pronounce that, I went with simple."

I headed in the direction of the garage, searching for the laundry room and large board. Hopefully, she will give me a tour of this place because it is huge. Although it's only one story, it has to be at least seven thousand square feet.

As I navigate through the hallway, I can't help but admire the black and white photos of the kids hanging in the hallway. They're candid photos of the three of them playing out in a field. It must have been taken somewhat recently because Ellie and Ben appear to be close to the same age as now.

I open the door by the garage and walk into the laundry room, only to realize she is surely trying to drive me insane. It's a spacious room with an enormous washer and dryer, a wash-sink, and lingerie everywhere. I inhale a sharp breath as I take note of the sexiest clothing I've ever seen. Bright and nude colors are folded neatly on the large countertop. Thongs, bikinis, and everything in between. Dangling right in front of my face are lace bras and a red bustier that has my mouth watering at the thought of seeing her in. I feel like a fourteen-year-old boy in Victoria's Secret right now.

I'm still frozen in lust when she comes running in behind me, as if she just realized she sent me into her underwear drawer to find this fucking plate. Her face is as red as the bustier, and I can't help but grin.

"I, uhh.. laundry day." She sneaks her arm around me and pulls out the massive board.

I didn't move an inch, loving the feeling of her being so close to me. A few days ago, I was shutting down any sexual thoughts before they even occurred. Now I can't stop imagining her in every single piece hanging up around us, and I can't say I hate the visual.

I smirked at her. "All good. Just had a hard time seeing through all the lace." I add a wink to really lay it on thick.

A tiny squeak escapes from her, and her eyes meet mine. Then she's turning and high-tailing it back to the kitchen.

Oh, this is going to be fun.

I take one more look around. It's probably a good thing that I hadn't known that the little miss covered up had such a naughty wardrobe. I would've never been able to look her in the eye had I known.

She has the "movie night plate" on the ottoman which sits in the middle of their oversized sectional. It's quite possibly the biggest couch I've ever seen, and it looks small in the living room. A stone fireplace sits to the left of the 85-inch TV. This room is a man's dream—better than, actually.

Sometimes, I forget just how much money she actually has. She never flaunts it or shows off. Her wardrobe doesn't ever seem to be anything outrageous or covered in designer logos. The kids are well-adjusted, not demanding, or snotty. But here we are in her multi-million-dollar home, living a life of luxury.

I look over at her as she's rearranging snacks on the board. "This house, it's amazing. Charlie mentioned you had it built a few years ago, and you were the genius behind it."

She nods, her face slightly flushing. "Right after Dan," she takes a deep breath through her nose, gathering her thoughts: "I just needed a fresh start and something to focus on, I guess. I'm sure I drove the contractor crazy, but we didn't miss a single deadline. It was done in a year."

I smile back at her and say, "Impressive; you must be a magician to get that done."

She shrugs one shoulder. "Just determined. And I know how to use some power tools."

Ellie and Ben come running out in their pajamas and start pulling me in different directions.

Olivia steps in before I get pulled apart. "Woah, slow down, children! We are starting this movie night in five minutes, so whatever you need to do, do it now."

Then she looked at me and frowned. "You can't movie night in your work clothes. Come on, Levi leaves stuff in the guest room for when he stays with the kids."

My teeth clench together as my mind derails into an endless number of questions I won't ask. How often is Levi staying here while she is out? Does she date? Is she just casually seeing someone? Is it Luke?

I finally mustered up some courage when I opened the dresser to find a full wardrobe. I glance at her and then point to everything: "Does he stay here often?"

She shakes her head no but then admits, "He did at first. The kids struggled. I struggled. Having Dan's exact twin helped more than it hurt. I think he needed to be here too. He was the first medic on scene when Dan was shot."

I stare at her solemn face, wondering why tragedies happen to such good people. "Fate can be cruel sometimes."

"Yeah. I think he's holding on to a lot of guilt. He blames himself for not being able to save Dan. It's maddening. The only one responsible is the woman who shot him."

Hayes filled me in on the details of Dan's murder after the rodeo. An unhinged woman went into the local grocery store and got into an altercation over them not carrying a brand of gluten-free bread that she likes anymore. She waved the gun around, threatening the employees, and then stormed out. When she ripped out of the parking lot and sped down the road, Dan saw her erratic driving and pulled her over. The store hadn't called it in yet, so he had no idea she had a gun. Dan had his right hand on the roof of her car, and when he turned to look back at his vehicle, she shot him. The bullet went through his armpit, not even an inch above his bulletproof vest. It was one of the worst places to get shot, and just by dumb luck, this untrained civilian hit her mark. She left him laying there. A good samaritan saw and called it in before she had sped off.

"It's heartbreaking, knowing that you followed everything exactly by the book. Yet, the outcome is still death."

She nods and searches my eyes. "It sounds like you speak from experience."

"Yeah." I offer her a small smile. I'm not ready to dive deep into that conversation yet, so I choose to change the subject, hoping she will drop it.

"So, he doesn't stay here as often anymore?"

"No, not so much lately. They typically stay over at Pops when I need a night to just..." She trails off as the blush on her cheeks turns rosy.

"Have some "Olivia" time?" I finish her sentence and wink.

The tiny squeal comes out again, and her eyes squeeze shut. Turning to escape, she says, "Wear whatever!" Then she closed the door behind her, and I let out a loud laugh.

Getting her to make that noise is definitely my new favorite hobby.

Chapter Fifteen

Olivia

I'm going insane. No, scratch that. Andrew is making me go insane. I spent the entire week avoiding him. I decided on Saturday after he left that there would be no more—no more trying to be friends, no more talking, no more crushing. Yet, here he is! In. my. house. Watching Despicable Me with me and my kids.

The worst part is how normal it all feels. He's sprawled out in the middle of the sectional, acting as if he's done it a million times. He's taking up so much room that I had to curl myself into the corner to avoid touching him. I can't even focus on the movie because I swear he's gravitating toward me.

The kids have been so excited before any funny scene that they both just stare at him and wait for the big, burly laugh they know is about to come. Not that I have any room to talk; that laugh of his is intoxicating. I'm fighting a grin every time I hear it. *Like music to my ears.*

He taps my thigh with the back of his hand, and his shoulder slags in my direction. "You're the only one not eating.

Is there a reason for that?" His husky voice is barely above a whisper, but I don't miss the insinuation in his tone.

I'm not exactly about to share the truth. His girlfriend gave me a slight complex about the "baby weight" that I haven't lost yet. I'm also trying to be cautious with what I say in front of the kids; just because I feel insecure doesn't mean I want them to ever pick up on that.

So, I lie, like the big coward I am. "No reason, just not very hungry after my workout."

He gives me a look that says, "you're fucking lying, and I know it," but I turn my attention back to the TV and try to refocus on the movie I've seen a hundred times.

Three minutes later, he puts a slice of my favorite pizza on a plate- combination with extra olives. Then he hands it to me without even looking, just expecting me to take it.

Feeling resigned, I accepted it without hesitation. I've been eyeing the pizza for so long that I was bound to give in sooner than later, anyway. I was already justifying it by telling myself that 80/20 healthy is more sustainable anyway.

"Thanks." He still doesn't look at me, so I lightly touch his elbow. His head turns, and those green eyes make me dizzy with all the attention. I clear my throat and retreat just a bit. "Thanks for all this; the kids love having you here."

The corner of his mouth quirked up. "I'm happy to be here. But I didn't have much of a choice. You've been avoiding me."

His bluntness makes my jaw drop, and I can't help but take a sharp breath in surprise.

Well, technically, yes. However, I'm not going to admit that to him. My pride can't take any more hits when it comes to this man. I already feel like the desperate widow begging for any scraps of attention he gives me.

I try to quickly recover and play innocent. "Been busy. The kids have a lot going on right now."

Oof, the "you're a dirty liar look' is back, and I can't help but laugh.

His eyebrow raises, but I see the hint of a smile in there somewhere. "You can avoid it now, but we are talking about last weekend. Tonight."

A thrill and a chill simultaneously ran down my spine. I'm much more of an avoider. I have no problem apologizing, but I hate being on the receiving end. Honestly, brushing it under the rug is way more my style.

The last movie finally plays, and both kids are asleep on the couch. I carry Ellie to her bed, and right behind me is Andrew with Ben. I almost get a little teary-eyed seeing Ben carried in; he looks so small, and I'm reminded of when Dan would carry him to bed a few years ago.

Quickly blinking the tears away, I tuck Ben in and give him a kiss. He barely notices and snuggles deeper under his covers.

Squaring my shoulders, I turn to walk out of Ben's room and see Andrew watching from the doorway. "You're a good mom. I know I've said it before, but you should hear it often. You're a good mom, Boots."

Thank God it's still a little dark because my eyes are instantly turning misty.

I swallowed down the emotion building. "Thank you; it's nice to hear. I feel like I'm just surviving day by day, trying not to fuck it up."

"Psh, you? Never!" He grabs my upper arms and pulls me into a hug. It feels natural to melt into him as I wrap my arms around his waist. *Holy moly, it's like hugging a solid, warm boulder that smells incredible.* I've only ever caught small whiffs of his cologne, and now that I'm up close and personal, I think I'm addicted. It's both floral and woodsy, creating a manly scent that has me feeling weak in the knees. I could almost orgasm just at the smell of him.

I pull away and let my hands fall to my sides.

The emotion from when he called me a good mom morphed into an entirely different feeling pretty quickly. My body's hormonal response to a hug is almost cringe-worthy. It's been so long that I probably just need to get laid. A primal itch that craves to be scratched. It has nothing to do with the gorgeous man in front of me. *Ha. Ha. Yeah, right.*

I clear my throat, trying to stuff those hormones back into the dusty box they came out of. "Let's go out to the patio. It should be a nice evening, and we can turn the fire pit on. Want a drink? I think I need a drink. Wine? Beer? Liquor?" I end up talking so fast that it all comes out as one big sentence.

Chuckling, he says, "Beer's good for me."

I start walking out the door and mention over my shoulder, "I've got that ale from Sunmountain Brewing still on tap from the party; want that?"

"Sure, that sounds perfect.' He pauses and looks around the patio. "Boots, this backyard is insane. Pool, gas fireplace—hell, you even have a kegerator with my favorite beer. I might move in."

My stomach instantly squeezes. Tonight feels different. He's been light and carefree, easy to talk to, and unguarded. I don't know what changed to have him be so casual toward me. I can't help but wonder if it's just because he feels bad about Saturday and how awful his witch of a girlfriend was towards me.

Thankfully, that thought brings me back to reality. Just because he's being less guarded doesn't mean I should be. I need to throw those walls back up fast. His undeniable way of waltzing and tearing them down in a blink should be the biggest red flag.

I forced a smile. "Thanks; I love it too."

I pour his beer and then reach for a glass to pour myself some wine.

We haven't even sat down yet, and he's already champing at the bit to say his peace. "Are you ready to talk about why you've been avoiding me?"

A small, humorless laugh pops out. "I learned from the best," I say, pointedly looking at him.

He nods, and I see his throat bob up and down. "Fair. I've been an asshole. I'm sorry about that."

I chew on my bottom lip as I stare at the wine glass I'm pouring into. His apologies seem to come by the dozen. At what point do we just accept that we shouldn't be friends? I wouldn't be surprised if he's back to ignoring me tomorrow.

"Okay. I appreciate the apology, Andrew." I shrug my shoulders and grab my filled wine glass, gesturing toward the patio furniture for us to sit on.

He strolls over and plants himself on the loveseat. "I sense there's a 'but' in there.

I sit down in the chair closest to him and pull my legs up so they're tucked underneath me. When I glance up at him, he's already looking like I broke his heart.

"But, maybe we aren't meant to be friends."

Hurt and confusion flicker across his face as he processes my words. He softly begins rubbing at his sternum, and it almost makes me lose my confidence.

I take a deep breath, trying to find the right way to explain myself. "It's just that we seem to constantly clash and have misunderstandings. Maybe we would be better off as acquaintances. Without so much back and forth."

He's already shaking his head before I finish my sentence. "No."

I feel my eyebrows rise to the ceiling. "No?"

"No." He shrugs, like it's a matter of fact, and sets his beer on the fire pit ledge. "I have fucked up time and time again at being your friend, and I own that. But tonight? Being with you and the kids? That was the most fun I've had in years. Years, Boots!" He looks at me with such sincerity that he's left me speechless.

"Being around you and your family, it's easy. I feel like I can breathe and let go. I don't take that lightly. I promise you, I will be a better friend than I have been. You deserve that. The kids deserve that."

Each of his declarations loosens the knot in my stomach, until all my resolve disappears. He has a way with words that creates a buzz in my body, surpassing any caffeine high I've ever experienced. I do want to be friends; I've always wanted to be friends with him.

Except there's still one little problem. I hate his girlfriend.

"What about Heather? She obviously doesn't like me, and the feeling is mutual."

He rubs his hand down the back of his neck and sinks back into the loveseat, looking up at the ceiling. "Heather and I, we... broke up?"

"Wait. Are you asking me or telling me?"

"Ha. Telling." He sits back up and puts his elbows on his knees while he starts to explain. "It's complicated; we've been together off and on for most of our adult lives. It felt weird for both of us to just end it in a big fight, and I'm in her sister's wedding as a groomsman in a few months. We both agreed it wasn't working, and we needed to figure our shit out. So taking a break seemed like a good option at the time."

"Very Ross and Rachel of you."

Chuckling, he says, "I thought the same thing myself, even clarified." His tone turns melancholy. "She told me I could fuck whoever I wanted, but nothing further than that."

I grimaced, "Wow. That's..."

His mouth quirks up at the side. "Controlling?" He finishes my sentence for me.

"You said it, not me," I said with a smirk.

He nods and drums his thumbs on his knees, almost looking nervous now. "I talked to Hayes. He filled me in on everything she said to you."

I roll my eyes dramatically and scoff, "Such a fucking blabbermouth."

He shrugs, but I see the smile he's trying to hold back. "He's got a soft spot for you, and he's always been indifferent toward Heather."

I gathered as much. He gave me an earful of ranting the next morning. I'd say he went from indifferent to hate pretty fast by the way she treated me. Hayes quickly became like a brother to me. He wasn't just there for us when we lost Dan. He was the glue that kept us together most of the time. Between him and Charlie, they made sure we had good days. Levi and Pop were always around, but they were grieving themselves and carrying guilt they shouldn't have been. Hayes, though, walked into the room with a smile every time. He'd wrestle with Ben or dance with Ellie, allowing me the opportunity to cry on Charlie's shoulder.

I turned my face toward the fire, preparing to pick at the scab that is Dan. "Hayes and Charlie, they both just accepted us—after Dan died, they rode the roller coaster and let us feel how we needed to feel. Every time Ben cried, Hayes would just hold him, tell him how strong he was, that grieving comes in all shapes and forms, and if he needed to cry, he would be there. Ellie didn't really understand much because she was so little, but Hayes would just sit and play with her for hours. And for me, well, I was angry, so he bought some boxing gloves and hung the bag, so I could get it all out.

Andrew's gazing at me with a small smile. "He's the best—

always has been. His mom did something like that for me when I lost my parents. I was a shithead teenager who wanted to rage at the world. She gave me a sledgehammer and told me to take out the wall in her dining room, saying she always wanted an open concept."

"Momma Carrington, master of the whole two birds, one stone thing."

His whole face smiles back. "She sure is. Hayes and I remodeled the entire dining room and kitchen with her supervision. She pushed us both to follow in our dad's footsteps. Join the Navy and become SEALs. It seemed like an easy choice at the time."

"Not anymore?"

He lets out a breath through his nose and huffs, "No."

I stay quiet, allowing him a second to gather his thoughts. I've known from the beginning that his time in the Navy was anything but easy, but he needs to work through everything on his own.

"The Navy, being a SEAL. I'm proud of that. It doesn't make some of the losses any easier, though."

"The losses. Is that what you were talking about earlier? Doing things by the book and the outcome is still death."

His head nods, but he glances away as the color drains from his face.

He clears his throat and takes a big breath, letting it out slowly. "My last mission. Our target killed his little girl right in front of us. She wasn't much older than Ben. I did everything I could to try to save her, but she was too far gone."

The look on his face is pure anguish. I can't begin to imagine the heartbreak that comes from seeing someone do that to their own child.

"The mission started off like any other raid, and we were

prepared for it. Five other SEALs and I approached the compound in unison, looking for our target. A high-profile terrorist had been hiding out for years with his family. I was set as the point when we hit the fourth floor, and when I breached through the door, he was crouching behind his young daughter. He set a knife against her throat and slashed it before I took my first step. In a breath, I fired two shots, hitting him in the forehead. He crumpled behind her, and we cleared the room. By the time we got to the girl, it was too late."

I stand up and move to sit by him on the loveseat, taking his hand in mine.

"It was the day I realized this may not be the career for me anymore. I can't get those little girls' scared eyes out of my brain—scared of us, scared of her dad. It wasn't just heartbreaking; it was life-altering.

I stare at him through sorrowful eyes, wishing I could take the pain away. "The decisions of others don't rest on your shoulders."

"She just stared at me, choking on her blood, and I couldn't do anything. How anyone could do that to their own child is beyond me. For no other reason than to fuck with us."

I sit up on my knees and wrap my arms around his shoulders. "The last thing she saw was someone good. Someone who was trying to help after she was betrayed by her own father. No one could look into those emeralds and not realize they're only trying to help."

He pulls me flush against his chest while wrapping his arms around my waist. He sets his cheek on my shoulder, and I hold onto him tightly. "You're one of the good ones, Andrew. Don't forget that."

He pulls back, quickly blinking, and then smiles. "Thanks for listening to me ramble on."

I let out a small chuckle and returned to my spot in the other chair. Being that close to him messes with my senses

"I'm around any time you need me."

Chapter Sixteen

Olivia

The last few weeks have been full of fun and adventure. Summer is in full swing, and I've been enjoying every minute of only working part-time. Charlie and Isla have been handling everything in the office like true professionals. If it weren't for the fact that I needed to sign their paychecks, I'd say they didn't need me around at all.

The kids and I have been all over Oregon, hiking to waterfalls, exploring the forests, and even spending a long weekend at the beach. Sporadically, Charlie and Hayes would come, or Everett, but no matter what, Andrew was right there with us. He even bought the right car seat for Ellie and a booster for Ben just to keep in his truck so that I didn't have to drive every time.

The Friday night movie night became such a hit that Andrew has spent the last five Fridays at my house. Ellie and Ben just expect him to be there now, and I'm starting to as well. We work out together in the office at least four times a week as well. Well, mainly, he guides me through an easier version of what he does, and I try not to make myself look like a fool in front of him. Even that only seems to be a warmup before his actual workout that he does with all the guys on his team.

His single status has changed things, yet nothing at all. He will always be out of my league, single or not. I'll be stuck in the friend zone, praying for those few uninterrupted hours after we put the kids to bed on Friday night. We sit outside and just talk about everything. Our struggles, our hopes, funny memories, or even just random thoughts that pop into our heads. It's the one time during the week it gets to just be us.

Even though I cherish those moments, I'm also terrified. Terrified of the feelings I have for him. The tiny crush has morphed into a full on infatuation, and I wasn't ready for it. I was content to just be the mom my kids needed me to be. The mom who puts them first and doesn't worry about dating or what some guy is thinking about what she's wearing. Yet, here I am, dragging Isla and Charlie shopping for new outfits on a workday.

We drove thirty minutes to Bend, where there is much better shopping, and hit a few stores. I feel like I'm buying everything they say looks good and just hoping I find the confidence to pull it off.

Isla's the first to mention it; they're sitting in the lounge chairs while I try on a few dresses. "So what's with the wardrobe overhaul? You've been shopping like a housewife that just got cheated on."

I laugh while trying to shimmy my way into a leather skirt.

I'm not ready to admit to them, or even myself, that I'm trying to impress Andrew. So I use the kids as my excuse. "I'm just starting to feel more like my old pre-kid self. They're getting older. I don't have to hover over them while they play. I can actually put some time into myself and not worry about them." Well, not be completely worried. I still peek in every so often because motherhood hit me with a big dose of anxiety. Tack on the horror stories from Pops, Dan, and Levi, and I can be a spiraling mess of worst-case scenarios in two seconds.

"I already can't wait for that day, and I'm barely pregnant," Charlie adds with a grumble and a slight huff. She's just starting to show at nearly 14 weeks, with the tiniest little bump. I'm surprised she's complaining at all; so far, it seems like her pregnancy has been rainbows and sunshine.

I open the door to peek out at her, and I see she has a playful smile.

I point at her and say, "It flies by in a blink. The days are long, but the years are short. One minute they need you for everything, the next they're asking for cell phones to talk to their friends."

Charlie gasps. "Ben asked for a phone?"

I scoff back, "No, Ellie! Five-year-olds with cell phones!"

"Stop it! That's crazy."

"I know! I told her absolutely not, but she could use mine to call her friends sometimes." I close the door to finish trying on the dresses I have left.

I hear what sounds like whispers, and then one of them clears their throat.

Charlie speaks up now, "So back to the original subject, are you sure it has nothing to do with the fact that a certain someone, possibly related to me, has been following you around like a lost little puppy?"

I inhaled sharply, caught off guard. Has he? No, I mean yes, he's been around more and hanging with the kids and me. I wouldn't say that means he's a lost puppy.

"He has not," I say, suddenly feeling a little defensive. Like-minded people just gravitate toward each other. All of our Friday late-night talks have only confirmed that. Our journeys haven't been the same, but the result is still two broken people who need to focus on finding themselves again. "Everyone else is just in a relationship or an employee of his."

I hear Isla snort. "Ahh, so that's why he stares at your ass every chance he gets."

I pause, mid-arm, through the sleeve. *Wait, they think he's into me?*

I try to think about the last few times we've hung out. He does compliment me often, but never has it been about my appearance. It's actually the only thing keeping me grounded, reminding me that our friendship is strictly platonic.

"Now I know you two are crazy. I'm not his type."

Charlie lets out a loud guffaw. "Why? Because you're not a blonde bimbo? Trust me, you're everyone's type."

"Not to mention, he doesn't take his lusty eyes off you when you're in the room." Isla adds on.

"Mhm. Connie and Odessa both say that every time they talk to him, he raves about you and the kids."

My stomach clenches hearing Charlie say that. I know he talks to them often and values their opinions, so hearing that he speaks highly of me to them is reassuring. Yet still, that doesn't mean he's interested in me as anything besides a friend.

"That's just because he thinks I'm a good mom."

"Everett thinks you're a good mom, and he doesn't look at you like that."

"Nope, or Hayes." Charlie adds, and I can almost hear her evil smirk.

I exaggerate an eye roll, even though they can't see it, but I can't help but feel a flutter of excitement at their words.

I walk out in a tiny black bodycon dress that has short off-the-shoulder sleeves and a deep v-neckline. "What do you think? Too slutty for Everett's birthday party next weekend?"

Charlie's eyes light up as she raves. "Move over, Princess Diana; that is the hottest dress I've ever seen you in."

Isla nods excitedly. "Seriously, you have to buy that!"

I glance back at Charlie, and she's pursing her lips while staring at my cleavage. "and show off those boobs more. Seriously, you're doing yourself a disservice by keeping those beauties hidden away."

Giggling as I check myself out in the full-length mirror, I have to agree with them. It's tight but supportive, and it gives me curves in all the right places. The cleavage is a little much, but it doesn't look like anything is going to fall out. Sexy, definitely, but still chic.

Isla makes eye contact with me through the mirror and waggles her eyebrows. "Lost puppy will be drooling over that."

I can't stop the grin that hits my face, clearly revealing that I'm crushing on Andrew. Thankfully, they dropped the subject, though. These girls know me well enough to know not to push too hard. They understand that I need my space when it comes to matters of the heart. Time to process whatever I'm feeling before I'm ready to admit it to myself, let alone anyone else.

Isla hands me a pair of heels to try on, distracting me from my thoughts. As I slip them on, a surge of confidence hits me. My legs look long and toned, thanks to the workouts Andrew has been helping me with. I feel more confident than I have in years as I smooth the dress down. She's right; this dress is definitely drool-worthy.

***

I can feel sweat dripping everywhere down my body. I'm officially starting to regret having Andrew workout with me. Not only does he push me harder than I've ever been pushed before, but he looks like a Greek god while he does it and doesn't even break a sweat. I, however, have a red, splotchy face, patchy makeup, and smeared eyeliner. *Hot mess, express.*

He's a surprisingly good trainer. Patient but assertive, and he knows exactly what I should be doing to get maximum results.

The problem is that I can't focus any time he's within two feet of me, let alone when he touches me to show me something. He'll barely touch my elbow, and I have a full-body shiver.

I lie on the cushiony gym floor mats, staring up at the ceiling. I've done more burpees in the last five minutes than most people do in an entire year.

Andrew sits next to me with his knees up, still looking like he should be on the cover of a sports magazine. His small chuckle is deep when I let out a mock groan in pain.

I close my eyes and grumble at him. "My leg is cramping; why did you do that to me?"

"Nope, that was all you. I would've had you stopped halfway through, but you just kept going."

Gasping, I sit up on my forearms and look at him with wide eyes. "I could've stopped?!"

He smirks in return. "Yes, here, let me help you stretch it."

Before I can protest, he leans down and picks up my right leg, gently pushing it back toward my head.

I take a deep breath and lay back flat again so that I don't openly gawk at him.

He always looks good, but right now, with his hair a little messy and his shirt stretched tightly across his chest, he looks phenomenal. His massive frame kneels in front of me as he pushes my leg out to the right while gently pushing down on my left hip.

I moan, both in pleasure and a little pain.

"Damn, I haven't been in this position in a while." I try to joke to make light of the situation because obviously, we've never been this close and personal, but it doesn't land. If anything, it almost looked like I pissed him off, the way he immediately clenched his jaw.

"Hmph." He doesn't even look at me as he keeps gently maneuvering my leg.

"Switch," he says, taking my other leg and bending it while repeating the same move.

I moan again as I feel the stretch in my hamstring. "Fuck, that feels good."

Another tick in his jaw as I hear the audible sound of his teeth grinding together.

He puts my leg down, centering himself in between them, but doesn't move. I try to stay perfectly still, waiting for him to make the first move.

My breath comes out in little pants as I feel the heat from him so intimately close to me.

His nostrils only give off a slight flare as he intensely gazes down at me.

Lust overtakes my normal senses, and I decide to take matters into my own hands. I reach up and grab the back of his neck, trying to pull him down to me.

His pupils flared a touch, and I heard him say, "Fuck it," before sealing his mouth to mine in a fit of passion. Our tongues sweep together in perfect synchrony, exploring each other's mouths. One of his hands roams up and down my thigh while the other laces through my hair.

It's by far the hottest kiss I've ever had. Every touch and every taste ignite a wildfire of desire within us as he rubs his hard body into mine.

I let out a tiny mewl when I felt him grind into me. Within a millisecond, the weight of him was gone as he propelled himself off of me.

I laid there, trying to catch my breath and figure out what just happened for a few seconds. I had no idea I could be that turned on by a sweaty floor make-out session, but that was nearly porn worthy.

Finally, I lift myself up onto my elbows so that I can see him.

We're both panting at the same rhythm, but his face is clearly showing signs of guilt and shame. As he digs his fingers into his eyes and I hear him mumble out a string of profanities, it hits me.

Oh, fuck. Either he didn't want to kiss me, or it wasn't good for him.

He grimaced, and his eyes flashed to mine. "Shit! I'm sorry, Olivia. That shouldn't have happened. I can't... I'm not..."

My hand shoots up, palm out, hoping he'll stop talking. I don't need to hear him say anything more. He's not interested in me that way. I understood that pretty loud and clear by the way he nearly broke his back trying to get off me.

Swallowing hard, I looked anywhere in the room but at him. I need to get out of here before I start crying.

I jump up and nearly trip over myself as I try to get to the bag I left by the door. "Let's just forget it happened."

"Boots..." I can hear the hurt in his voice, but I refuse to look at him. I know that if I do, I will cry all over this gym floor.

I grab my bag and reach for the door in the same step. "All good, I gotta go. Thanks for the lesson."

With my heart pounding so loud, I couldn't hear, I sprinted through the lobby.

The first tear falls the second I open the front door, and the hot summer air blasts me. I feel a small sob trying to work its way up my chest, but I refuse to let it out until I'm safely hidden behind my tinted windows. Andrew's truck is the only other one parked in the lot, so at least I know I haven't humiliated myself to anyone else here today.

I peel out of the parking lot before I even have my seat belt on. I know I need to drive somewhere that I can pull over and park, but I can't think of where to go. If I go home, the kids could be there, and everyone in this town knows what kind of vehicle I drive, so I can't just park on a side street.

For a little while, I drove around mindlessly, not knowing where to go. It wasn't until I spotted the long driveway that I realized my subconscious somehow brought me to the cemetery where Dan is buried.

Slowly, I cruised down the driveway, making my way down the familiar curves. The kids and I visit a few times a year, but we've never felt close to him here. Normally, I hate this place. Just because his body is here doesn't mean that he is. Not when I can feel his presence everywhere else—all the lake trips we took as a family, every festival or town event. Hell, anytime I see Ben or hear Ellie laugh, I'm reminded of the best parts of him.

Today, though, I just need a place where I can go and cry. Somewhere, no one will wonder why, and I can just get it all out. This place seems as good as any.

Surprisingly, there weren't any other mourners around today, though. Granting me the peace and solitude I so desperately crave.

I made my way to his headstone and sat on the lush, freshly mowed grass. The town pulled together and donated a beautiful standing headstone that has a large Cascadia County Sheriff badge on it. A portrait of him in his uniform is placed above a prayer, and it guts me every time I look at it. I know Dan would have loved it, but it's not lost on me that the thing that took him away from us is now forever memorialized on his headstone.

I bury my head into my knees and just cry.

I cry for Dan, who was robbed of his time here.

I cry for the kids, losing their dad, who loved them.

I cry for myself, losing my friend and husband.

I cry from guilt, wanting someone who isn't Dan.

I cry from humiliation, knowing what I'm feeling for Andrew isn't reciprocated.

I just cry.

I cry until I don't have any more tears left in me.

Then, I wipe my snotty face on my tank and pick myself up.

I know what I need to do and sitting here is only going to make it harder.

Chapter Seventeen

Olivia

I left the cemetery and was relieved to see that Levi sent me a text saying that he was taking the kids into town for dinner. I guarantee my face is red and puffy, and I don't want the kids to see that.

Making my way home, I drove past the sprawling hay fields and open pastures. The hot sun is still beating down on the landscape, casting long shadows across the fields. The vibrant colors of wildflowers and the sweet scent of freshly cut grass filled the air, providing a momentary distraction from my grief.

I pull into my garage and stare at my wedding ring, the ring Dan gave me when he promised me forever. The ring Pops proposed to Anne with. I loved that ring from the moment I got it, knowing how much it meant to the Turner family.

I know that it's time to take it off. I probably should've taken it off years ago, but every time I tried, it felt like the end of my marriage.

Lately, though, it felt more like a security blanket. The last thing keeping me from exploring new relationships.

I walk into the house, surprised that it's still relatively clean.

Usually, when Levi offers to hang with the kids, it looks like a tornado ripped through the house.

Letting out a heavy sigh, I opened the door to my closet. Dan left a large gun safe that houses a security box inside of it. I don't keep much in there—a few expensive pieces of Lovey's jewelry that she left to me, our passports, and some valuables that were Dans.

Taking the ring off, I hold it delicately between my index finger and thumb. I close my eyes and whisper to Dan, "I loved you so much, even when we weren't as close as we should have been. Thank you for giving me the two very best things I could ever ask for, Ellie and Ben. I miss you every day, but it's time for me to let you go."

I set the ring in the box that Dan proposed with and placed it into the security box, locking it away.

Someday, Ben may ask to give it to his future wife, or maybe I'll give it to the man who proposes to Ellie. Either way, it belongs on the finger of someone who will cherish the Turner legacy as much as I did.

As I walk away from the security box, a sense of closure washes over me. It's time to move forward and embrace the new chapter of my life, knowing that love will always find its way to those who deserve it.

My goal for the week was to act naturally, but try to avoid any one-on-one time with Andrew. I've done a pretty good job at making myself scarce around the office, but I make sure to still nod hello and smile whenever I come and go.

By Wednesday, my stomach was still in knots, trying to let go of the mortification I felt from our kiss a few days ago. The office feels busy today, so at least I don't have to worry about any awkward run-ins.

It's almost lunchtime when a very enthusiastic Everett waltzes into our office. I've been stuck at my desk most of the morning while Isla and Charlie scour over new investment prospects. They have at least fifteen properties laid out on our circular conference table, trying to weigh the pros and cons of each.

"Hello, beautiful ladies! Are we excited about my birthday party on Saturday?" Everett is truly just one of those men who walk in with lightness. His infectious energy charges up the room, but I don't miss how, when he talks to Isla, Charlie, and me, his eyes never leave Isla.

Isla's returning grin is equally bright. "Almost as excited as you are."

Subtly, I scoot my chair away from my desk so that I can see Charlie. She locks eyes with me and smirks, confirming she sees the sparks flying between the two of them like I do.

I shake my head subtly and let out a little laugh. They've been circling each other for months, but Isla is still in a relationship with Jeff. Even though most of us consider him to be the epitome of a douche, we are trying not to pressure her about it. The last time they got into a fight, he cursed her out and called her every name in the book. We tried to convince her to end things, but she ended up just shutting us out. Although it's difficult to watch her in such an emotionally abusive relationship, we know it's ultimately her decision to make. All we can do is be there for her and make sure she knows we are a safe place for her when she needs us.

Smiling at Everett, I turn toward him. "I don't know; I may be more excited! Pop's is taking the kids for a four-day weekend to his beach house. And Charlie and Isla helped me find the best dress, so I'm rewarding them with a full spa day on Friday beforehand to get all dolled up."

Everett raises his eyebrows and sassily says, "All for me? You don't have to do all that for little old me."

Charlie protests, "You insisted we go all out for this." Before Everett can protest, Charlie puts her hands up and backtracks, "Not that I'm complaining! I'm so excited for a facial and maternity massage."

Isla chimes in, "And the mani/pedis! My nails are in dire need of some TLC."

I glance down at my cuticles, feeling the same way. "Same. I also need to ask you guys for a favor."

"What's the favor?" Hayes inquires as he strolls into our office, planting a kiss on Charlie and then looking at me expectantly.

I feel heat rush to my cheeks now that they're all around and staring at me. I know that I need to rip the bandage off and just tell them, but the words suddenly feel stuck in my throat. "I, uhm..."

Glancing between the four of them, the nerves hit me about getting this out for the first time. In the past, I've been pretty persistent that dating wasn't for me. I know that these are my safe people, but I'm still afraid they'll think it's too soon.

My cheeks puffed out as I let out a loud breath of air and then mumbled, "I joined a dating site last night."

Four gasps sound at the same time.

"You what?!" Charlie shouts across the small room.

I quickly glance over at the other office, making sure no one else is listening. Specifically, Andrew—I don't need him weighing in on this topic. He's still looking at his computer, so I know that I'm in the clear.

"I joined Bumble." I cringe, waiting for their reactions.

Isla beams and rushes over to give me a hug. I'm still sitting, but that doesn't stop her from throwing her arms around me. "I'm so proud of you!"

Over the top of Isla's head, I didn't miss the worried exchange of glances between the others.

Hayes clears his throat first. "So what's the favor, then?"

My bottom lip worries through my teeth. "I was hoping you guys would vet any potentials before I actually go on a date with them." We all know firsthand how stalkers can appear out of thin air, and putting myself out there on a dating app feels risky.

Isla pulls away from the hug, her eyes sparkling with concern. "That's a smart idea, actually."

Hayes nods in agreement, his expression serious. "Consider it done."

Everett visibly winces and then asks. "What about Drew?"

Shock and frustration roll through my body. "What about him?" I snap a little too aggressively.

They all exchange another set of worried glances, and then Hayes finally relents. "He's going to want to know about this. He cares about you."

I know he cares about me, but he has no say in my dating life.

My shoulder lifts defiantly, before dropping. "That's fine. He's probably going to be happy to hear it after..." Oh, shit.

I just almost revealed way more than I intended to. I try to think of something to say, anything to say, but my mind comes up blank.

"After what?" Charlie asks, leaning in with curiosity.

I shift, uncomfortable in my seat. I know they won't drop it, and I guess it's better coming directly from me. "I kissed Andrew the other day, and he stopped it."

"No!" Isla gasps. I had a feeling she would be bummed.

Both she and Charlie were both rooting for us, but it turns out that just wasn't in the cards for us.

Taking a deep breath, I feel a mixture of relief and disappointment. It's nice to have this off my chest and be able to talk about it.

"It's okay. I had a feeling he wasn't attracted to me."

I notice Everett's head rearing back in denial and his mouth open, but I keep forging on so that I don't lose my courage. "I kind of surprised him with the kiss, and he jumped back like I was on fire. It was... mortifying, to say the least. But it also helped me realize that I was ready to move on."

I hold up my now ringless left hand and wiggle my fingers.

Charlie's eyes swarm with tears as she gives me a big hug. "I'm sorry my brother is a dumbass, but I'm so happy for you! We will find you the perfect guy!"

Chuckling, I pull back. Hayes and Everett look concerned, but they both hug me and tell me they think it's good that I'm taking the next step.

It feels good to finally start the next chapter of my life. I was honestly shocked this morning when I woke up to see so many matches on my account. It's nice to feel wanted, and some of the guys I matched with seemed like good prospects. I'm not ready to be in a fully committed relationship, but going on a few dates or having a casual hookup with someone seems harmless.

Chapter Eighteen

Andrew

I called Olivia the morning after our ill-timed make-out session and was shocked when she answered. She did steam-roll the entire conversation, but at least I know there hasn't been permanent damage to our friendship.

By Friday, I hadn't seen much of her, except for the few smiles and waves she made on her way in and out of the office. It feels like a lifetime since I've spent any real time with her, and I'm starting to feel on edge. All that I want is to talk to her, let her know where my head is, and see where hers is.

We both got caught up in the moment, and seeing her almost in tears wrecked me. I know she hasn't been with anyone since Dan, and I'm sure me mauling her only freaked her out more. We both need to slow down and pace ourselves if we want this to work.

The problem is, that was the best kiss I've ever had. It damn near killed me to pull away. But our timing is so far off right now, and I'm terrified I'll screw it all up.

She's still wearing her wedding ring, so I know she isn't

ready to date, and I still have four and a half months left in my prison sentence. I mean, promise to Heather.

Everett went all out for his birthday. He reserved a badass party bus to drive us into Bend and then drop us all off at our houses after. He insisted we all dress up too, so I threw on a pair of light gray slacks and a black button-down and rolled the sleeves up. It's still hot as hell here, but the evenings cool down tremendously when the sun goes down.

Hayes and I are standing by the party bus, waiting outside of Olivia's house when I hear Everett loudly exclaim. "Damn, Mamacita! Lookin' fire today."

I glance over, thankful my sunglasses are shielding my eyes from the bright sun, and she can't see my reaction. The sight of her almost knocks the breath right out of me.

She's wearing a tiny black dress that shows far too much leg and cleavage. Her deep brown hair is pulled back into a low ponytail and has curls falling down her back. Her makeup looks dramatic, and the dark red lips do things to me, they shouldn't.

Somehow, the sight of her has me both turned on and pissed off at the same time. I don't want any of these other assholes staring at her all night. She's turned me into a caveman with one outfit. It has me itching to throw her over my shoulder and take her back into the house.

Her smile falters a bit when she sees me, but she keeps walking toward us. Her matching black heels look better suited for a runway than walking down her driveway. However, I can't help but admire how sexy her legs look.

Everett steps toward her and wraps her up in a hug. "Hottest one here, Liv." He winks at her and then kisses her on the cheek. I can't stop the "hmph" that comes out of my mouth, but I do contain the eye roll that threatens to escape.

Hayes ignores the both of us, giving her a brotherly hug. "You look lovely, Liv."

He steps out of the way so that I can give her a hug. Right as I'm about to step toward her, she gives me a small one-handed wave.

That's different. We hug all the time now. Maybe she's feeling weirder than I thought about last weekend. I narrow my eyes and step toward her. Her breath hitches, but she doesn't move.

I try to go in for a full hug, but she shuts me down. She puts one arm around my waist but holds her head and chest back. It barely lasted two seconds and she was quickly trying to step back. The same way she did with the other guys, only I didn't let her go.

Without releasing my grip on her, I tilted my head back to look at her face. I scrambled to find the right words, desperately trying to avoid sounding sleazy or jealous, but somehow, I only managed to make things worse. "You really went all out..."

The fake smile she plastered on her face falls a touch, and then she steps back quickly. "Thanks guys! I'm going to get out of this heat."

She walks away, stepping onto the bus, and Everett and Hayes both turn in unison. Looking pissed off and shocked at the same time.

Everett's eyes are wide, and he's looking at me like I might be the dumbest person that he's ever seen. "What is your fucking problem? 'You really went all out?' Are you a fucking moron? She looks fucking gorgeous, and you just blow it like that?!"

Surprised by his outburst, I stare back at Everett before stammering, "I didn't mean it like that."

He shakes his head back at me, and then I see his thumb start to rub circles with his index finger. "No. No. Just no. Did you see it? She's moving on, and you don't even realize it."

I glanced at Hayes, hoping for some backup, but instead he

blindsided me. "She mentioned to us that she joined a dating site."

It would've felt better if he had just punched me in the gut.

I splutter at him, trying to make sense of what he's saying. "No fucking way." She told me she didn't want to date. It would be too hard for the kids. Sure, that was a few weeks ago, but it couldn't have changed that fast. Right?

Everett slaps me in the arm—not hard, but enough to bring me back to reality. "She also told us you weren't attracted to her. Leapt off her like a little bitch the second she kissed you."

I feel a sudden burst of rage. "That's not what fucking happened!" I leapt off her because if I hadn't, I would've stripped her naked and fucked her right there in that gym. I wasn't going to take the chance of anyone walking in.

He looks at me incredulously. "Tell her that then! Because I'm done defending your dumbass when you can't even fucking compliment her."

I stare back at him dumbfoundedly. I've complimented her. I know I have. I tell her she's a good mom and a hard worker. I'm sure I've told her how beautiful I think she is. Right?

Everett turns and stalks back onto the bus. Hayes gives me a sympathetic look and sighs. "He's working through his own shit. You have what he wants, but you're blowing it. The dream girl right in front of you, who we all know wants you, and she's saying she's ready. His dream girl is..." He trails off and looks at the bus.

I know exactly who he's talking about. Isla.

I nod quickly, showing him I'm understanding what he's saying. "Not available?"

He looks back at me with sadness in his eyes. "Yeah. Don't lose her before you even have her."

I follow him onto the bus on autopilot, replaying Everett's rant through my mind. I try to think of every compliment that

I've given Olivia, but I come up blank. I've had a million dirty thoughts about her. I've wanted to say how sexy she is more than that, but I was so careful not to cross any lines that I may have inadvertently led her to think I'm not attracted to her.

Delta sits at the front of the bus with his phone plugged into the stereo, being DJ. Cooper, Lincoln, and Everett take up the end seat. Charlie, Olivia, and Isla sit on one side of the aisle, and Hayes sits on the other. I plant my ass next to Hayes, directly across from Olivia. Not once has she looked my way, and it's starting to drive me crazy.

Her phone dings, and she pulls it out, smiling at a text. It kills me that I can't ask her who it's from, but the music is too loud for me to say it without shouting. She quickly types something back and then puts her phone back in her purse. Her eyes glance at me, but when she catches me staring, something crosses her face. Guilt, maybe.

The girls talk and sing as the music blares on. All that I want to do is pull Olivia aside, but at least this gives me time to formulate a plan. I need to know how serious she is about dating. Surely, she would wait a few months until I could commit to her. I just need to convince her that it's a small wait for potentially a lifetime together.

I can't lose her to a fucking dating site.

The restaurant Everett picked is one of the fanciest I've ever been to. The dimly lit ambiance and elegant decor make it feel like we should be somewhere in Europe. Each table is set up in smaller rooms, creating an intimate atmosphere, regardless of the group size.

I don't leave her side as the hostess walks our group to the table. I need her next to me. It feels like she's slipping away faster than I can catch on.

I pull out her chair, and she gives me a small, reserved smile before sitting down. She politely sets her hands in her lap and shifts her shoulders slightly to the right toward Isla.

My jaw clenches together at the unmistakable cold shoulder she is giving me.

I decided to try to let it go and coax her back to me. We have all night to work this out, anyway.

It isn't until everyone has finished eating, and she reaches for her glass of wine to finish it, that I notice the "it" that Everett was referring to.

The ring is gone.

I reach out and snatch her hand before she grabs the glass. Pulling her hand back, I set it on my thigh. Her eyes snap to mine, wide and confused.

The only thing I can do is take a deep breath through my nose to control my temper. I hadn't realized the sight of her "on the market" would set me off like this. She wasn't mine, but she sure as hell wasn't anyone else's either.

We aren't even dating, but the insanity I'm feeling has me itching to buy a ring to stick on her finger right now.

"You took the ring off." I try to keep my voice low, but I think it comes out more like a growl.

She nibbles on her bottom lip and stumbles through her words, "Uhm, yeah. Well.. It just felt like time."

My heart clenches, trying to figure out what changed. "Why now?"

She lifts the shoulder closest to me nonchalantly and glances around the table to see if anyone is paying attention. They're all either unaware of what's happening or choosing to ignore us.

I still haven't let go of her hand, so I give it a little squeeze to encourage her to keep talking.

She takes a shaky breath and then looks me dead in the eye

while squaring her shoulders. "I'm going on a date tomorrow night."

The fuck you are.

My eyes and temper flare. "With who?!"

"A guy I met on a dating app a few days ago."

She must sense my rage because she squeezes my fingers, trying to give me reassurance. "I already asked the guys to vet him, and they said he checked out."

Those fuckers. I made a mental note to kick each of their asses.

It's not lost on me that she thinks I'm only being protective of her, but that will change soon.

I must be a masochist because I keep pressing. "Why now? The kiss?"

"Yeah, I mean, it's been a long time, but that kind of ignited something. I'm not looking for anything serious, but..."

"But what? You want a fuck buddy?" I ask sarcastically, expecting her to deny it.

A smile tugs at her lip. "Maybe."

My teeth gnash together so hard, I'm sure I'll chip a tooth. She can't seriously be looking for someone random to hook up with. What about the kids? What about me?

"Are you stupid?"

Her eyes go wide, and she snatches her hand out of mine. The hurt on her face says it all: I fucked up. Again.

I barely notice everyone standing to leave, but she does. She's on her feet, pushing her chair in, and walking outside before I can stop her. She doesn't even stumble on those four-inch heels.

"Are we heading to that rooftop bar above the hotel? We can walk from here; it's just up a block." Charlie asks everyone.

Olivia latches her arm around Isla, stopping me from continuing the conversation.

Hayes slows his pace and walks with me, behind the girls. "You good?"

I shake my head at him. "Nope. She told me about the date. You fucking trying to kill me?"

"It's not like that. I couldn't just let her date some sleazeball! I dismissed a handful of guys before I approved that one. What would you have done?"

"Called you."

He scoffs back. "Yeah, and said what? Hey, the girl you won't admit you're in love with thinks you don't find her attractive and wants to date some other dude?"

I pondered that for a second. In love with? I don't think I'm ready to admit that to myself just yet. I won't deny that my feelings for her are tenfold greater than anything I've ever felt before. She's everything I could want in a person, and more. I'm not scared often, but right now, I'm terrified that I've already lost her to someone else.

"Yep. That would've been better than me finding out in a restaurant full of people." I could have processed everything in private and then figured out a way to talk her out of it. One that didn't include me insulting her in the process.

"Okay," he grabs my shoulder and holds me back from walking into the hotel lobby. "I'm sorry. I should have told you."

"Thanks." I slumped back under the weight of his hand, suddenly feeling defeated. I know he's not the enemy; he's trying to be a good friend to both Olivia and me. It's not his fault that I'm always a step behind Olivia.

I haven't forgotten about the promise to Heather, but I'm so scattered that I don't know what to do. My moral compass feels like it's spinning out of control.

Hayes' eyes are filled with sympathy as he watches me reel. "Do you want advice?"

A small chuckle that almost sounds like a sob escapes: "Not sure even the wise Hayes can help me out of this one."

He smirks at me like he's about to prove me wrong. "Go up there; apologize. Trust me when I say, it goes a long way. Then you whisk her ass out of there and into one of those hotel rooms. We all know you want to. Don't define any relationship stuff tonight. Admit to yourself that you want her, and then tell her that. Not every relationship starts out perfect and wrapped in a pretty bow. Sometimes they start rocky and with a lot of uncertainties, but you need to think about the long game."

I narrow my eyes back at him, both annoyed and relieved that he's always the sound of reason. Hayes has always been the coolheaded one of the group, looking at every angle before deciding. I have a feeling he knew I would react like this and already had a speech planned.

"That could work." I'm not sure if I'm fully convinced, but Hayes has a way of making things sound logical and practical. Plus, he knows me and her better than anyone else, so maybe he's onto something.

His blank stare tells me he knows I'm just messing with him. I'm still a little annoyed that he didn't tell me sooner about Olivia. He's evidently known how I feel about her for longer than I have.

"Let's go; I've got a girl to win over." I grumble back.

We caught up to everyone at the elevator, waiting to ride up. I hang back once the cart opens, though. I need to book a room and brainstorm how I'm going to convince Olivia to give us a shot.

As soon as the elevator doors closed, I hit the front desk and got a room. I don't even care how much it costs or what the view is; just give me a private room and a locking door.

Chapter Nineteen

Andrew

With the room procured, I took the elevator to the roof. Nerves and excitement swirl in my stomach as I see the numbers approaching. Olivia has been more than forgiving to me in the past, but at some point, that's going to run out.

The doors open, and I step out onto the rooftop terrace. The city skyline stretches out before me, and beyond that is just black desert air. Bend may be much larger than Three Sisters, but it's still small enough that you can see the city limits; where wilderness and mountains meet an abrupt edge to the town.

Taking a deep breath, I remind myself to stay confident and genuine when I finally approach Olivia. She deserves the truth; I'm crazy about her and the kids. I want her and only her. I will beat the shit out of anyone who touches her.

I glance around and look for our group. Charlie, Isla, and Everett are standing around a tall table, sipping their drinks. Lincoln, Cooper, and Delta are flirting with a bachelorette party by the stage. I scan a little harder, looking for Olivia. A small flare of panic rises through my chest when I don't find her immediately.

Hayes slips up by my side, and before I have to ask, he nods his head toward a smaller bar off to the side. Olivia is standing by a group of at least four guys. One asshole is standing a little too close and laughing a little too hard at what she's saying. He screams fuckboy with his cocky demeanor and perfectly gelled hair.

I start to move, but Hayes throws his arm across my chest. "Calm the fuck down. It won't do any good to go over there raging. Ask her *politely* to talk."

Gritting my teeth, I take a deep breath through my nose, but unfortunately, it does little to calm my racing mind. When things are off with Olivia, my entire body goes into fight or flight mode, and right now, it's fight.

I focus solely on her as I approach, and the guys surrounding her notice me first, instantly puffing out their chests as if they can assert some kind of dominance. Olivia must sense their shift in demeanor because her posture tenses, yet she doesn't turn to look at me.

I gently place my hand on the small of her back, claiming what's mine—or what will be."Hey Boots, can we talk for a moment?" I ask, trying to keep my voice steady despite the adrenaline coursing through my veins.

Those brown eyes flash with annoyance, but I don't miss the curiosity lingering behind them. She looks directly at one of the guys, smiles politely, and apologizes.

He smiles back at her, graciously allowing it, but I don't miss the flare of his nostrils or the side glare he gives me. "No worries, Olivia. It was great running into you tonight. Maybe we can get that drink soon."

Over my dead body.

I grumble out, "She can't make it." I watch her mouth pop

open and her eyes go wide, but I gently grab her hand and loop our fingers together as I pull her back toward the elevator.

Hayes stands near the doors, already holding them open, waiting for us to get on. A damn good best friend.

I hit the button for the two floors below us and watched as the doors closed.

Letting go of her hand, I turn to look at her. Finally getting a chance to admire her without everyone watching me. She looks sexy as hell, the dress fitting her perfectly, her perfect tits rising and falling with every breath, and her lips slightly parted with confusion mixed with a little anger.

She's a goddamn wet dream.

She fiddles with her bare ring finger, twisting a ring that isn't there any longer out of habit.

"Where are we going?"

Giving her a half-smile, I try to keep it short. "To talk."

The elevator doors open, and I gently grab her hand this time, pulling her toward our room. Praying it's going to be our room. She hasn't agreed to anything yet, but I'm still hopeful I can convince her.

Opening the door, I guided her in. I'm too nervous to notice the grandiosity of the room, but I do spot sliding doors that open up to a balcony. Seems fitting since balconies are my go-to for apologies.

I pull her toward it, and she hesitates briefly before following me out the door and on to the balcony. "When did you get this room?"

"Right when we got here. We need to talk, and it shouldn't be around all of our friends."

A small nervous hitch of breath comes out before she asks, "About the kiss, or you calling me stupid?"

I wince but turn to stand fully in front of her. "Both. I'm

sorry I ever said that to you. I was caught off guard and was a jealous asshole. There's no excuse."

She tries to yank her hand out of mine, but I hold on to it. "Jealous?"

I nod, my heart pounding in my chest. "Not sure I've ever been more jealous than I have been tonight."

"I don't understand."

I let go of her hand but reached down to pull her waist flush to mine. "You said the kiss ignited something in you? Same. I've been obsessed with that kiss for days. Analyzed every part of it. Dreamt of it every night."

Her eyes softened in response. "It was a good kiss."

"The fucking best."

Olivia

My heart feels like it's going to pound out of my chest. Once again, back on the roller coaster that is Andrew. He pulls away, just to jump in further.

"I don't understand what you want right now." I tell him honestly.

He pulls his head back, but he keeps my body pinned to his. "All that I know is that I want you. I know you aren't looking for a committed relationship right now. I'm not in a position for that either. However, the thought of you with another man has me crawling out of my skin. I want a future with you. I want to be in your life. In the kids' lives. I want to kiss you, hold you, and fuck you every chance I get."

Goosebumps break out across my arms. Within seconds, he goes from sweet and sentimental to dirty—and I'm here for it.

It's been a long time since I've felt truly desired, and right now, in the dim light of this small balcony, it's all I feel.

"Would you be willing to take this slow with me? We can keep it between us for a while if you'd like. That way, there's no expectation and no pressure. I can't get that kiss out of my mind, and I would love nothing more than to strip you down right here and appreciate that sexy body."

"What does that look like, Friends with Benefits?" I feel too old to be getting tangled up in something so juvenile, but on the other hand, I'm not sure I'm ready to commit to a relationship. One of the main driving forces that made me think I was ready to date again was Andrew's hot body writhing into mine.

I can acknowledge that this may be the best of both worlds.

He shrugs one shoulder and grins with the most seductive smirk I have ever seen. "For now. Until we are both ready to take the next step."

I don't even have to think about it anymore; I've been hot and bothered by this man for months. I need the release, and I'm dying to see if he lives up to the expectations my mind has conjured up.

I lean up on my toes and press my lips against his, feeling the electricity surge through my body. The kiss is everything I hoped for and more, igniting that same fire within me from before.

Consequences be damned, I'm ready to explore every inch of his body while he does the same to mine.

He pulls back and grins from ear to ear. "Feels like I'm living a dream, Boots." He places soft kisses up the side of my jaw until he gets to my ear. "You in this dress? If I had known you were ready to start something, I would've never let you on that bus. I would've just carried you back into your house and locked the door."

"Good thing we have that big empty room right there,

then." I gesture with my head, and he swoops me into his arm's bridal style.

He sets me down at the edge of the bed, his hand roaming down my sides as he kisses me breathless. I don't even realize he has my dress unzipped until it's falling to the ground. He leans his head back and groans as he sees my black strapless bra and matching lacy thong. "Fuck *me*, Olivia. You naked is even sexier than I imagined, and I've imagined it a lot."

I lock my lips to his again as he grabs a fist full of ass, moaning into my lips. That sound alone spurs me on; it might be the sexiest sound I've ever heard.

I unbutton his shirt slowly and untuck it out of his suit pants. I take a second to admire his toned chest and abs as my hand traces the contours of his muscles. "Keep looking at me like that, and you'll give me an ego."

I reach down and palm him through his pants. "You're a 6'3" Navy SEAL, and obviously well-endowed. If your ego isn't the size of Texas already, you're insane."

"You forgot about my chiseled jaw and stunning eyes." He says as he wriggles his eyebrows at me.

With a smirk and a fingertip sweep across that impeccable jaw, I remark, "There's the cocky attitude that turns me on."

His eyes darken with desire as he pulls me in closer. His kiss turns ravenous as we shed the rest of our clothes. The rest of our night is spent in a blur of passion and pleasure—forgetting all the reasons that kept us apart.

Chapter Twenty

Olivia

Light snoring startles me awake out of what felt like a deep sleep. Panic immediately ensues until I look around the room, remembering everything that happened last night. It's been a long time since I've had anyone other than one of the kids sleeping in bed next to me, and apparently I'm out of touch.

Andrew pulls me in closer to him and kisses across my bare shoulder. "Good morning, Boots."

When he rolls over on top of me, continuing our escapades from the night before, I can't help but feel a rush of something that feels a lot like hope. Part of me was expecting him to pull away again in his signature Andrew style. Instead, he seems as desperate as I am to keep whatever this is going.

It isn't until it's close to time to check out of our room that we finally go back to the real world.

"Are we ubering it, taxi ride, or calling a friend?" I ask Drew while slipping back into my dress. Nothing like the walk of shame at 10a.m on a Saturday morning.

"Hayes and Charlie are on their way." *Lovely.*

My shoulders slump in response. They're going to lose their damn minds over this. Charlie is going to get her hopes up and assume we are together now. She's probably already planning the wedding, babies, and lifelong happiness. While I'm still trying to process the fact that I just had the most mind-blowing sex I've ever had.

Andrew walks up behind me, wrapping his arms around my waist and setting his forehead on my shoulder. "You don't want them to know?"

"I don't mind if they know. It'll just be hard for them to understand that we are keeping this casual for a little while."

"Hayes gets it. He was the one who convinced me to get the room and worry about the details later."

"He's not the one I was worried about. Your sister will be over the moon about this. She's probably picking out baby names for us as we speak."

"Is that something you'd want again? More kids? A wedding?" He almost sounds melancholy while he asks, like he's afraid of my answer.

"Someday? Maybe. I'd be happy either way, but if the right person came along and wanted kids, then yeah, I'd be all for it. I love being a mom and watching Ellie and Ben grow into who they are."

I feel his head nod, and then he kisses my shoulder. "Good to know."

I'm dying to ask him what he wants, but something holds me back. This is casual for now; if things grow into more, we can talk about it then.

His phone beeps with a text. "They're downstairs, you ready to go?"

Ready as I'll ever be.

The shit-eating grin on Charlie's face confirms what I

already knew. She tries to purse her lips as I climb into the back of Hayes truck, but she's smiling too hard for it to work.

I point my finger at her, "Not a word, Carrington."

She cackles and turns back to the front. "Told ya so!"

Andrew scoots to the middle from the other side so that he's sitting right next to me. "Told her what?"

Charlie turns around again. "Told her you had the hots for her and wanted to do dirty-dirty things."

Rolling my eyes while shaking my head, I look out the window, trying to hide my grin.

He places his hand on my bare thigh. "No denying that. Only wish I had done it sooner."

You and me, both.

The kids spent three days plotting and planning the most "epic" movie night they could think of. We even drove to Bend to shop for the coziest blankets, pillows, and pajamas we could find. This morning they woke up, champing at the bit, to get everything set up for Andrew. If I'm being honest, I was just as excited as they were. Our new "arrangement" has transformed into a lot of sneaking around after the movie ends and the kids go to bed.

In hindsight, I shouldn't have let them get so excited about it and start so early, but Andrew had never canceled before. This would have made the ninth movie night in a row—excluding the weekend of Everett's birthday. Not that I'm counting, but I figured there wasn't any harm in letting them stay busy arranging and rearranging everything. Right? Wrong.

I told the kids that Andrew had to work late today, and it set the kids off. Ellie went into full-on rant mode, stomping her little foot and shouting, "Are you kidding me? After all this work!" Her tantrum was raging until she noticed how quiet Ben was being. He had retreated into that shell of his so fast that I barely blinked.

Ellie must have noticed too because she immediately stopped her rant to comfort him. "Well, Benny! That just means more smores for us!"

"Yeah," he mustered a smile for her, and then solemnly asked if he could go build legos in his room. Knife to gut. I knew better than this; I shouldn't have let them get their hopes up.

I try to give him my best, reassuring smile. "Sure, buddy! Is it okay with you two if I invite Pop's tonight? He's going to love all the work you two did!"

Ellie's face lit up in support. "Yes! Good idea, mommy!"

Ben nodded his head and mumbled something, but he was already walking through the door back inside the house.

Just after six o'clock, Pop arrived bearing four enormous pizzas, and I couldn't help but groan when he entered the room. I'm going to gain fifteen pounds by the winter if these men keep bringing enough food to feed a frat house.

We settled outside at the patio table, scarfing down pizza and laughing with Pop. Ellie has done nothing but rave about the new s'mores maker they got and the popcorn machine. Even Ben's funky mood didn't last long after Pop's arrival.

It's just been a nice, relaxing summer evening, and I've almost put Andrew completely out of my mind. Almost.

The sun is finally getting close to setting, so I send the kids to get their pajamas on while Pop's helps me clean up the dinner plates in the outside kitchen.

He's been so different since his retirement—where he used to see the kids a few times a month, he's now helping me out almost daily with them. I know he misses Dan and holds on to a lot of guilt, but his attitude around the kids never reflects that.

It's like he flips a switch whenever they're around and is precisely who he needs to be for them. I have a small inkling that Hayes was the one who knocked some sense into him about retiring, but I've never outright asked.

I'm washing the last plate, a little lost in thought, when he hits me with a question out of left field: "You ever think about dating, Liv?"

My eyes darted to his as I inhaled sharply. "What? Why?" We don't normally talk about this stuff. Sure, we've talked about Dan and missing him, but never about me moving on.

His eyes are filled with so much sadness that my heart clenches for him. "The kids are getting older, but you're still young. Your life didn't end with Dan." He takes a deep breath in and then huffs it out. "I don't want you to end up like me."

"What do you mean, end up like you?"

"After I lost Anne, I lost myself too. I focused on the boys and my career, and that was it. I kept telling myself I'd date later on. But later on, it never came, and now I look back and wonder what the hell I was thinking."

I let out a resigned laugh. I know exactly what he was thinking. I've been thinking the same thing for years. "It's hard to put that trust in someone again. Especially because it's not just me I have to think about anymore. The kids take things harder than I do sometimes. They've already been through so much, and I don't want to expose them to any more heartbreak."

He nods his head in response. "You can't control their heartbreaks. People will disappoint them, you'll disappoint them, and life will disappoint them. You just need to keep showing them how to grieve that heartbreak and come out of it stronger. You, of all people, know how to navigate through difficult situations. You're resilient, Liv. There's no one else I'd rather have as a role model for my grandkids."

Tears threaten to spill out of my overflowing eyes. *Damn, Pop's, for hitting me with the sentimental shit tonight.* I've been concerned all day about my situation with Andrew and how it will affect the kids.

"I'm scared to commit to anything serious. I thought something was going on with Andrew, but I'm not sure he's ready to take on a widow and her two kids." I tell him honestly. I never thought I'd find myself in this kind of situation, trying to navigate a complicated relationship while also being a single parent. It's overwhelming, wondering where his head is while trying to figure out where mine is as well.

"What makes you think that?"

"It seems like he carries as much baggage as I do. On top of that, I think he may have Levi's stance on marriage and kids."

Pop's grumbles out a curse worse. "I'm not sure where I went wrong with that boy. He always had to beat to his own drum." He shakes his head in mock disapproval and then pulls me into a hug. "You've always been a daughter to me; losing Dan doesn't change that. He'd have wanted you and the kids to be happy; however that looks. He pulls back, still holding on to my arms. "And I want more grandkids! Levi isn't ready yet, so that leaves you."

I laugh and give him a playful shove. "Don't you put that out into the universe, Ezekiel Turner!"

He winks back, looking so much like an older version of Dan that it almost hurts.

The kids come running in, chanting, "Movie night! Movie night!" in perfect unison. I swear they practice that or something.

Chapter Twenty-One

Andrew

"Get me eyes on Delta!" Hayes bellows toward the table. We have our team setup at the conference table; a projector on the wall shows satellite footage of a remote town in Brazil. Three of the guys, Delta, Leo, and Cooper, are trying to extract men from the country they are being held hostage in.

I grit my teeth, waiting for the all-clear sign. We've been in the office for the last eighteen hours, trying to evac men who were on Delta's team when they were all in the army. Delta insisted he go to Brazil, saying he owes one of the guys his life.

Not only am I tired, but I'm also fuming that I had to bail on Friday night movie night with Olivia and the kids. I sent her a text a few hours ago, but I haven't even had an opportunity to check to see if she responded. It's been controlled chaos.

Two men, Delta Force Operators, Dylan Jones and Keith Monroe are currently being held by a ruthless cartel, and three of my best guys are risking their lives to get them out. Even though these men received special forces training, I'm beginning to wonder how they ever made it through boot camp, given that they allowed themselves to be kidnapped in Brazil.

If it weren't for Jones getting a call-out to Delta before all hell broke out, and he disappeared off the map, we would have had no idea they were even down there. The news would have ruled it as two discharged American soldiers victimized by a mysterious disappearance in South America.

They are actually the perfect example of why Hayes and I started our Elite Forces Security and Contracting business. We deal in iron-clad contracts that support our guys and ensure their safety and success on missions. We pride ourselves on selecting only the most skilled and disciplined individuals to join our team. It's frustrating to see others in the field who lack the same level of professionalism and commitment. Nonetheless, we remain dedicated to our mission of providing top-notch security services to clients worldwide.

A tiny agency tucked away so deeply in our government that it is unheard of has hired them to get information on a new cartel trying to work its way into North America.

These dumbasses went in blind, without support, and with no backup plan or official contract, expecting they would have all the necessary resources and support. The agency claims to know nothing about what's going on or even who these guys are, and without a paper trail, they're trying to wash their hands clean of responsibility.

Hayes spent three hours speaking to every contact he could find at the agency, all of them claiming the same thing: they're not investigating anyone or anything in South America. Luckily, between the seven of us here and our connections, we were able to reach out to someone high enough to figure out what was going on.

It was actually Everett who saved the day. He made one call, and within twenty minutes, the agency was forced to come clean and offer us any support we needed. Delta, Leo, and Cooper were already on a flight there by that point.

Once the team was there, it took four hours to find Jones and Monroe's location, two hours to come up with a plan, and fifteen minutes to implement it. They were in and out without being seen or heard, with no casualties, and no record of them even being in Brazil.

A total of twenty-two hours, from start to finish. I'm beyond proud of how the team handled this. Even though a few of the guys were trained in different branches of the military, we all worked seamlessly together. Each guy had an input, an idea, or a skill that contributed to the mission, and to say I'm impressed is an understatement.

My eyes feel like they're bleeding from all the computer work and phone calls, though. It's difficult to believe that only seven months ago, this was my daily life. I was itching to be on that plane with them, but at the same time, I knew I was better suited here. This cozy office has begun to grow on me.

Checking the clock on my screen, I'm shocked to see it's only 1800. I could easily run home and shower, put on something comfy, and head to Olivia's to be with her and the kids. I probably wouldn't make the start of the movie, but at least I'd get a little time with them.

I glance down the table at Hayes, who looks as worn out as I feel. "Time to pack it up? The guys just boarded their flight stateside and should arrive in the morning; everything else is looking quiet."

Hayes nods his head and starts packing up his stuff. "Sounds good; I'll finish everything up with our contact at the agency tomorrow."

"Excited to get home to Char?"

He chuckles, "Fuck yeah, I missed my girl and my bed. I can't believe we used to do this shit all the time. You should take the guys out for a beer; y'all deserve it after the last 24."

Liam glances up from his screen. "I'm in." Joined the team

less than a week ago. He's a big dude, with a very slight Russian accent. We've known him for years, served with him, and still don't know much about his history. But, we trust him with our lives.

"I'll text Everett; he was the one who called the VP, anyway." Lincoln adds.

Shit, there goes my evening for the second time. It's not their fault; they've worked their asses off to get this done, and they deserve it.

I let out a dramatic sigh. "Fine, but I need a shower first. I'll meet y'all there in an hour."

On the drive home, I take my time, windows down, enjoying the warm August evening. The sun is starting to set earlier, a sign that summer is coming to an end soon. It's bitter-sweet; this has been the best summer of my life. Spending time with Olivia and the kids, my best friend and sister, and even having Everett as a roommate. But I'd be lying if I said I wasn't excited to get closer to making things official with Olivia. We've only been hooking up for a few weeks now, but every time it gets better and better.

When I drive past Olivia's driveway, and it nearly kills me to not pull down it. The last bit of the drive is consumed with thoughts of them. What movie and takeout they pick, if Ellie convinces her mom to let her wear her tutu to bed, or if Ben finally mastered the move he was working on at Jits last week. I thought about calling them the second I got into the truck, but I'm sure they're already halfway into the movie by now, and I didn't want to disrupt that.

The second I park and get out, I notice Everett standing in the doorway. He looks like a kid on Christmas morning, bouncing up and down with a shit-eating grin on his face. Then he throws his hands out and says, "I'm waiting" with a high-tone pitch.

My face must conveyed that I have no idea what movie he's referring to now because he says, "Come on! Vizzini? Princess Bride!" He lets out a dramatic sigh when I only shake my head at him. "Whatever. Hurry the fuck up; we've got beers to drink and women to chase. I'll even drive if you can be ready in 10 minutes."

I roll my eyes and walk a little slower. I'm not interested in chasing any other woman than Olivia, but we are still trying to keep everything on the down-low, so I choose to ignore his comment. "You'll drive either way; I haven't slept more than two hours since Wednesday night."

I'm pretty sure he called me a pussy, but I've already slammed my bedroom door. I shower and change into my boots and wranglers on autopilot. The outfit has surprisingly grown on me the last few months, becoming the only one I wear outside of work.

I don't even look in the mirror after I throw on my clothes; I just walk out to his 4Runner and get in the passenger seat. The only woman I care to impress isn't going to be there tonight.

Damnit, I miss her.

I unlock my phone to see if she's texted and notice I have a few unread. One from Connie checking in, Heather's sister Kara confirming wedding details, and the last one is a picture from Olivia.

Her patio is set up with a projector and screen; fairy lights dangle around the pool; pillows and blankets make a giant bed on the pool deck cover. They went all out on this movie night; there's even an old-timey popcorn maker. The text beneath read, "Aww, the kids have been working on this all week to surprise you! Bummed that you have to work late, but we understand. I told them we can leave it up for a while, so maybe we can rain check."

Fuck, fuck, fuck.

Now I feel like the biggest asshole. She sent that text a little after I texted her, nearly five hours ago. I typed out and retyped out an apology, but nothing seems right.

A loud groan escapes as I try to think of what to say.

"What's got your panties in a twist over there?" Everett chides.

"I canceled on Olivia and the kids when I thought we would be working late. Then I got sucked into going out tonight."

He glances over at me, eyebrows knitting together.

I cringe as I say, "I didn't know it, but they set up a whole thing for me. She said they've been working on it all week."

"Oof, fuck man. You want me to turn around and drop you off?"

"Yes, but no, I shouldn't. I owe the guys a beer; they kicked ass and didn't complain."

He shakes his head at me and whips the 4Runner around. "You're an idiot, but at least you have me to set you straight."

"What the fuck are you doing?"

"Not one of those guys would want you to choose that family over them. I guarantee if Olivia looked at any of them the way she looks at you, they wouldn't have even thought twice."

He's right, of course. She's the best, and so are her kids. The thought of disappointing them kills me.

Five minutes later, I'm knocking on Olivia's door empty-handed. My stomach is in knots when I realize no one is coming to open it. Zeke's truck is in the driveway, so I try the handle and pray they are just in the back watching a movie and not out at dinner somewhere.

I open the door, and make my way through the house, calling for them. I spot them outside on the pool deck and instantly smile.

"Hey y'all! Mind if I crash your party?"

I'm met with two giant grins and kids throwing blankets around to run to me.

They both collide with my legs. "Sorry, I'm late! Do you mind if I finish the movie?"

Zeke grins at me like the kids just were—a first, if I'm being honest. He's always been cordial toward me, but I think he knew I had feelings for his son's wife.

Olivia's wide eyes stare at me, and she rolls her lips together before looking away.

"Of course, come sit with us!" Ellie pulls me toward the makeshift bed they have on the pool cover and sets me right in between her and her mom. She's only five and by far the best wingman I've ever had.

I turn to Olivia and give her my most charming smile. "Hi, Boots."

Her shoulders fall a touch, and she shakes her head, but a very tiny smile plays on her perfect lips. All I want to do is kiss her hello, but I don't want to confuse the kids or myself. Instead, I settle for sneaking my hand under the blanket to hold her hand.

The movie is over too soon, and Zeke helps me carry the kids into their rooms while Olivia picks up the blankets from outside.

We end up walking out of the kids rooms at the same time, almost running into each other.

A corner of his mouth lifts, and he sets his hand on my shoulder as we walk through the hall.

"You seem like a good man, Reynolds. Don't fuck it up."

The uptick in my heartbeat is instantaneous as his words sink in. The realization that Dan's father just gave me his permission to date his daughter-in-law. Gratitude and immense pressure hit my chest in tandem. I want nothing more than to be the man she deserves, but I can't promise her the world yet.

"Alright, kids. I'm outta here. See ya out at the lake tomorrow!" Zeke hugs Olivia when we make it back to the kitchen and then winks at me as he walks by to leave.

I shake my head and chuckle once he passes, and Olivia raises an eyebrow in question.

"I think I just got the 'dad talk' and 'approval' in two sentences."

She groans in response and spins to put away the rest of the snacks that were left out.

"He gave me the 'you should get back on the horse' speech before you got here."

Wrapping my hands around her waist, I pull her back flush with me and kiss her neck. "You should. Right now, to be specific."

"How about in twenty minutes? I need to get some stuff put away and a few things ready for tomorrow. Luke is riding with me and the kids, and he said he would be here before lunch."

My hands tightened into fists automatically at the mention of Luke's name. We haven't talked about what is going on with them, and it's been driving me crazy.

"Why is he riding with you?" I ask, trying to hide the jealousy in my voice.

She turns around with an evil glint in her eye. "Are you *jealous* of Luke?"

I shrug, making sure to keep her caged in between me and the countertop.

She places her palm on the side of my cheek, and I lean into it. "You have nothing to worry about with Luke. He was not only Dan's best friend mentor, but his girlfriend, Madelyn, was in a car accident the day that Dan was murdered. I call it our doomsday. He goes to visit Maddy at the memory care facility almost every morning. Anterograde Amnesia. She lives each day like it was the day before the car accident."

My shoulders slump as I lean my forehead against hers. I feel like the biggest asshole out there. I can't begin to imagine the heartache that must be for him. To essentially lose your best friend and girlfriend on the same day.

"I didn't know. I should've asked sooner."

She lets out a soft chuckle. "He doesn't talk about it, or her, really. Every man in my life seems to carry an unusual amount of guilt on his shoulders."

I nodded in return. She's got that right.

She leans on her tiptoes and plants a chaste kiss on my lips, which I immediately deepen. Picking her up, I carried her out of the kitchen. Hoping she would forget about whatever she wanted to get done tonight.

I need her in her bed, behind that locked door, and on top of me.

Chapter Twenty-Two

Olivia

October rolled around faster than I expected. The chill is finally in the air most mornings, and today is no exception. The kids are beyond excited for Halloween in a few weeks, though. They're planning costumes that include the entire family, plus Charlie, Hayes, Everett, and Andrew. That last one gives me butterflies every time.

We've been together for a few months now, and the kids still seem blissfully unaware. Thank God they're still young and naive because I'm in a constant state of blush and freshly fucked glow. Charlie, Hayes, and Everett noticed within the first 24 hours, but luckily all agreed it was best to keep it from the kids until we were serious.

Andrew spends most of his evenings at our house now. We still do Friday night movie nights, but instead of talking for hours after the kids go to bed, we are locked away in my bedroom. The talking still happens, just with more benefits.

Overall, Friends with Benefits turned out to be a damn good decision. I've been tempted for weeks now to ask him if he's ready to turn it into a full relationship. That talk with Pop's about dating has been weighing heavily on my mind. I'm tired of hiding everything, and I know the kids will be thrilled. We've also never discussed seeing other people. Are we allowed to? Should I be keeping my options open still? I don't want that; I want him.

I glance over at Andrew. He's still smiling as his head bops to the beat of the country song we are listening to.

"How much shit do you think we're going to get for walking back in all post-sex glow?" He's driving us back to the office after our "lunch date." Which mainly consisted of him bending me over my kitchen counter and then grabbing a protein bar from the pantry as we left.

"Probably about the usual amount," he says with a smirk. "It wouldn't be so obvious if you could wipe that smile off your face."

I scoff back, "Me? You're the one who went from never cracking a smile to always looking like that damn smirking emoji."

He laughs and kisses my hand. "True, I wouldn't change a thing about it, though."

"No? I was thinking maybe we switch up to mornings." I innocently shrug when he glances over at me.

His grin falters just a bit. "As in, meet-up after you drop the kids off?'

I do my best to muster up all the courage I have. I've never exactly asked a man to be my boyfriend before. It seems so juvenile, but I'm itching to announce to everyone that we are together.

"Or you could just stay the night? You're over most evenings anyway." I risk taking a glance at him; his eyebrows are drawn together, the little wrinkle between them becoming prominent, but he hasn't taken his focus off the road. I'm not sure what his silence means, but I soldier on: "The kids probably wouldn't even notice a difference, but we can ease them into it; maybe go on some official dates."

Occasionally, Pop will take the kids overnight so that we can have some adult time. He's one of the few who knows we are trying things out, but since the rest of the town doesn't, we've never left the house. Usually, we are too consumed with each other to want to leave the house. On the off chance we do go out, it's always with the group, and we still act as only friends. This town is too small and has too many gossips for us to think we could get away with flirting in public.

He clears his throat and sits up a little straighter. His jaw is tightening and loosening as he thinks of what to say. I can't tell whether I'm reading into it or not, but he's almost starting to look nervous. "Maybe. I just..." he pauses to clear his throat. "I want to make sure the timing is right. Keep us on solid ground before the kids know everything."

His hesitancy is a major letdown, but I understand where he's coming from. We are still relatively new, and maybe he's just not ready to fully commit to a mom and her kids. I'd rather he is 100% in before we talk to them anyway, so I'm glad he's being honest. It still feels like a punch to the gut, though.

My shoulders droop, but I force a smile. "That sounds good. I know we started this with an agreement to go slow because of our histories, but I wanted to let you know I'm ready when you are."

He nods his head but doesn't look at me or smile; his brows are still furrowed. I feel like I'm walking a tightrope right now, trying to confess that I've fallen for him without outright admitting it. Instead of giving me the reassurance I crave, though, we drove the rest of the way into the office in silence. Thank goodness it's a short drive because, by the end of it, the inside of my lip is raw and bleeding from chewing on it so hard.

"Hold on..." He hops out of his truck and jogs over to my side, opening the door for me. He doesn't back up; he just helps me out, enveloping his body in mine in a tight hug. Slightly concealed by the open door, he kisses me—one of those knock-you-on-your-ass kisses. One arm wraps around my waist, keeping me up, and his right hand tilts my chin up so that his mouth can meet mine.

Damn, I really don't know how to read him. One minute, I feel like we are heading into deeper water, and the next, I feel like we will always be stuck in the shallow end.

<hr>

Halloween finally arrives without any more hiccups, but I've also tried to cut back on our lunch rendezvous. I don't have much of a guard left up, but I'd be lying if I said his reservations didn't erect some walls.

We decided to go to the kids' elementary school instead of normal trick or treating; they have a full trunk or treat outside in the parking lot, and inside the school is a big party.

Ben and Ellie wanted to be Ant-Man and The Wasp, wearing a full mask and suit. I can hardly recognize them, but they are committed to their costumes.

I, on the other hand, am starting to feel a little self-conscious in my Wonder Woman costume. I tried to tame it down, opting for jeans instead of the skirt it came with, but the red corset top is a little PG-13 for a kids' event; the thigh-high boots and lasso aren't exactly helping either.

The parking lot is crazy; kids are running everywhere trying to get the most candy, and by the time we get inside, I'm overwhelmed.

We spot the rest of the group chatting with Luke, still in his uniform from work that day, manning the Sheriff's Department Dunk Tank booth. Everyone else is dressed up as superheroes, though.

"I can't believe you didn't write "Get Dunked, not Drunk!" Charlie mocks Luke. She's dressed up as "Fat Thor," rocking sweatpants, a crop top sweatshirt that accentuates her growing belly, a red cut-off robe, and a full beard.

"I agree with pregnant Thor; you really missed an opportunity there." I wink at Luke while I give Charlie a hug.

"Holy shit, Liv! You look amazing!" Charlie raves at me.

"Same to you!"

"Yeah, but oh my god, I love this new you!" She waves her hand up and down my body and grins.

It's true; I've definitely started to dress up a bit more. I like feeling good and looking good. I'm not as stuck in my standard old ways anymore.

I glance over at Hayes, covered in green body paint and shredded clothes, throwing the ball and trying to dunk a new deputy recruit.

Everett is talking shit, as always, while dressed as Wolverine in a wife beater and jeans. He even has the iconic mutton-chop/ducktail combination going for him.

"Where's the claws at Wolverine?" I shout at him.

He looks at me, just now noticing we got here, and lets out a low whistle. "Damn. You are a *wonder* woman."

"Watch it, Astor." Snaps from behind me, and I instantly feel my knees go a little weak at that growly tone.

I already knew it was Andrew behind me. However, I wasn't prepared to swoon as hard as I did when I turned around. He's down on one knee, admiring the kids' costumes, no doubt making them feel like they have the best ones in the room.

His eyes light up when Ellie shows him her bag of candy and offers to share it with him tomorrow at Movie Night.

I let my eyes roam over his entire body, savoring each moment while he gave them his undivided attention.

Superman has never looked so good. He opted for the full suit and cape. Filling it out better than Henry Cavill ever did. He's freshly shaved and showing off his killer jawline. That alone has me fanning myself thinking about all the naughty things it does to me. I used to think role-playing was cheesy, but damn if I don't want to be a damsel in distress right about now.

He stands and takes a step closer to me as the kids run over to Hayes and Everett to show off their costumes.

"Looking good, Wonder Woman. I might need saving later on," he winks at me.

The kids are only a few feet away, so I try to keep my voice low, but still flirty. "I was thinking the same thing. You should keep that costume; it might come in handy." I waggle my brows a little.

"Only if I can borrow that lasso," he says, tugging lightly on it. My body wants to give in and close the distance, but before I can, he lets go and takes a step back.

Damn him. He makes me simultaneously turned on and disappointed at the same time.

Another reminder why I wish the kids knew: I'm so tired of pretending we are strictly friends in public. My traitorous body gives me away every time anyway. If he wasn't so good at putting space between us, I would've caved a hundred times already.

"Pop's having any sleepovers soon?" He asks, breaking me out of my momentary discontentment.

Since I've been avoiding "lunch dates," it's been almost a week since we last had sex. Friday movie night is the only time he stays until the kids go to bed during the week. Giving us just a bit of time to have some very quiet, sexy time.

I shrug noncommittally. "Not sure; I'll have to ask him what his schedule is like." The sparkle in his eyes dims, just enough that I feel guilty for being so harsh. "Maybe you could stay a little after the movie, though?"

He gives that signature smirk, "I'd like that."

I'm such a sucker; it takes one look and a promise of unlimited orgasms, and I've forgotten all about whatever distance he keeps firmly between us.

Charlie pulls us out of our little flirt bubble by grabbing my elbow. "Let's get a group picture!"

We all stand together, with the kids in the front, and I'm flanked by Everett and Charlie, with Hayes and Andrew on the opposite side. I can't help but feel a little disappointed that he chose to stand next to Hayes and not me. We don't have a single picture, just the two of us. I'm increasingly feeling like the dirty little secret he is hiding. The only thing keeping me sane is that our friends know about us and support us being together.

The night continues; we all separate a few times, with Andrew sticking with the other adults while I follow Ellie around. Ben is around here somewhere too, under strict orders not to leave the gym, but I allowed him to go hang out with his friends.

Ellie races off to do the small hay maze they have set up, and I stand by the exit waiting for her. I'm admiring my shoes when a tingle runs down my spine, and I get goosebumps on my arms—that same feeling of being watched.

I quickly look around, hoping it's just Andrew, but he's with Ben, shooting baskets. I scanned through the crowd but didn't notice anyone out of the ordinary. Either way, I'm thankful that Ellie pops out and can stick close to my side.

I convince her to head toward the basketball court and

immediately regret it. Our friends are standing there, saying their goodbyes so that they can head to the 21+ Costume Party at Ponderosa Pine.

Andrew hangs back a second after they leave, hugging Ellie. "Thanks for the invite, little Wasp! I had the best time!"

She beams that radiant smile at him, then without being prompted thanks him for dressing up with her. When he looks at me, I'm already smiling.

He stands up, puts his hands in his pockets, and offers me a goodbye nod with a sad smile. "I wish you could make it tonight."

Oof, that hurt a little. Ellie gets a hug, while I'm reduced to a head nod.

Jealous of a five-year-old in a wasp costume. A new low, even for me.

Feeling about the size of an actual wasp right now, I fake a smile, trying not to show how much his dismissal affected me. "Thanks for coming tonight! We owe you one, huh, Els?" I bump her with my hip, and she grins.

She nods at both of us and says, "Sure do! We had the best costumes!"

His brow furrows, and he looks like he wants to ask something, but instead, he just shakes his head. "Ok, see ya'll later then..."

I point her in the opposite direction and try to remember that being a mom is the most important thing in my life. Sure, I'm bummed that I don't get to hang out and drink with them at the bar, but that's not my life. Never has been.

Seeing Ellie try to eat a donut off a string faster than all the other kids? That's my life, and I'm damn proud of it. She keeps me laughing so hard that I almost stop dwelling on Andrew. Almost.

While she's collecting her prize, more candy—big shocker—

I post the video I just took of her annihilating her opponents. Her entire face is covered in chocolate and sprinkles after practically inhaling that donut.

A few hours later, the kids are in bed, and I'm sipping a glass of wine and tapping my fingers on my kitchen island when my phone beeps with a notification from Andrew. The insecurities have run rampant through my mind since we left the Halloween party, and I hate that I'm even contemplating opening it.

I've analyzed every minute detail about my relationship—or lack thereof—with Andrew, and then compared it to my marriage with Dan.

A laugh bubbles up as I take a sip of my wine. I can't believe how opposite my situationship with Andrew is from my marriage with Dan.

Dan and I barely spent any quality time together in private; our sex life was nearly nonexistent. Between chasing toddlers around and our work schedules, we just never made the time for it. I didn't mind it though, not that the sex wasn't good; it just wasn't mind-blowing enough to drop everything. In public, though, he paraded me around, showering me with compliments and affection. I realize now that I only felt loved when he was telling everyone he loved me.

Andrew, however, treats me like a goddess in private, worshiping my mind and body every chance he gets. We can't keep our hands off each other. Our connection feels like the complete package. That is, until we are out in public, and he treats me like every other friend in our group, and I'm often left feeling a little neglected.

I finally decided to open the message; we agreed to no longer avoid each other.

"Dammit! I knew I should've driven myself. I can't believe I missed that!"

As I'm trying to decide what to say back, the three dots appear, and another message comes through.

"You looked beautiful tonight, Boots. Can't get you off my mind."

Yep. In private, he certainly says plenty of things to keep me hooked on that line.

Chapter Twenty-Three

Andrew

It feels like the weather changed in a blink, going from sunny 70-degree October days to barely above 45 degrees most days in November. The cold, high desert air has me breathing in a little deeper, the smell of Juniper trees hanging in the air.

Everett and I still run most mornings before work, pushing ourselves in the nearly ten-degree weather. He finally landed the pilot job at the sheriff's department, so his new schedule can be a little irregular.

Occasionally, Hayes will meet us at the end of his driveway to run with us, but that's getting few and far between with the progression of Charlie's pregnancy. She's almost in her third trimester and acting like she's miserable, so Hayes is on high alert, making sure she gets whatever she wants.

Today, it's just Everett and me, though. Running at a decent pace, but neither of our heads seemed to be in it.

I can't think of anything but Olivia these days. It's been a few weeks since she's brought up the fact that she's ready to take the next step and start publicly dating. One side of me wanted to scream from the rooftops. Yes, thank God! The other side was reminded that I stupidly made that promise to Heather.

I tried and failed to think of the right thing to say to her, but ended up with an excuse that I don't even believe. Then seeing her face fall damn near gutted me.

I just need to get through the next four and a half weeks, and we can put this all behind us. I'll go to that wedding, officially tell Heather we aren't getting back together, and then ask Olivia to be in a committed relationship.

Everett trips a little over his own feet, clearly lost in his thoughts as well. He won't talk about what's eating at him, but if I had to guess, it's Isla's growing withdrawal from the group. She barely spends any time with us outside when she's at work, and she makes a point to avoid Everett if he comes into the building. It's not just him she's avoiding, though; Olivia mentioned that she's growing worried about her as well.

I clear my throat, hoping if I mention Olivia's side of things, he will open up. "Olivia mentioned she's worried about Isla."

"Hmph."

Ok, maybe not.

"Something happen between y'all?"

"Nope," he says as he picks up his pace.

"Then why are you actin' like a sad sack of shit?"

"Leave it the fuck alone," his tone leaving no room for argument, as he once again picks up his pace.

Great! I guess we are sprinting the rest of the way home.

He sets a brutal pace, but I don't know whether it's to punish me or himself. At this point, I'm not sure who he is more pissed at.

Finally, four miles later, our feet hit the gravel, and he slows down. We are both huffing and puffing as we walk the rest of the way to the house. He stops at the top of the steps but doesn't look over at me. Chest heaving, he says, "She won't let me help her."

"Is it that bad?"

Any one of us will go to hell to help her; not only is she Charlie and Olivia's best friend, but we all know how Everett feels about her.

"I don't know, man. It isn't good; I know that much."

I grab his shoulder and say, "Call me anytime. Alibi and hide the body; no questions asked."

We started saying that at age 15, when his dad started doing the same shit to his mom that we suspect is going on with Isla. A slight escalation from verbal abuse to physical. We could never prove it, but we are a lot older and smarter now.

He lets out a humorless laugh. "Thanks, man. Sorry, I had to smoke you back there. You pissed me off, though."

"You call that smoking? Just an average day as BTF."

"Yeah, Big Tough Frogman, my ass."

***

That run this morning didn't do much to quell my anxiety with Olivia, but I'm hoping seeing her will put me at ease. We agreed to keep things professional at the office, but it gets exponentially harder, *pun intended,* the longer we go. Especially now that we aren't sneaking off at lunch anymore. She ended those after I told her I thought we should wait to tell the kids. I can't blame her. She still has her guard up, and every time she lets it down, I end up letting her down.

Today, she's wearing a white blouse tucked into her black pencil skirt with stockings that I want to tear off. It's been almost two weeks since we last hooked up.

Last weekend, the kids caught a stomach virus, so she canceled Friday Night Movie Night. It took all of me not to drive over there and try to help, not expecting anything apart from just being there for them, but she insisted on quarantining them in.

I sent her a text instead of going over there and doing just that.

"I can't get any work done when you're over there looking like every man's office fantasy."

I watch her pick up her phone and smile while she reads the text. She looks up at me and, catching me watching, starts typing.

"Yeah? If only you knew what was underneath..."

Tease. "Please, do tell. Or show. Preferably show. Lunch today? I miss you."

I see her smile, but it doesn't reach her eyes. "I can't today, sorry!"

I knew that was coming, but it didn't make it hurt any less.

Another text comes through, attached with a picture. "At least you can still see it, though." She's wearing black lace lingerie, a piece I haven't seen yet.

Holy shit.

She's the sexiest woman I've ever seen.

My second thought isn't my proudest moment, for sure. Jealousy ripples through me, and I can't help but wonder if I'm the only one she's sending that to. She's grown so distant that I wouldn't be surprised if she decided to let me go and find someone else.

My text goes out before I have a chance to think about what I'm saying. "Just had that waiting to be sent, did ya?"

"Kind of? I took it this morning and was waiting for you to text so that I could send it."

I don't respond for a few minutes; I just stare at my blank computer screen, pretending to work. I know that I'm being a jealous asshole, but I'm so fucking afraid I'm losing her that I'm not thinking clearly. It isn't fair to her, though; she asked me to commit to her and I came up with some bullshit reason to postpone it rather than just bringing up the stupid promise I made to Heather.

I haven't even talked to Heather since she went back to L.A. but for some reason I'm terrified to even mention her to Olivia. I don't want her to read into anything that isn't there.

"You look amazing! I should've said that first. It caught me off guard, is all. My head went to some dark places."

I immediately followed that up with another one.

"Can we please have lunch soon? Just lunch, I promise."

Even from here, I can see her chewing on her bottom lip as she types, surely about to say she can't. *Fuck this.*

Standing up, I storm out of my office. My phone vibrates, but I'm too chicken shit to look at it.

I throw open the door to their office.

Both girls nearly jumped in shock. Charlie's the first to say, "Andrew Roger Reynolds! You scared the daylights out of us!" Her southern accent has mostly faded, but occasionally, it slips out, like now.

"Boots, take a break and walk with me to get a coffee."

She points toward the window. "It's like 20 degrees out there."

"I'll drive then, please." I'm not above begging or fireman carrying her out of this place. I just need to spend five minutes alone with her.

"It's actually a good time," Charlie says with a shrug. "I'll finish paying these invoices, and you could grab me peppermint tea, too!

I grin at Charlie. She must see the desperation on my face and is taking pity on me, knowing that Olivia would never deny her pregnant friend peppermint tea.

With a sigh, she grabs her purse, a small smile tugging at her lips.

She walks out of the door I held open for her, brushing by me to get through, smelling like my favorite scents, jasmine, and vanilla.

I touch the small part of her back, just enough to feel like I have some contact with her.

We get to the truck, and I open the door for her, letting her climb in, but I don't close the door yet. Just stand there staring at this beautiful woman, who is so obviously pulling away from me. Her hands are clasped politely in her lap, and I try to keep my breathing even until she looks at me.

Finally, she turns her head, eyebrows raised.

I smile, grab her chin, and crash my mouth into hers. It's not the most eloquent way, but I'm desperate for the connection. It takes a second, but she finally opens, letting me in, and I take full advantage.

By the time I pull away, we are both breathless. Her lipstick is smeared, and it must have transferred onto my face as well because she takes her thumb and brushes my lips.

Her smile is genuine now, unraveling some of the knots in my stomach.

"You're so fucking beautiful, Boots."

"Thank you. Come on, if we don't leave now, I may just go for another round of that kiss, and it's freezing out here."

I could go for that, but I see her shiver a bit. I press a light kiss on her perfectly plump lips and close the door. Hustling to my side so that I'm not losing any more time with her.

I climb in, and she smiles, "Can we go to Maisie's? I know it's across town, but she may still have some treats." Maisie is a friend of Olivia; they don't spend much time together, something to do with a falling out with Ethan and sides being chosen, but Olivia always chooses to go there over the bigger drive-thru coffee huts.

"Sure, more time with you is never a bad thing."

Her face lights up. *Damn, I missed that.* It feels so good to have her with me. I reach over and grab her hand, pull it to the center console, and just hold on.

"What's new with Ellie and Ben? Are they feeling better after last weekend?"

"They're good now, but it was 62 hours of puke fest. I ended up catching it on Saturday night and didn't get off the bathroom floor until Sunday afternoon."

My head rears back, anger and frustration hitting me hard. "You didn't tell me that. I would've come over and helped!"

She laughs, brushing it off. "So you could catch it too? No way, it was miserable!" She squeezes my hand and smiles. "Levi came over and helped with the kids anyway; his immune system is unparalleled."

My entire body stiffened. Levi shouldn't be there helping them. I should have been. "I at least would have liked the option."

"Okay."

"Okay?" It's probably not the right time to question her, but I'm shocked there isn't any pushback.

"Yeah, okay. If you want to risk your health to watch me puke my guts out, then I'm not going to stop you."

"Thank you." I sigh and squeeze her hand. "Sorry I reacted that way; I'm having a shit time today expressing my feelings to you."

She nods an exaggerated nod, so I continue, "Boots, it feels like I'm losing you before I even really have you."

Her intake of breath as she releases my hand has me glancing at her. I can't do much, though, because we pull into the drive-thru and right up to the window.

"Hey guys! It's so good to see you!" Maisie is a short, natural blonde who is always full of energy and loves to chat—but not in an annoying way, just friendly.

I pretend to smile and refrain from grumbling as I say, "Hey Maisie, how's it going today? This is the first time I've been here, and there hasn't been a line." This place always has a line of cars, and I was counting on it today.

"I know, slow day! It won't be like this next week, though. Thanksgiving week brings out the crazies! Hey, Livy, how are the kids?"

"Wild as always, Ellie's birthday falls on Thanksgiving this year, so she's pretending everyone is celebrating her that day."

"That's amazing! Swing her by, and I'll give her a birthday treat on the house!"

"She'll love that!"

Another car pulls into the window opposite us, and Maisie turns to greet them and ask them for a minute.

"What can I get for you two?"

Olivia orders for her and Charlie, throwing in a few treats, and then I order a simple black coffee and hand Maisie my card. Olivia missed the whole transaction while still trying to get her card out of her wallet.

I smirk at her and say, "Put it away; I already paid."

Shock registers on her face. "You did? You didn't have to do that!"

It takes me a second to realize that she's shocked because we've never been in this situation before. Sure, I've brought plenty of dinners over and a few coffees here and there, but we've never been on an official date.

"It was my idea to come here, Boots. Stop worrying about it."

She nods her head once and glances out the passenger window.

Maisie is quick, already handing us our drinks and food. We thank her, and Olivia promises to come in next week with Ellie and Ben.

She takes a sip of her dirty chai and moans. Blood rushes instantly south at that noise, and I have to try to readjust without her noticing.

"Good?" I ask, my throat suddenly dry.

"The best, Maisie has perfected a good chai. If it wasn't a million calories, I would drink one of these every day."

I make a mental note to start surprising her with these more often.

She's quiet for a second, and then she finally looks at me again. "So Sunday is a weird day for us, but the kids asked me to invite you all."

"Okay? Why is it weird?"

"It's Dan and Levi's birthday."

Shit. I can't imagine how hard that is for all of them, Levi especially.

"I'll be there." I don't even have to think about it. If they want me there, I'm there.

She laughs a little. "You don't even know what it is."

I shrug. "It doesn't matter; I want to be there for them." *And you.*

"Good, they'll love that. We start the morning at Mountain Lion Cafe at 9 a.m. for Dan's birthday breakfast and then go to Ponderosa Pine at 5:30 p.m. for Levi's birthday dinner. Pop's and Annie started this when Dan and Levi were little. That way, they each had their own parties. It made it easy that Dan loved breakfast and Levi loved dinner."

"It's nice you keep doing it."

She sighs, "Yeah, it was hard at first, very awkward, but the kids enjoy it. We make sure to tell the kids all the good memories we have. Once word caught around town, people started stopping by our booth and sharing their favorite stories too. If you only want to come to Levi's dinner, I understand."

"No, I'd like to hear the stories." I don't add how intimidating it is that I have enormous shoes to fill. The man was the town martyr, and to them, I'll always be second best. I just hope Olivia never feels that way about me.

We pull into the parking lot, and I back into my spot, once again asking her to wait. Without even grabbing my coffee, I hustle around the truck to get my kiss. This one is far less passionate, but still enough to leave me aching for the next.

We part as I grab my coffee, and we head into the office.

I already miss her.

The distance between us feels like it's back in full force.

Chapter Twenty-Four

Olivia

Dan and Levi's birthday is always exhausting. I throw on a brave face and perma smile and pray the day flies by.

Ellie usually does okay, but it's hit or miss with Ben as to how he handles it.

Ellie, Ben, and I got to the diner earlier than everyone else and picked the corner booth that's big enough to fit our large crew. Hayes, Charlie, Andrew, and Everett were the next to arrive, followed by Levi and then Pops.

Hello, awkward. Only, it wasn't for anyone but me. Levi and Pop love Andrew and Everett. They make it seem like they've been around for every birthday breakfast.

"Pop! Start us off!" Ellie demands of her grandpa after our food has been dropped off. Now that we have a couple of these under our belts, we start the same way. Pop tells us how the whole breakfast/dinner thing started, and then everyone goes around to tell their favorite Dan story.

Pop grins at Ellie. "I'd love to. Well, it all started when the boys were just babies. Dan was an early riser, wanting breakfast first thing. Levi was the opposite, a night owl that only cared about dinner."

Levi sticks his finger in the air and interjects, "Still do!"

Chuckling, pop continues. "Annie and I quickly learned that we had to divide and conquer. I took the morning shift, and she took lates. It was her idea to split up the day so they each got their own special party, and the tradition just stuck."

"You two never wanted to switch when you got older?" Everett asks.

Levi takes a sip of his coffee and then smiles broadly. "Nope. Either way, we got ate out twice in one day."

Calvin and Elise step over to our booth, grinning.

"Story time?" Elise asks in her singsong voice.

"Hey, you two! Just in time." They've never missed a breakfast or dinner, showing support to both Dan and Levi.

Cal pats Zeke on the back and gives him a nod. "Mind if we go next? We are on our way to church."

I motion for them to take the floor. It's the same story every year, and the tears start welling before he even starts to talk. The story of Dan asking the three of them for their permission to propose to me. I have no idea how Andrew will feel about this, but this moment isn't about him.

"Our favorite Dan memory started right here in this booth. Lovey, Lise, and I sat sharing a cup of coffee when Dan marched in. He was in his full uniform, and the cruiser was parked half-hazardously in the parking lot. He marched in, slid next to Lovey, and gave the three of us a wobbly smile."

Elise takes over. "We knew right then what he was going to ask, but Lovey wanted to make him work for it."

Cal grins in response. "And work for it, he did. She arched one brow at him before he even opened his mouth. 'So you think you're good enough to marry our girl?'"

I bite my cheek as hard as I can to keep the tears at

236

bay, but one slips out. No matter how many times I hear this story, I get choked up. Lovey was the best, and Dan fought so hard to get her to like him. She always had, but never let him know that. She wanted him to prove himself to her.

Elise places her fingertips delicately on her chin. "He looked her dead in the eye and said, "No, ma'am. But no one on this earth is good enough for her. I promise you all that I'll do everything I can to be deserving of her, though.""

Calvin wraps his arm around Elise and holds her. "For speeches, I'd say that was a pretty darn good one. A few days later, they were engaged. Then what, a month after that, you were married?"

Blinking away tears, I smile and nod. "Close to." I don't add that it was because Dan told me he was too afraid he'd lose me to someone else. Andrew apparently doesn't have that same stance, and I'm trying not to let it bother me.

Pop stands up to give them both a hug, and then they wave their goodbyes to the rest of us.

Ellie bounces in her seat and looks at me. "Mommy, your turn!"

I let out a heavy sigh and tried to think of a favorite Dan memory. I change it up every year so that I hopefully don't forget any of our best times.

"This seems like a good birthday to share the story of when Dan sent me my very best friend."

I smile at the kids and look between them. "Your dad called me one morning, and we had just found out that I was pregnant with you," I say as I tickle Ellie's side.

"He said, 'Hey, babe. I'm sending you the answer to your prayers. A nanny. I don't know the whole story of why she's in Three Sisters, but she's got a good heart and I think you'll really like her.'"

I glance at Charlie, which is a bad idea. Tears are already spilling out of her eyes as she fans her face.

"I had no idea he was sending me this gorgeous strawberry-blonde woman who would end up being better at my job than I am. Sure enough, though, Charlie walked in and said, "I heard you needed me." She has no idea how true that statement was. I didn't even know how much I needed her at the time. How much I needed her to bring her people into my life.

Charlie reached across the table and patted my arm. "It was all false bravado. I was the one that needed you."

"I think we both needed each other. Anyway, I immediately called him after she left and told him she was way too hot and educated to be our nanny, but that I had hired her to be my assistant."

"It took approximately five minutes for me to know that she was going to be my best friend. The surprising part was all the amazing people she's brought into our lives since then."

Hayes holds up his coffee mug, and the rest of us do as well, "Cheers to Dan bringing us all together. Happy birthday, friend."

Ellie, being our ring leader, takes that moment to quiz Hayes. "What's your story, Uncle Hayesy?"

"Probably when he tried to arrest me for talking to Charlie."

Ellie giggles back, "I love that story!" She looks at Everett and Andrew. "Daddy almost took Hayesy to jail because he thought he was a bad guy."

Charlie laughs, "Another at this diner story. Hayes slid into my booth one day, shocking me. I hadn't even known he was looking for me, let alone that he was in town. Dan knew my history, and when he saw this big guy sitting with me and that I was crying, he yanked him out of the booth. He had him handcuffed before Hayes even saw him coming."

Hayes throws his hands up in defense. "First of all, I was too distracted by finding you. Second. Well, I don't have a second."

Everett chuckles. "Sounds like he must have been good at his job. I'd arrest Hayes if he ever came into my town, too."

Everyone laughs, even Andrew. He's been a little quieter than normal—well, a lot quieter. He hasn't said a single thing to me, but he's been having side conversations with the kids throughout the meal and has smiled the entire time.

I'd say all the Dan memories aren't affecting him, but he hasn't looked at me once. It's ironic considering the other day, he said he felt like *he* was losing *me* before he even really got me. Yet here I am, with all my baggage laid out on the table, waiting for him to jump in, but he won't.

<hr>

Andrew

"Thanks for coming, man. This morning and tonight. It means a lot to me and Olivia." Levi pats me on the back as I walk into his birthday party at Ponderosa Pine. Somehow, there are even more people here than those who popped in at breakfast. It just goes to show that the Turners are loved beyond measure. Between breakfast and now dinner, I'm beginning to feel very inconsequential.

"Happy birthday, Levi. Thanks for the invite. I know—" I rub the back of my neck, trying to decide how best to say this. "I know that you know about Olivia and my situation."

He nods, smirking, waiting for me to spit the sentence out. "I appreciate that you've been so understanding and haven't shoved me out. I need you to know that I only want the best for her and the kids. It seems daunting to try to live up to Dan's legacy. But I'd like to try."

Levi clears his throat, the smirk falling off his face. "Dan would have wanted them to be loved, happy, and protected. As long as you do that, no one's going to have a problem with the two of you together. They're treated like royalty around here. If you fuck it up, it's not only me you'll have to worry about."

"Let's hope I don't fuck it up then."

He laughs and walks away, giving me an opportunity to look for my girl. I'm not going to lie and say today wasn't hard. I couldn't even look at Olivia this morning, too afraid I'd see the yearning she carries for Dan. I know they didn't have a perfect marriage, but when you only hear good stories about someone for hours, I'm sure it's easy to forget the difficult memories.

Sneaking up behind her as she talks to Charlie and Hayes, I whisper in her ear. "Hey, beautiful."

A full-body shiver runs down her spine, and she turns around, smiling. "Hey. You made it!"

She's smiling, but it doesn't quite meet her eyes. All I want to do is pull her into me and kiss her. To hell with the promise, but I've already waited this long, and I don't want to go back on my word. It wasn't surprising to hear that Dan married her as quickly as he did. It's killing me that no one knows she's mine.

"I wouldn't have missed it. You look incredible. " She has on tight jeans that mold perfectly to her ass and a black, long-sleeved, lacy bodysuit. It shows just enough to have me itching to tear it off, but not so much that I want to throw my jacket on over it.

"Oh, hello to you too, brother dearest!" Charlie sarcastically chides me.

I don't even look up from Olivia's eyes as I say, "Hi, Carrington's." Olivia rolls her lips together, fighting off a laugh.

"Boots, come with me to get a drink?"

She nods, a blush already hitting her cheeks.

Ethan is helping bartend the party. So far, he's the only one I haven't won over. I don't think it has anything to do with Olivia, though. He's more guarded than I was when I first moved here, but he's been here a hell of a lot longer.

Olivia sidles up to the bar in front of him. "Hey, Eth. Did someone call out today?"

He rolls his eyes and throws the towel he was cleaning with over his shoulder. "Someone calls out every day. Today, four people called out."

"Damn, let me know if I can help." I offer. I don't have much bartending experience, but I do have a lot of drinking experience and the uncanny ability to schmooze.

His head cocked to the side, surprised that I even offered. "I may take you up on that."

"Good. Want me to get my own beer?"

He chuckles and grabs a glass to pour my regular drink.

Olivia beams at me, hopefully happy that I'm trying to make an effort with Ethan. They've been friends since she first moved here, so I know his approval is one of the big ones to win over.

I took a drink of my ale and set it back on the bar before looking at Olivia. "Thanks for inviting me this morning to Dan's birthday breakfast."

She nods before offering me a small smile. "I appreciate you coming. I know it's... a complicated situation, but it meant a lot to the kids to share those stories with you."

"Not complicated." I reach my arm out to pull her into me, but quickly remember we are out in public, and let it fall. "It's unique, for sure, but I wouldn't have missed it. Being there for the kids and honoring their dad was a special moment. I know firsthand how easy it is to lose memories of loved ones that have passed away." It's been over a decade since I lost my own parents. The memories fade away slowly and unless someone mentions them, I rarely think about all the good times we had as a family.

"You're a stand-up guy, Andrew Roger Carrington. I'm glad we have you in our lives—in whatever capacity that ends up being."

Something about the way she says it throws a knot in my stomach. I'm so damn tired of the distance she's put between us, but there isn't anything I can do about it yet. I have less than a handful of weeks until I'm out of purgatory and can make her mine. I only need her to hold on a little while longer, and then everything will be as it should.

Chapter Twenty-Five

Olivia

The next few days flew by. Ellie wanted to go all out for her birthday party and Thanksgiving this year. We spent days decorating, baking, and preparing to have a house full of people.

The night before the party, I barely slept, stressing about everything I needed to get done before the party. I was already half-awake at 6:30 a.m., contemplating just getting up, when I heard my phone beep and then saw an alert that Andrew was pulling into the driveway.

I quickly threw on a robe and tried to smooth out my hair as I ran to the front door. I threw the door open, and there he was, holding birthday balloons and giant gift bags. The porch light was the only thing illuminating him in the dark morning.

"What are you doing here?" I whisper-shouted while holding the door open for him. He hasn't been coming over as much in the evenings. To be honest, I've been mostly avoiding him. We still do movie night, but I've been trying to keep a wall up while he figures out what he wants with us.

He steps inside and sets everything down. Turning, he

pulls me into him and wraps his arm around my waist. The twinkle in his eye tells me he's been planning this for a while.

He sears his mouth to mine, trying to dive in, even though I try to keep mine closed. I'm sure I have morning breath. He's relentless until I finally let him, and then he pulls away, grinning.

"Good morning, beautiful!"

"Good morning. Whatcha doing on my doorstep before the sun is even up?"

"I'm helping." He says with a shrug. "I have stuff for breakfast in the truck and a few more things. I hope you don't mind. I bought a new Lego set for Ben too. I know it's Ellie's birthday, so I'll give it to him in private, but I wanted him to feel special too, and I wasn't here for his birthday."

My jaw drops, and he lightly sets his fingertips under it, closing it. Every guard I have set up comes crashing down at that moment. My eyes feel a little extra watery when I say, "Thank you."

He smiles and admonishes me to get ready for the day so he can prepare the balloons and breakfast.

I get ready, taking a little extra time on my hair and makeup, and then throw on a pair of skintight jeans and a tucked-in tank. I'll be cooking most of the afternoon, so I don't want to get my Thanksgiving outfit dirty.

Sauntering out with a little extra sway in my hips, I see him flipping the French toast he made. "Smells amazing! I didn't know you were such a chef."

He glances up, and his mouth drops. "Fuck, Boots. You're killing me in those jeans."

I wink and grab a coffee mug from the cupboard, knowing he's been staring at my ass the entire time I do a little shimmy. "What? The pajamas and morning breath weren't doing it for ya?

He darts behind me, placing his hands on either side of me, caging me in from behind. "You kidding? The sexiest version of you is first thing in the morning, especially when you have that freshly fucked glow."

I set my mug down and turned, tipping my head back so I could see him. "Kids are still sleeping."

The next second, his lips are on mine, and his hands are on my ass, lifting me onto the counter. I can feel him grinding into me when we both hear a door opening and jump apart.

Ellie comes running out of her room, yelling, "It's my birthday!" Thank goodness that little girl doesn't have a quiet bone in her body.

My face feels warm to the touch, and I'm a little breathless in the best way possible. Andrew just stares at me, his eyes widening and his lips puffy.

"You're burning the French toast." I say with a smirk.

He looks over quickly and then jumps into action, a small murmur of curse words flowing out as he does it.

I can't help the giggle that escapes as I hop down and walk to the edge of the kitchen, right as Ellie runs in.

I scoop her into my arms and squeeze. "Happy Birthday, Little Turkey! Can you believe you're six whole years old today?"

"It's the bestest day ever!" She hugs me close and then must notice the male presence in our house because she screams "DREWY!" in my ear and is scrambling down to get him.

Same, girl, same.

He picks her up with one arm and beams at her. "Happy Birthday, My Els!"

Damn, if that isn't the cutest thing I've ever seen or heard.

Ben saunters out of his room, sleepy-eyed and looking mildly annoyed that Ellie woke him up. The second he sees

Andrew, though, his face lights up, and he bypasses me to run over to hug him as well.

After breakfast, the kids are hopped up on sugar and the attention Andrew gives them. He plays games, reads books, builds Lego sets with Ben, and watches Ellie do a million dance moves. Effectively letting me get everything I need to get done for the Thanksgiving feast and birthday party done. He even manages to sneak an ass grab or kiss whenever the kids aren't looking.

Our friends start to slowly trickle in around two, so I go to get changed into my Thanksgiving outfit: a white skirt with a slit and a slightly oversized, off-the-shoulder, tan sweater tucked in. I paired it all with my brick-colored cowboy boots that have little white flowers on them.

Andrew sees me first as I walk out, and within a blink, he's pushing me back into my bedroom and kissing me. He closes the door behind him, mumbling through kisses that the kids are outside, with Hayes showing him something. He picks me up, and my legs wrap around his waist as he turns us so that my back is against the door.

"You can't wear this tonight," kiss. "Too sexy," kiss.

I laugh. "You said the jeans were killin' you, so."

"Everything you wear is too sexy; you could wear a trash bag, and I'd say it's too sexy."

He kisses me again as his hand slides up my leg through the slit of the skirt. He groans when he feels the lace on my panties, and then he dives under, grabbing a handful of cheek.

He pulls back, and those emerald eyes are so full of lust that I can't believe he's able to stop now. "Later? Can we finish this later? If we don't stop now, I'm going to fuck you against this door and all of our friends will hear."

He sets me down and helps readjust my skirt, then grabs my chin and tilts it up to give me a sweet kiss. "You're beautiful, always. Seeing you fluttering around the kitchen today baking and cooking, making sure Ellie's birthday isn't overshadowed by Thanksgiving, all while still giving Ben and I enough attention...You're a real-life Wonder Woman."

I grin back at him. "I've got the costume around here somewhere; should I break it out again?"

"Just the lasso," he murmurs while peppering my neck and exposed shoulder with kisses.

Taking a deep breath through his nose, he takes a step back and asks, "Can I stay and help get the kids to bed tonight?"

I nod. "I'd love that; it's been too long..." It hasn't even been a week, but before Halloween, we were having sex almost every day. I miss that. Not just the daily orgasms. The connection, too. But, I'm trying so hard not to lose myself in him. I need the commitment before I can fully let myself go.

"You're telling me I only have one picture of you to work with, and it's committed to memory by now."

I never thought a guy telling me he uses my picture to get off would be such a turn-on, but here we are.

"I'll make sure to send more," I say with a wink.

The rest of their day is filled with long looks and hidden touches; I almost forget that I'm supposed to be pulling away, preparing for him to end this. He's just so good at sucking me back in.

Ellie and Ben both fall asleep twenty minutes into the movie; we fast-forward through most of it in case they wake up when we try to move them ten minutes after that.

They don't even open their eyes, though; they just snuggle into their beds and snore away.

I get a pit of nervousness in my stomach when I turn around to see Andrew's eyes blazing at me.

He motions with the crook of his finger for me to follow him, and I do so willingly. Each step filled with anticipation and nerves. I wasn't even this nervous the first time we did it, but for some reason tonight feels different. Maybe because I know my walls are down tonight.

I don't even make it into my bedroom before he has me pushed up against my door, like he did a few hours ago. Kissing the nerves away until we are tearing at each other's clothes.

After what feels like hours of sweaty, dirty sex, I walk him to the front door. He kisses me again and snuggles his nose into my neck. "You're the best thing that's ever happened to me, Boots. You, Ellie, Ben... I'm making you mine, all of you, when I get back in a few weeks. I just need you to wait until then."

Goosebumps erupt all over my skin, at first from the loving declaration, and then it feels like I've been hit with ice water. He wants me to wait a few weeks. *For what?*

"What do you mean, wait until you get back?" I take an abrupt step back, severing the contact we had.

He rubs his hand down his face and sighs. "I have to go to Kara's wedding; officially end things with Heather."

My heart sinks as I process his words. "Officially end things?! What the fuck does that mean?" I cry out hysterically.

"I told you, I told you that first movie night." He looks at me with a mixture of regret and sorrow. "I promised Heather that at Kara's wedding we would have a healthy conversation and end things. She told me I owed her a proper breakup, and I promised I wouldn't get into a relationship until then."

His words hit me hard as the puzzle pieces started locking together tightly. The Ross and Rachel conversation. She didn't care if he only fucked someone else, but he wasn't allowed to date. Heather is the reason that we've only ever fucked in the privacy of my home—no dates, no public outings, no steps forward. Friends with benefits.

It feels like the wind got knocked out of me and nausea swirls in my stomach. "You should go."

"Please, Boots."

"No," I say, holding my hand up. "I can't right now."

He shakes his head and reaches for me again. "Me going there doesn't change my feelings for you. It's just to end this stupid promise and to support Kara and John. That's it!"

"JUST GO!" I haven't been this confused, hurt, or mad since the last time I kicked him out of my house over Heather.

The pain on his face is excruciating to look at, so I turn and open the front door.

He doesn't move, and it takes all of me to keep the tears at bay. When the first one leaks out, he moves to stand in front of me, taking his thumb to brush it away.

"This isn't over. Please just wait for me." He tries to kiss me, but I turn, so he only kisses my cheek.

With a sigh, he walks out the door, and I slam it behind him. Locking it. It feels a little representative of what I should be doing with my heart, too.

I sink to the floor and cry. I don't hear his truck start until after my phone has beeped a few times. I know it's him texting me, but I can't look at them right now.

This has to be it for us. He just asked me to wait for him until after he talks to his ex-girlfriend.

The ex-girlfriend, who is not only a terrible fucking human being but apparently still controls his every move, and I have to just wait around for her to decide if it's okay we date.

Irrational? Maybe. But I'm not trying to be rational right now.

I want to call Charlie and Hayes, but I know they would rush over here and try to fix everything. It's not fair to pit them against their family, either. Andrew will need them, too. I saw it on his face—the hurt and rejection. Our pain mirrored each other so much that I almost wanted to give in.

Isla has been too distant lately for me to call her. I know

she's going through something, even though she won't talk about it. It seems cruel to pile any of my emotions on her. The same is true for Ethan; between being a single parent and running the bar, he's juggling a lot.

I place my cheek on my knee and stare at the photos in the entryway. I don't know if I've ever felt as alone as I do right now.

Before I was married to Dan, I always had Lovey to rely on. She just had a way of making everything okay. Making me feel like the most important person in the world. I guarantee she would've told me to get off my ass and show that dumbass what he's missing. To hell with the ex. If he doesn't choose me, he isn't worth the tears.

I can almost hear her saying, "Don't let anyone treat you like a discount bag. You are Hermes. Birkin, baby! Act like it."

So instead of wallowing on the floor, I pick myself up and cry in the shower until the water runs cold. I remind myself that I need to be with someone who chooses me above everything else. The standard needs to be set that I am the first choice prize. If Andrew can't see that, then I'm not the one for him.

Chapter Twenty-Six

Olivia

I ignored Drew's call most of the weekend. Hell, I ignored everyone's calls. Only sending proof of life texts so that no one showed up at our door. Not that we were even there if they had.

I packed the kids up early Friday morning with our snow gear and some overnight clothes and booked two nights at a ski resort near Bachelor in Bend.

We spent three full days playing in the snow, snowboarding, and drinking hot chocolate by the fire in the resort. The kids were on cloud nine, treating it like a proper vacation, and not somewhere only thirty minutes from our house.

By the time we got home late Sunday evening, we were all well and exhausted. Even my phone looked tired from all the missed calls and texts.

I sent the kids to shower, and get ready for bed, thankful we grabbed burgers on the way home, so I didn't have to cook.

I'm still unpacking my roof rack when I hear the familiar rumble of Andrew's truck pulling in behind my SUV.

Fuck. Fuck. Fuck

The door slams shut, the sound banging through the quiet night. Guess he's pissed, too. At least we are on the same page here. I've had a lot of time to process everything, and I'm feeling more annoyed than sad right now.

I turn around, still standing on the running boards of my SUV, ready for an epic showdown, but lose steam when I see how miserable he looks.

"Where the fuck have you been?" It's not quite a yell, but his tone sounds harsh and filled with frustration.

"Bachelor," I say indifferently as I pull down Ben's snowboard.

"For three fucking days?!"

I nod, rolling my lips together. "We stayed at the resort; I needed to clear my head."

"And you couldn't have told me that? Charlie wouldn't tell me anything. Hayes either! I was fucking worried about you!"

Shrugging, noncommittally. "I didn't tell them not to tell you. I'm sorry they didn't."

"They shouldn't have had to!" His chest is rising and falling with every angry word. "You should have told me!"

I'm about to respond that he needs not to be so damn entitled, when a little voice pipes up from the other side of the car: "Mom, what's going on?"

Shit. Ben.

The color of Andrew's face pales as he realizes he was caught venting out three days of angry emotions. I understand why he needed to let it out. I put a lot of anger into snowboarding down that hill while the kids were in the kids club.

"Hey, bud. I'll be in soon. Just unloading the car and I gotta get the cargo box off." I offer a smile as I peek over the windshield to see him.

His face looks incredibly stoic, for an eight-year-old. "Are you sure you're okay? Should I call Hayes?"

I give him my best, reassuring smile. "Nah, Andrew's going to help me, and then I'll park in the garage. Head inside and keep El in there, please."

He goes inside, albeit reluctantly, without another word.

I look toward Andrew. His eyes are closed, the gravity of the situation weighing him down.

"Sucks when they catch you being a normal human, doesn't it?"

His eyes pop open, filled with regret. "I shouldn't have been yelling at you like that to begin with."

"You were worried; three days of festering emotion can come out in shitty ways. He'll understand. He's seen me have some pretty epic meltdowns."

"I don't believe that."

I give a small laugh. "Punching bag, remember? We had it hanging in the living room at your house."

He nodded, but changed the subject: "Can we talk about the other night?"

I sigh, better now than later: "Sure, help me get this damn thing down and put the kids to bed."

It takes all of thirty minutes for the kids to crash into bed. Ellie was first after filling Andrew in on everything we did on the mountain. I take her to her room, get her snuggled in, and then close the door behind me as I leave.

I'm about to go wait in the kitchen when I overhear Andrew apologizing to Ben for losing his temper with me. He explains how worried he was, without throwing me under the bus for not talking to him, and lets him know that the way he expressed it was wrong.

I had to walk away from the door when I heard him tell me he promised to do better with me in the future. Nausea swirls again, knowing that I'm about to tell him that the future he wants doesn't exist.

I sit at the kitchen island and try to distract myself by reading through three days of missed messages. Ninety percent end up being from Andrew, so I ignore those.

Charlie sent a few, telling me she didn't know what was going on but she had my back. Hayes even offered to throw up the punching bag again if I needed it.

There's one from a number I don't recognize, just simply saying, "Hello, please call me when you get a chance." I'm not sure who it's from—possibly a renter or Andrew having one of his guy's messages for him. Either way, I don't read too much into it. It can wait until tomorrow.

Andrew walks out of the hall, directly to me, a look of sadness clouding his features. He pulls my legs toward him, and the swivel seat has me facing him. He parts my legs so he can stand as close as possible.

"Can we restart that conversation from Thursday night?"

"Sure, but I don't think the outcome will be much different."

His frown deepens as his eyebrows pinch together with disappointment. "Just hear me out, please."

I nod my head, encouraging him to go on. I'm having a hard time trusting myself to speak around him. "When I made that promise to Heather, it was just to end the fight. We had been arguing in circles for so long, and the conversation wasn't going anywhere. I had already known I wanted to end it before she even got to town, but I was hoping, by some miracle, she would show up, and I'd change my mind."

He lightly rubs his thumb along my thigh. "We were together off-and-on for twelve years. Her family was there for me during the darkest times. Kara was always like a little sister to me; it just made sense to say yes when she asked me to be a groomsman. I didn't think I'd fall for you during that time. Six months seemed easy; I'd get my head on straight and focus on building the business with Hayes. I knew there was something between us, but I had no idea how quickly I'd fall for you. Then you decided you wanted to date, and I went a little crazy."

"I'm not arguing with any of that; I know why you made the promise and want to fulfill it. I can see your side; I know how important your word is to you. However, you just said it yourself: Twelve years. Twelve years of birthdays, holidays, weddings, missed calls, texts, sex... Who is to say all that won't come back the second you see her? Does her family even know you aren't together?"

"It's not like that. I swear to you. I haven't even talked to her since she left. I only owe her this conversation in person."

"Okay, and what about what you owe me?"

His face tightened with a mixture of guilt and hurt. I soldier on, though, not giving him a second to respond. "I keep asking myself the same thing: If Ellie came to me and said, "I'm falling in love with this guy. He is everything I have ever wanted in a partner. But he wants me to wait for him until after he takes care of the emotional needs of his ex. I'd tell her to find someone who is so afraid of losing her that he would *never* have asked her to wait in the first place."

For a moment, he closes his eyes and stays silent. "This... It can't be the end of us. I don't want to lose what we have."

"I don't, either," I say with a shrug, "but I won't be the girl waiting around for a guy to love her back. You drew your line in the sand, honoring a promise to an ex. I drew mine—not being put in second place."

"You feel like I'm putting you second?"

"How could I not? I'm your dirty little secret, and it was fun —so much fun, at first. But then it just got sad."

His entire expression hardened. "You are not a dirty little secret."

"No? So you've told people about your feelings for me?

Everett?" His brow furrows, trying to think, so I continue on, "Hayes? Charlie? Connie? Have you told anyone that you have real feelings for me?"

"They know. They knew before I did. I don't have to say it."

"Do they? Because I'm the one in this with you, and I don't even know! You've told me *once* that you plan on making me yours. Just enough to keep me dangling on the line."

"I've shown you, though. I've shown you how committed I am."

"To what? Friends with benefits?" I know it's a low blow, but I'm so tired of beating around the bush. I've kept my feelings so locked up tight, but I can't keep pretending this is okay anymore.

His entire body rocks back when he whispers, "that's not fair."

I reach for his hand and lace our fingers together, trying to offer some comfort in a really shitty situation. "You're not ready to be in a relationship with me yet. I'm asking what you're committed to. If it's being a good friend, then, yeah, you've shown that. But beyond that? Showing your feelings toward me? You haven't. Half the time, I don't know if you're falling for me or if I'm just a good fuck."

Pain streaks across his face. "That's not all you are to me."

I give a small shrug of one shoulder and look away. This conversation is way harder than I thought it would be. The exhaustion from the weekend is finally hitting me.

He tips my chin back to look at him. "Will you let me fix this?"

"I don't know if there is a fix."

"But you'll let me try?"

"Sure." He kisses me with a slow kiss. His fingers wrap through my hair, keeping me to him. I put everything into that kiss. The love, the heartbreak, the longing.

Then he gently places his forehead on mine. He untangles his fingers from my hair and uses them to tilt my chin up.

He said he was going to try to fix it, but that kiss felt like goodbye.

I stood up and guided him to the front door; at least this talk went better than the last one. I'm sure I'll make it to the shower before I start crying this time.

"If you can't, though, please don't let it affect your relationship with the kids. They love you; they talked about you all weekend."

"I won't let anything come between that. I love them, too."

At least he's willing to admit that.

"See ya tomorrow at work," I say, reaching on my tiptoes to kiss his cheek. The kiss in the kitchen needs to be the last one.

"Bye, Boots."

I watch him walk to his truck, offer a small wave, and close the door. It's just as hard as it was the other night, but the time to think things over has softened the blow this time.

I shower and cry; it feels like the dam of emotions has finally broken since Andrew came into my life. As the water cascades over me, I let my tears mingle with it, a mixture of relief and sadness.

Chapter Twenty-Seven

Olivia

I haven't slept much since my conversation with Andrew at the beginning of the week, which has left me completely unable to concentrate at work. All of my energy goes into not looking at him in his office. The few times my resolve slipped, I noticed he looked just as miserable as I felt.

"I need a coffee," I say to no one in particular as I stand from my desk to grab my purse. Sure, we have coffee here, but I need to get out of this building.

Charlie looks up and spots my purse. "Ooh, can you please go to Maisie's? I'm dying for that cream cheese brownie she makes."

"Sure thing, tea too?"

"Yes, you're the bestest friend ever... and boss." She adds with a wink.

I skillfully avoid looking over at the guys by checking my phone as I walk to the stairs. Really, in hindsight, my idea for an open-concept office space with glass windows and doors was dumb. Then again, never in my wildest dreams would I have expected I'd have fallen for someone in the office. At the time, it was just Charlie and me trying to work while also keeping an eye on the kids.

I get to my SUV and see a small manila envelope tucked into the windshield wiper with my name on it. Olivia Lynne Williams. My birth name, to be specific. A name I haven't gone by since Lovey adopted me and changed it to Ellison.

I look around, trying to find the person who left it, but the parking lot is empty.

Climbing in, I lock the doors and say a silent little prayer that this isn't a Charlie situation.

I peek into the unsealed envelope to see a blank white card. Plucking it out gingerly, I open it, barely registering a photo strip that falls out onto my lap.

The card simply says, "It's imperative you call me. I have information on your mother and father," followed by a phone number. I just stared at the number—the same area code from the text I received over the weekend. Which means that it wasn't Andrew or a renter.

I glance at my lap, the photo strip laying up right. It must have been torn in half a long time ago; the edges weathered, leaving only two pictures—both of my birth mom and a man I've never seen before. One photo shows them smiling at the camera, and the other shows them kissing. I flipped it over, but the back was blank.

I don't think. I just put my SUV in drive and hit the gas. I made it to the sheriff department in under two minutes. Nothing good could come from my mother reaching out, or even worse, a father I was told wanted nothing to do with me. I put them both in the past at five years old and locked that box up tight.

Damn near sprinting through the front doors, I spot Jill sitting at the front desk.

"Liv! What are you doing here?" She's worked here for

almost my entire life, dropped off countless casseroles after Dan, and knows everything about everyone in town.

I make a conscious effort to slow down and smile so that she doesn't suspect anything. The whole town will be out front of my house, guarding the doors if they think something is wrong. Pitchforks and all.

"Sorry, I'm in a hurry! I just need to chat with Luke... He in his office?" She nods, starting to say something, but I'm already moving.

Knocking twice on the door, I let myself in and closed the door behind me.

Luke looks up, eyes wide with surprise. He scans my face for two seconds, scrutinizing every detail.

"What's wrong?" His deep timber would scare most people, but it surprisingly comforts me.

"Probably nothing, maybe something. I don't know!"

"Take a deep breath. Sit down." He gestures with a head nod toward the chair opposite him.

All sheriff mode right now.

I breathe in through my nose and out through my mouth, just like the Lamaze teacher taught me. I know it was to help with labor, but I'm freaking out, and that's all I can think to do to calm down.

"This," holding up the envelope, "was left on my windshield today."

He scowled at the envelope. "Do I need gloves? I don't want to tamper with something I may need to fingerprint."

I shake my head, no. "It's just a picture of my mom—my bio mom—and a man, with a note that says to call."

"Nothing threatening?" He asks as he reaches over the desk to grab it from my outstretched hand,

"No, but the number called me a few times over the weekend and texted once."

"Show me."

I pull out my phone, showing him the missed calls and wincing at the number of times they blend with Andrew.

He raises an eyebrow in silent question.

"Andrew and I were..."

"Hooking up." He finishes the sentence for me.

"You knew?!"

"I'm the goddamn Sheriff; I know everything," he grumbles. "It's also not hard to miss the glare he shot at every man who talked to you on Thanksgiving. Ethan and I had a bet on which of us could piss him off the most."

I narrowed my eyes on him. "Ahh, I was wondering why you two were so helpful."

"So, what's with the harassment level of calls?"

Shifting uncomfortably in my seat, I can feel the weight of his gaze. "We ended it that night—Thanksgiving. He isn't ready to take the next step, and I'm not willing to wait."

He nods and says, "Good for you. I'm glad you're finally standing up for yourself."

The corner of my mouth lifts. "Thanks, Luke."

I open up the text from the unknown number and hand him my phone again.

He reads it over: "Do you want me to call for you?"

"I don't know; I just have a bad feeling. I've... fuck. I don't know! I've had a weird feeling that someone's watching me. I thought it was just in my head, but when I got the note, it was the first thing I thought of."

"Let me look into the number, see who it belongs to, do some digging of my own. I'm swamped right now, though, so give me a day or two."

I nod; that sounds reasonable.

"But you're telling Hayes. Right now. I need to know

someone in that office is watching out for you, and I'll need him to pull the security footage to see who left the note."

Shit.

I know he's right, but that doesn't make it any easier. Hayes is going to go all-protector, and if he tells Andrew, I'm screwed.

"I was going to get a coffee when I found the note. I'll let him know when I get back."

"Fine, one hour, then I'm calling him to get that video." His tone left no room for argument.

It looks like I have to get Hayes alone and on my side to keep this quiet as fast as I can.

I shoot Hayes a quick text: "Ran to get coffee. Do you or any of the guys need a pick me up?"

His text back comes right in time as I pull into Maisie's, ordering two black coffees.

"Hey, I was just starting to worry about you!" Charlie says this as I walk through the door. I glance at the clock; it's been over an hour since I left.

I cringe, but try to laugh to play it off. "Sorry, I got distracted. Your brownie and tea."

She gives me a quizzical look but takes a bite of her brownie and moans loudly. "Best fucking thing I've ever had in my mouth."

I giggle. "I'll make sure not to tell Hayes that."

"Tell Hayes what?" Speak of the devil; he walks into our office. So much for trying to get him to the kitchen to grab his coffee.

Charlie cackles, "Nothing, dear sweet husband of mine."

I hand him both the black coffees, and he says, "Thanks! Andrew says thank you as well. He's on some important private call."

I don't even want to know what the call is or why Hayes is saying it like that.

Okay, maybe I do, but I'm pretending that I don't.

"Hey. Can we go talk about the secret-not-so-secret baby shower? The one that Charlie is pretending she doesn't know about?"

Charlie mocks innocence as she places her fingertips on her chest. "Who? Me?"

"Sure," he says, pointing toward the kitchen, "away from prying ears." He bends down to kiss her and picks off a piece of her brownie without her noticing.

"Love you, Sunshine." He plops the bite into his mouth as he walks away.

"Hey! You thief!" I overhear her yelling from her desk.

I walk in first and sit at the kitchen island, tapping my fingers on the lid of my Dirty Chai. I needed the comfort and calories after the stressful week it's been.

Hayes stands at the sink, washing the chocolate off his fingers.

"So I actually need to talk to you about something else," I say nervously.

He keeps scrubbing his hands, but his eyebrows furrow and his lips press into a thin line when he says, "Go ahead."

"I need your word; you won't tell anyone. Luke is handling it." His eyes quickly flash up to mine in fear, and his lips part a bit as he inhales deeply.

"Start talking now." *A man of such few words sometimes.* All of these guys are straight-to-the point during serious conversations. No fluff. Just tell them the facts and let them process them.

I let out a sigh that sounded more like a huff. "I had a weird feeling that I was being watched a few weeks ago, and then over the weekend I got a few calls and a text from a number I didn't recognize. This morning, someone left a note on my windshield with a picture of my bio mom and a man. Maybe my dad? I don't know who he was or why anyone would be reaching out about them now."

"Lukes running the number?"

I nod. "Yeah, and he wants you to pull the security footage from this morning and send it to him."

He walks over to sit in the chair next to mine and pulls out his phone to open the app that we use to store the security footage.

"It's probably nothing bad, but... After all the Charlie stuff, my head just always goes to the worst-case scenario. Luke was the first person I thought to go to. Candace, my bio mom used to be involved with some sketchy people."

He doesn't look up as I ramble on. Finally, he says, "You did the right thing; there's not much on the camera. A black sedan pulled in. It looks like a male, wearing a baseball cap and puffer jacket, probably about 5'10". He put the envelope on your windshield around 0930. He keeps his head down, though."

Great, the standard outfit of 75% of the population in Central Oregon.

"Will you send it to Luke?"

He nods. "Already did. Are you going to tell Drew?"

I shake my head and roll my lips together. "No, we ended the benefits, part of our friendship."

He winces. "I figured as much. He's going to be pissed if he finds out later."

Well, guess what? I'm pissed too.

"I know, but right now, there isn't much to tell. Once Luke figures out what's going on, I'll fill everyone in."

His jaw tightened as he threaded a hand through his hair. "Alright. But if I at all think that you or the kids are in jeopardy, I'm telling him."

"That's fair. Thanks, Hayes."

He hugs me just as Andrew walks through the door.

Oof, I hope these butterflies go away soon. Just seeing him makes my stomach do nervous flips.

I give a small smile and stand up to get out of here as fast as I can.

"Hey. There's your coffee."

His thumbs drum on the countertop as he stares at me, not saying anything. I don't miss the shadows under his eyes or the sag to his normally straight shoulders. He looks about as shitty as I feel.

Hayes clears his throat, reminding us we aren't the only ones in here.

"So, I should get back to work." I give a little wave as I walk away.

I try to remind myself that it'll get easier. It's only been a few days. We can go back to being friends. It just takes time. *Ha, Ha. Yeah, right.*

Chapter Twenty-Eight

Olivia

The relief that I feel that it's Friday afternoon is beyond measure. Pops left this morning with the kids to spend the weekend at his vacation house along the Oregon Coast. It wasn't planned, but when I broke down and told him what happened with Andrew, he offered to let me have some "Liv time." A weekend to cry, lick my wounds, and drink copious amounts of wine. Thank the Lord for that man.

Charlie begged me most of the day to go out for dinner with her and Hayes, but the weather forecast calls for snow later this evening, and I don't have it in me to drive in that later on. This morning the roads were already slick, and I don't want to white-knuckle it, especially after a drink. Isla called in today because of a migraine and said she would rather not brave the roads as well.

I'm finishing the last bit of emails, trying to make it to the last fifteen minutes, until I can leave at 4:30 without being eyed, when I hear the undeniable click of heels walking up the stairs.

I glance up at Charlie, an eyebrow raised in question, and she shrugs.

We both looked over just in time to see the back of a long-haired blonde walk into the guy's office, wearing a long fur jacket and heels.

Heather.

Andrew looks up, shock covering his face, as he stands to hug her.

And that's my cue to get the fuck out of here.

Slamming my laptop closed, I unplug it, grab my purse, phone, and keys, and throw my jacket over my arm. I turn to escape and hear Charlie say, "Love you, Livy. Drive safe!" I throw open the door to the back stairs, taking them down two at a time, and rush to my car.

I peel out of the parking lot and don't remember that the roads are slick until I slide a bit when I turn onto the main road.

Taking a deep, shaky breath, I slow down. It's already dark, and I don't need to get into an accident over Heather's sudden appearance in town.

The roads are relatively empty, so it's a little shocking when a car comes speeding up behind me.

Slow down, asshole.

I keep driving at a snail pace, hoping the idiot driver will pass me. It's all open roads here, hay fields for miles, but the car won't pass; it just stays glued to my bumper.

If I go faster, then they go faster. If I slow down, they'll slow down—just enough that they are practically kissing my bumper. Most of this road is a passing lane, and I haven't passed a single car coming from the other way, so I don't understand why they haven't just gone around. Clearly, they're just trying to fuck with me.

Ice runs through my veins when I remember the note on my car. The two things can't be related. Right?

I hit the call button on my steering wheel and yell at it to call Luke; if he doesn't answer, I'm calling dispatch. This car is seriously freaking me out. My palms are sweaty, and my jaw is starting to hurt from clenching it so hard.

The highway splits, and I veer off to the road I take home, praying they'll continue on the highway. I try to ease off the gas to slow down, but the car behind me doesn't, and I feel a small jolt as it grazes my bumper as we both take the other road. I clench the wheel tighter, trying to will the car to keep going forward and not spin out.

What *the fuck? Damn it, Luke, answer!*

He answers on the last ring, "Hey Livy, I was just about to call you."

"Okay, well, it's going to have to wait. Someone is following me and really fucking with my head. They just hit me. Well bumped."

"Where are you? What's the vehicle description?"

"Barely off Highway 126, heading home on Johnson. I don't know. A smaller SUV or a bigger car? It's dark, and I didn't really get a good look. But it sits lower than my SUV."

"I'm about five minutes away. Just drive slowly and don't stop. I'll catch up to you."

I hear him radio to his deputies to see if anyone is close, but I can't hear their responses.

I'm only doing about 30 mph, but the car is close enough that I can't even see them in my rearview mirror. If I even brake at all, they're hitting me again.

I could probably just keep driving until Luke could catch up, but I'm almost at an intersection that requires me to stop and yield to oncoming traffic.

"Luke, I'm almost to the intersection of Johnson and Whitemore! What do I do?!"

"Run it. If it's clear, just fucking go through it."

"Okay, Sheriff. Can I get that in writing?"

"Ha fucking ha, Olivia."

I can see the intersection, and there isn't anyone stopped on Johnson, but I see a vehicle's headlights coming in from the right side on Whitemore. They seem far enough away, but I really don't want to go blaring through this intersection.

I attempt to slow down again, and this time the car behind me lets off as well.

"Holy shit, they're backing off."

"Can you make it through without stopping?"

I glanced behind me again. "Maybe, but I think they're going to let me stop. They've backed way off."

The stop sign approaches, and I'm able to come to a full stop. My heart is pounding as I glance in the rearview mirror to make sure the car behind me has stopped too.

"They stopped like thirty feet back. What the fuck are they doing?" I half wonder aloud and ask Luke.

I start to lean forward to see how far out the headlights of the other car are on Whitemore.

"I don't know, Li..." He doesn't get to finish that sentence because the deafening sound of metal on metal fills the air as I'm jerked forward.

My chest hits the steering wheel, and I scramble, trying to lean back in my seat as I'm suddenly barreling into the intersection.

I almost have my whereabouts when the glow of headlights blinds me from the right side. The large vehicle I was waiting for is now plowing into my passenger side. Instead of the forward motion I was just trying to gain control of, I'm thrown into my driver's side door as my SUV is forced to the side.

The airbags begin exploding around me, and I know I am royally and truly fucked right now.

Time doesn't stand still, and I don't see my life flash before my eyes. One second, it feels like I'm flying through the air, and the next second, I'm crashing back down to the earth.

Logically, I know what happened, but my brain is having a hard time making sense of it. The ringing in my ears is deafening and distracting. I try to shake my head a few times to clear it, but it doesn't do anything but bring blinding waves of pain and nausea.

The airbags had already started to deflate as I started to get my bearings. My SUV is on its side, and gravity is trying to pull me down into my driver-side door, but my seatbelt keeps me locked in place. The smell of chemical smoke fills my lungs, but I'm able to resist coughing.

I think I hear the sirens of the first responders start to fade in, but not only do they sound far away, the ringing is drowning them out.

Everything is hazy, but the glow of headlights begins to filter through the spiderweb cracks on my shattered windshield. I can't focus on anything, though. The ringing just won't stop.

Why won't the ringing stop?

People start yelling from a distance, but they sound too far away for me to know what they're saying. The heat waves radiating from the dash have been hitting my cheeks for so long that it's starting to hurt, but I can't make my hands move to turn it off.

I glance down at my hands, willing them to move, but they're still in a death grip on the steering wheel. My jaw hurts from clenching it so hard, but my entire body feels like it's in a vice.

Breathe, just breathe, Olivia! *In through your nose, out through your mouth.* My body won't listen, so I settle on in through my nose and out through my nose.

My head is pounding, and the aches in my body are starting to take over. With the adrenaline crash hitting, I just want to sleep. The clock on my dash says 4:30, but surely that can't be right. I'm just too tired to read it correctly.

Maybe a nap will help.

My last thought as I drift off is of Ellie and Ben, thankful they aren't in this car.

I begin to stir when I feel hands on my face. My eyelids feel heavy as I try to get them open.

Dan is crouching down in my now torn-out windshield, and headlights illuminate the dark night behind him. His reflective snow gear has the Cascadia County Sheriff's Department badge front and center. His eyes look terrified as I try to focus on them, but they widen with relief when I smile at him. His mouth begins moving like he's yelling, but I can still only hear the ringing.

My head falls forward, but a rush of relief floods through me. It's all going to be okay. Dan's here. He's going to save me. He always saves me.

I feel hands go around my waist, just as the restraint of the seatbelt is cut loose, causing me to slump into him. I'm gently, but forcefully, pulled out of my SUV and laid on a stretcher.

I blink up at the dark sky as snow falls around me and begins to hit in wet splotches on my face. Hands are everywhere, strapping me down, and then I'm hoisted into the air.

I turn my head so that I can see Dan's face again as he carries one side of the stretcher out of the field. He's so beautiful when he works, a confidence about him most people lack. He looks like he's ready to burn the world down as he's saving it.

His black beanie is pulled down over his ears, and he looks furious. His lips are moving so fast that I can't tell what he's saying. People seem to be taking his orders, though, because I'm being lifted and placed onto a gurney and hauled into the back of the ambulance.

I can't help but just stare at him. The same silly question playing over and over in my head. Why is he wearing a beanie? He hates beanies. Levi likes beanies. Dan likes snapbacks.

I blink at him, just staring, until he finally looks at me. His eyes locked with mine, and that's all it took for me to realize I'm looking at Levi.

Not Dan.

His twin.

Levi.

The medic.

Not Dan.

Dan is dead.

The tears start falling on their own accord, and I'm hit again with the same impact I felt nearly three years ago. Dan is gone, but I still get to see his beautiful fucking face.

I'm so used to hearing Levi's voice while looking at him that the resemblance to his brother just faded away. Dan always had a serious tone, with a slightly deeper octave than Levi's jovial, lighter tone. Levi sports a slightly rounder "peach" face to Dan's slightly longer "pear" face. The dead giveaway is in their eye shape. I could never describe it; I could just look into his eyes and know it was Dan. Even from a distance.

But apparently, I lost the touch, or maybe my subconscious just wished so badly that Dan was there to save me. The fucking sheriff department jacket didn't help much either.

The ringing started to fade away but hasn't fully stopped. Levi hasn't stopped working and moving the entire time. Except for the pain in my head, ribs, and ankle, I feel okay. Nothing seems life-threatening.

I cough a bit, trying to talk, but the words barely come out. Levi's head snaps in my direction, eyes wide, like I just died on his gurney.

After clearing my throat, I tried again. "Thank you."

He just shakes his head and gets back to hanging an IV.

By the time we arrived at the hospital, I had an IV sticking out of my arm and my vital signs had been checked a hundred times. He's examined nearly every part of my body, taking note of the bruises, scratches, and a few burns. I've even heard him calling ahead and threatening every E.R. doctor with their lives if they weren't ready for us. He hasn't stopped moving; he hasn't stopped checking things on me; he's checked out.

His PTSD from Dan is showing loud and clear, and I can't help but shed a few tears for him.

He glances at me, and when he sees I'm crying, he freaks out even harder, begging me to tell him what's wrong.

"I'm okay! I'm okay! But you aren't." The tears flow out of my eyes like a waterfall. "You're going to therapy."

He looks at me like I've grown two heads. His chest began rising and falling rapidly as he tried to process my words.

"You were there when Dan died. In this ambulance! Driving to this hospital! You just pulled me out through my windshield. You are going to therapy!" I can't control the shout that flies out of me. It has nothing to do with my hearing and all to do with the broken man in front of me.

He nods solemnly as the ambulance slows to a stop and the doors are thrown open.

Chapter Twenty-Nine

Andrew

Heather's surprise showing up, not even ten minutes ago, is both welcome and extremely unwelcome. I'm thankful I get to have this conversation in person, but seeing Olivia run out of the office like that has me anxious to get this over with.

Grabbing my jacket and keys, I hurried her out of the office and to my truck. Hayes and Charlie both shooting death glares at me during the entire conversation would only be an added distraction. I need this conversation to go perfectly, I need Heather to let us go, and I need to fix things with Olivia.

Heather said she was dropped off, so she climbed into the passenger side of my truck.

Small snowflakes are already starting to fall, the first sign of the impending storm coming our way. Ponderosa Pine seemed like the safest bet to take her since it's close to everything, and it should be quiet enough at this time that we can talk in peace.

We make the quick trip over there, and I half pay attention to what Heather is jabbering about. Jesus. I forgot how much this woman can talk. Olivia and I spend just as much time in comfortable silence as we do in conversation. Neither of us ever felt the need to fill the space.

"Sorry, I know I'm talking a lot," she apologizes as we walk in. "I'm just nervous."

"It's okay. We have a lot to talk about."

"Yeah…"

The hostess guides us to our booth in the back. I throw my hand up to wave at Ethan, who is behind the bar cleaning, but he only shakes his head and gets back to wiping the same spot.

Fuck, nothing like pissing everyone off in one fell swoop.

At least, it's relatively empty in here; it's still too early for the dinner crowd. I don't need the town to start any rumors. They don't necessarily know Olivia and I have been hooking up, but I have had a few "big brother warning" talks over the last few months from more than one local.

I shrug off my jacket and take a seat, facing the entrance, as Heather slides in and sits opposite me.

Our server ends up being Ethan, and I wince when he walks over.

"Hey man. Short on staff again tonight?" It feels like weeks ago we were here for Levi's birthday party and not barely over a week.

"Yep."

"Okay. Water for me." I glance at Heather as she orders the same.

Ethan walks away, not sparing another glance my way.

"You can order a cocktail if you'd like. I'm just not drinking because of the snowstorm that's supposed to hit tonight."

Her body is visibly nervous, more nervous than before, as she says, "I can't. That's actually why I'm here."

My head cocks to the side. "You're here because you can't drink?" What does that mean?

She gives me a sheepish look and says, "I'm pregnant."

Only then does she take off her oversized jacket, and a very large, prominent bump sticks out.

Holy shit. She's as big as Charlie.

I must look like a fucking cartoon character as I try to process what she's saying. Math. I need to do math. When was the last time we had sex? She visited at the end of June, but we didn't have sex then. So, before I moved up here. April? That was.. I started ticking my fingers to count months, but thankfully she put me out of my misery.

She smirks at me. "They're not yours. Stop counting. I'm only four months along."

Shock ripples through me again. "They're?! Twins?"

She smiles, the first genuine smile I've seen from her in a long time. Her face is full of pride, and she says, "Yeah, identical girls."

"And the dad?"

The smile slips from her face. "He's..." she pauses and lets out a shaky breath. "It's a long story; I don't know what to say. It was a one-time thing that turned into... Something? I went home to help Kara with wedding planning, and he was there, and I was. Sad... I'm so, so sorry, Drew! You must hate me. I know we were going to wait until Kara's wedding to talk, but I didn't want to blindside you. I love him. We're getting married."

"Thank fuck." Maybe not the best response, but I'm so damn relieved.

She looks up, tears welling in her eyes. "What?"

"I'm in love with Olivia."

A laugh bubbles out of her, almost sounding more like a sob, but she smiles through it. "I knew she was it for you. I could tell the first time I met her. You were angry and smitten. You showed her more emotion the first time you met her than you showed me our entire relationship."

"Heather..." I run my hand down my face. "I'm sorry. I promise you that I had no idea that I would feel this way."

Her hand reaches across the table to pat mine. "I know, I was livid at first, but then Ledger. I just understood immediately."

"Ledger? As in Ledger Knight? The corn farmer?" Ledger was a few grades above us, but his younger brother Hudson was in our grade and his oldest brother hired Charlie when she was in college. Their family owned a large tobacco farm, but I had heard that Ledger had taken it over after he got back from ESU and turned it into a large-scale corn operation with the help of his older brother Noah.

She closes her eyes but giggles. "Yeah, can you believe it? Me. Moving to live on a farm. A real homesteader, I am."

I smile back, "You always did want a big family, though. I believe you even mentioned homeschooling a large brood at one point."

"I did. I always wanted that, but I got lost in L.A. chasing fame and money. It was all so dense; Ledger knocked me on my ass and helped me find myself again."

I get it. I lost myself in the Navy too. It took getting out to see how deep I was. "I'm happy for you, Heath."

"Me too. So, you and Olivia? Is it serious?"

"It's about to be, I hope. I was waiting until after the wedding."

She looks at me, confusion clouding her face. "Why?"

"The promise. We made a promise not to start a relationship."

"Oh shit! I forgot about that!"

"Yeah, clearly!" I say as I wave my hand down her front. I want to be pissed, but I'm just so damn excited to tell Olivia. The weight has been lifted from my shoulders.

Ethan comes back to take our food menu and openly glares at Heather's baby bump but doesn't say a single word. Heather, still being Heather, notices and cuts right to the chase. "Twins. Not his. Not getting back together. So *do not* spit in my food. I want a cheeseburger with bacon and extra fries." Damn, six months ago, she would have only eaten the lettuce off a burger. Ledger might be the best thing to ever happen to her.

"What she said." I pointed at her and handed him my menu.

"I'll get these in, but we are closing early because of the storm, so you won't have much time to eat it."

She smirks at him. "That's okay, I'm exhausted! Can we get it to go?" She looks at me as she asks, and I nod.

"Thanks, I just want to get back to my hotel and Ledge."

Twenty minutes later, she's safe and sound in her hotel, and I'm driving to Olivia's house. I need to explain the last hour to her, beg for her forgiveness, and hopefully spend the rest of the night reconciling.

I tap my fingers on the steering wheel as I approach a slew of cars stuck in a traffic jam. Sheriff vehicles are parked on the opposite side of the road, and down in the field, lights glow in the dark.

A few deputies are trying to direct traffic, but it's chaos down there; the snow is starting to come down hard. I should text Luke to see if there's anything I can do to help up there.

I reach for my phone in my pocket but come up empty. Looking around the truck, I'm trying to remember when I had it last. It must have been at the office before Heather waltzed in.

I'm only about three cars behind the stop sign when I can finally start to make sense of the scene. A white F-350 is parked off to the side of the road, blocking the vehicle it hit behind it. The front end of the truck is completely smashed in.

The cars in front of me start to creep forward, and I follow as the deputies try to direct us through the intersection. We all drive slowly, giving into that human urge to rubber-neck as we pass by the carnage of the accident.

Truck lights and flashlights illuminate the vehicle in the field. I see Luke out there, ordering his deputies around, looking every bit as in charge as he is.

I'm almost through the intersection when I finally get a good look at the vehicle on its side. It's just the underside of a large SUV, but my entire body runs cold.

I slam the wheel to the right and pull off the road, bailing out of my truck seconds later. I don't even shut the truck off or close the door. I'm just running across the road to Luke and sliding down the ditch.

"Luke!"

He looks my way, seeing me slip and slide as my feet try to get traction on the snow, and lets out a deep breath before laying into me. "Where the fuck have you been, Drew?"

"Is that hers?" I don't even care if I look insane right now, my gut is telling me that it's hers.

"IS THAT HER FUCKING SUV?"

He nods. "She was conscious when Levi loaded her up in the bus." He pauses to check his phone. "45 minutes ago. She has a possible TBI, broken ribs, stitches on her forehead, and a few burns from the airbag deployment. They're still going to run some scans, though. Overall, it's good news."

Good news? Is he fucking kidding me?

I gnash my fist into my chest, rubbing at my sternum.

She's alive, and she's going to be okay, but hearing it while still looking at that totaled SUV doesn't give me the reassurance it should.

All that I know is that I need to see her. I turn on my heels and start back toward my truck.

A large hand grabs my shoulder, forcing me to stop. "Hey, you're not driving right now."

If he wasn't the sheriff, I would have already knocked him on his ass.

"Hayes is on his way. Been driving all over, looking for your dumbass."

I don't even turn; I just growl out. "Listen, I respect you, but you need to let me go."

"Don't even fucking start with me, Drew. I don't need your bullshit right now, and if you even think about getting in that truck, I will have your ass sitting in a cell for the night."

I swing around with my fist's clenched. "What's your fucking problem, Luke? That's my girl's SUV right there, and I am going to check on her!"

He squares up against me. We are about the same height and build, nose to nose, right now. I never thought he was intimidating, but I can see how people would think so. Especially when he's looking at you like he wants to deck you. The thing is, I'm just as enraged as he is. If he thinks I'm backing down, he's wrong.

"Yeah, and that's my dead best friend's wife—that I just pulled out of it! You think you're the only one affected by this? You didn't hear the terror in her voice! You didn't hear her scream when that truck smashed into her! I did! She called me, and I wasn't here fast enough. So quit your fucking shit and let me process this goddamn scene!"

I take a step back, my shoulders going slack as I try to process everything he just said. He's right; she hadn't called me. I was too busy trying to rip the bandage off with Heather to be the one that Olivia called when she was upset. Hell, if Heather hadn't shown up like that, she wouldn't have even left the office in such a huff anyway.

"Reynolds! Let's go!" I turn to see Hayes. His truck is

parked behind mine; I'm barely aware that the door is now closed, and the truck is off. I'm sure that was Hayes.

I ambled back up the small slope, trying not to slip on the muddy field. I climb into the back of Hayes truck and see a red-faced, crying Charlie in the passenger seat. She doesn't even look at me; she only stares forward and sobs.

Chapter Thirty

Olivia

Besides the clock's ticks above the door, an occasional machine beep, and the hushed words of those in the hall, it's silent in this room. Deadly silent. Move an inch, and you can hear the sheets ruffling—silent.

The doctor was just in and informed me that he would be starting my discharge paperwork and releasing me to go home soon, so long as Levi stays overnight to monitor me. I tried to insist I didn't need a babysitter, but Levi shut that down with one look. He was there when the doctor went over my laundry list of ailments: a minor TBI, cracked and bruised ribs, three stitches above my left eyebrow, a few friction burns, and pregnancy.

Pregnancy. Pregnant. As in a baby in utero. Bun in the oven.

How did that happen? I mean, I know how—man and woman have unprotected sex, sperm meets egg, and a tiny little human starts to grow. I know all of this. I know how babies are made. I've made two of them. Yet, here I am, flabbergasted that I'm pregnant.

Me. A single, widowed mother, pregnant, even though I was taking my birth control regularly. Pregnant.

God truly has the best sense of humor.

The doctor confirmed gestation to be about 8–9 weeks, based on the ultrasound and blood work. Levi was witness to all of it and has been stunned into silence since the doctor was in here, a first for my normally chatty brother-in-law.

I can't stand the tension in this room. It's suffocating. What should be a wonderful, joyful, moment is brought down by the tragedy of earlier.

But I'm okay, and the baby is okay.

I look at Levi. "You know this is all you and your dad's fault, right?"

He glances up from his phone, his mouth parting in shock. "What? How?"

"Pop cornered me a few months ago. Told me he wanted more grandchildren, and you weren't going to give him any." I point at him like it's his fault as well.

The laugh oozes out of him slowly, but he's in hysterics trying to talk while laughing. "He fucking manifested... You having a baby!"

My entire body is shaking from trying to stop laughing, and my ribs hurt with every slight movement. I clutch them and say, "Stop making me laugh; it isn't funny!"

He stands up and shoves his phone in his pocket. He takes the two steps toward my bed and grabs my hand. His smile is still there, and the crinkle in his eyes gives me a little hope: "I'm going to be an uncle again. I know things are complicated with Drew." He looks at me with raised eyebrows. "I'm assuming he's the baby daddy."

I give him the side eye, and he laughs again. "But no matter what, that baby will be loved by me and treated no differently than Ben and Ellie."

I nod, tears welling in my eyes. "I appreciate you, Levi. You've been a really good brother to me and the best uncle to my kids."

"So, I take it you didn't know?"

I shake my head. "Nope, I had no idea. Things are complicated right now. I'm not ready to tell anyone yet."

He nods. "I get it. Just don't wait too long. I know it might not seem like it, but he loves you and has from the beginning. I think you two are the only ones that couldn't see it."

"I'm not sure about that but thanks."

"You're welcome. Now, chin up. They should be walking in here any minute."

I let out a small gasp as he retreats to his chair. "They? Who are they?"

Not even a second after the words are out, Andrew is walking into the room like a man on a mission, followed by Charlie and Hayes. He walks past Levi and comes to stand on the opposite side of the bed Levi was just on. He doesn't say anything. He just stands there, his jaw working double time as he grinds his teeth together.

I let out a string of silent curse words. Between the car accident and crying every two minutes, I guarantee I look like a disaster.

Andrew's eyes scan me from head to toe and back again, a cold, calculating look like he's trying to assess every injury. He's still in his work clothes, no jacket, and he looks soaking wet.

I glance at Charlie; her face is red and splotchy, but at least she has her big puffy jacket on. Hayes looks a lot like Andrew right now, always assessing. Both of their faces are a complete mask to hide the inner turmoil, but I catch just the slightest glimpse of relief in their eyes when they see I'm okay.

"You guys didn't need to come. I'm sure the storm is just really starting to hit."

Hayes lets out a little chuckle. "Actually, we did; I heard y'all need a ride home." He sets his palm on Levi's shoulder and gives him a reassuring squeeze.

Right. Levi brought me here in the back of an ambulance. Therefore, neither of us has a vehicle here.

That must have been why Levi was on his phone so much.

"Yeah, guess we do…"

Is it just me, or is this the most awkward moment of my life?

I just found out I'm having a baby with the man who hasn't said a damn thing since he walked in. Charlie also hasn't said a word, and that woman usually doesn't know when to stop. Hayes's eyes are bouncing between the three of us, trying to figure out who he needs to help first. And Levi. Levi's just sitting there with a smug smirk, like the jackass he is. At least he's back to normal.

I extend my right hand out to Charlie, and she walks to the side of the bed not occupied by her brother. "I'm okay. I'm so sorry. I know how scared you must feel, but I promise you, I look much worse than I feel."

Andrew lets out a scoff, but I don't even glance at him. Just try to hug Charlie and hide the wince as I do. She leans back and takes my hand, sniffling. "You're sure everything is okay? Levi told us it's just a minor TBI and some broken ribs, but are they sure there isn't anything else?"

Oh, girl. You have no idea.

I can't exactly tell her that, though. I need to talk to Andrew first, and then I can fill her in on the rest.

I nod my head, trying to think of a lie of omission: "Bumps and bruises. I'll be okay."

I glance at Andrew, the only one who hasn't said anything yet. The anger pours out of him, but once again, I can't tell if he's pissed at me or the situation I'm in.

Maybe he's just mad that it ruined his evening with Heather.

Hayes speaks up: "Everett wanted me to let you know that he's thinking about you and, if you need anything, to call. He's trying to help where he's needed with Luke."

Unconsciously, I began to chew on my lip as I gathered the courage to ask, "Did they ever find the car that hit me?"

Something snaps with Andrew, and he looks at Hayes and then back at me. "You mean the truck?"

I open my mouth and close it, trying to think of what to say as Hayes lets out a loud sigh.

Shaking my head, I explain, "No, uhm, the car that was following me? It slammed into me and sent me into oncoming traffic, where the truck hit."

Andrew crosses his arms across his chest, and he widens his stance. "Explain. From the beginning."

Should have kept my mouth shut.

I sigh and look at my hands while I talk. "I left the office, and when I got onto the highway, I noticed someone was following me and kind of messing with me. I called Luke when I turned onto Johnson, and the car continued to follow. The last thing I remember is the car stopping really far back at the intersection and then being propelled into oncoming traffic. Next thing I know, Dan is pulling me out, well, Levi. But I was a little out of it, and you know, twins." I try to shrug, but wince at the pain in my ribs.

When I glanced up to gauge his reaction, I noticed he had already turned his large frame toward Levi, eyebrows raised.

"We got a dispatch at 16:22 from Chief, motor vehicle accident, unknown injuries. We were there by 16:28; she was conscious, but out of it. Chief and Fire were already on the scene when we got there, working on getting her out. We had her here by 17:02."

He nods his approval and looks at Hayes. "And the car that was following her?"

Hayes fills in the rest: "Luke tried to set up a perimeter and box them in, but they must have hit a side road or squeezed by without someone noticing. I was all over town looking for you and didn't see a matching description either."

"Who the fuck would be following you?" He looks at me like I should have the answer.

I glance guiltily at Hayes. "Could it be related to the note left on my windshield the other day?"

I hear Charlie let out a small gasp and flinch when Andrew grinds out, "What note?"

"The other day, I went to get a coffee. I found a note that said 'Call me' and had a picture of my bio mom and a guy. I went straight to Luke, who told me he would look into it but insisted I tell someone at the office. I only chose Hayes because it was right after our fight."

A brief look of hurt washes over his features as he listens to me ramble on. The next second, it's gone, and left is unmistakable anger as he turns those glaring eyes on Hayes. He tips his jaw and then arches an eyebrow, prompting Hayes to fill in his side of events.

Shit, I knew I shouldn't have gotten Hayes involved.

Hayes squares his shoulders in response and looks like he's ready to go toe-to-toe right back. One look at these guys, and you'd never know they've been best friends for over thirty years.

"Olivia briefed me on the note and asked me not to say anything to anyone except Luke. Luke and I looked into the note, the calls, and the security footage. I'd like to speak to Olivia in private before I go into detail."

I hear another scoff from Andrew, clearly pissed that he is getting shut out of this. Hayes ignores him, though, and looks at me; his features soften when he sees the panic on my face. "I'm positive the person who left the note has nothing to do with the accident."

"Bullshit." Andrew looks like he's ready to punch Hayes. "You can't know that! Why the fuck am I just now hearing about all of this?!"

I reach out and grab his wrist, turning him to look at me. "Stop; it's not his fault. I asked him not to say anything."

"That's fucked up, Boots." His words crack with emotion: "You're my girl, and he should have told me."

I immediately let go of him, his careless choice of words snapping me back into reality. For months, I wished so desperately to hear those words from him, but now it just feels like a slap in the face. I was never his girl. His friend? Sure. Fuck buddy? Definitely. But I could never have been "his girl" while he was still emotionally tied to another.

"No, I'm not..." My eyebrows pinch together as I try to figure out how to get the rest out without being too harsh. I soften my tone, but it doesn't lighten the impact. "We ended the 'benefits' part of our friendship. Luke insisted I tell someone at the office, and Hayes has without a doubt been there for me and my kids. You're not going to make him or me feel guilty for the situation that you put us in."

His Adam's apple bobs as he swallows. The hurt on his face is evident, but before he can say anything, the discharge nurse with a wheelchair walks into the room. He has to be over six feet tall and bald, and he looks like he rivals the Bod Squad in the gym.

"Hello, I'm Derek. I'll be helping you get out of here tonight," he says with a killer smile aimed at me.

Damn, that would've been swoon-worthy if I wasn't so caught up in the brooding jerk next to me.

I hear the throaty growl from the other side and roll my

eyes. He can be jealous all he wants. Derek is doing his job, not trying to get in my pants. Even if he was, it isn't his problem.

I swing my legs to the right side of the bed as he wheels the wheelchair closer to me.

When he goes to grab my hand to assist, Andrew is already there on my left, lifting me into his arms. With one look, Derek has his hands up in surrender and takes a step back, a small smirk playing on his lips.

I'm gently placed on the seat, and while he's still leaning down, he brushes my hair back behind my shoulder. His knuckle gently grazes down the side of my jaw while his woodsy scent surrounds me.

I can't help but notice the look of longing that lights up those green eyes. The butterflies take flight at the contact, and I realize his face is still close enough that I could kiss him. A shiver runs down my spine at the thought, and I wince at the pain in my ribs. In a flash, he's standing and stepping behind the wheelchair, no doubt trying to be in control of the situation.

I take a deep breath, thankful that his scent and touch are no longer clouding my judgment. I do not need to kiss him. Heather was just parading her way through our office, and he looked pretty damn happy to see her. He decided to put her first, and I need to let him go.

The car accident didn't change that, and neither will the baby.

Chapter Thirty-One

Andrew

The drive back from the hospital is almost as tense as the drive there. Not only is the cab of the truck silent for almost the entire drive back to Three Sisters, but the roads are only getting worse. The snow is coming down hard, and the roads are mostly deserted except for a few snowplows. Despite our protests, Olivia insisted on sitting in the back, and once I lifted her in the truck, she scooted herself to the middle seat between Levi and me. Thankfully, she let me buckle her in without much complaint, but when I settled into my seat, her entire demeanor changed. She turned to sit sideways in the seat, giving me her back, facing Levi, and resting the side of her face on the seat.

I knew she would try to shut me out, but this feels fucking brutal. I haven't been able to talk to her about Heather yet, and it's eating at me.

I scoot so that her back is touching my arm and thigh; she recoils at the touch and then winces. I hold my breath, waiting, hoping she will relax into me. Finally, after what feels like an eternity, her shoulders sag, and she leans back. *Small victories.*

What I want to do is wrap her up in my arms and hold her the entire way home.

Hayes is the first to speak as we approach town, asking everyone, "What's the plan? Levi, do you need anything from your house?"

"Nah, I've got spare stuff at Liv's."

Hayes nods, barely visible in the dark cab. "Want me to drop you off at your truck?" He glances at me in his rearview mirror.

"Nope."

He raises his eyebrow as Olivia asks, "Where's your truck?"

I shrug and keep my mouth shut, hoping to avoid this topic.

"Side of the road on Johnson." Hayes decides to pipe up.

Olivia turns to face forward and inhales a sharp breath at the movement. "Why would you leave your truck there?"

"It'll be fine." I'm not letting Olivia out of my sight until they catch whoever hit her car.

"Or it'll get broken into..." Charlie has to add.

Maybe. Don't really give a fuck, though. They can take the whole damn truck, for all I care.

"It'll be fine. I'm not leaving Olivia." My tone leaves no room for discussion, but Olivia seems to ignore that.

Her face turns toward me. It's dark in here, but the lights from the town illuminate her beautiful face as she splutters out. "You're not staying with me."

Rather than respond, I lift my shoulders in a shrug. She's not going to change my mind, so it's not worth the argument.

"No, seriously." She gestures with her index finger between us. "This, us, no. You're not staying. Levi will be there to help, and I'll be fine after a shower and some sleep."

This time, I do loudly scoff in response. Not a chance in hell is he helping her shower. She can barely move without her ribs hurting. There is no way she will be able to get undressed by herself, and if he's the only one there? Nope, no way.

I gently rest my palm on the side of her face, and she leans into it, her eyes closing. "I'm staying. I'm helping. We are talking."

Her mouth opens and closes, gapping like a fish, but I continue, "It can wait until tomorrow. But I'm not leaving."

Her eyes are swimming with defiance, but finally, she relents and shakes her head at me.

"Levi, will you please drive his truck to the house?"

"Sure." I can tell he's pissed, but there's nothing he wouldn't do for her. He's a damn good brother to her. I actually respect the hell out of him, but I have a feeling it's going to be a while before he feels the same about me.

"Thanks, man." I try to look around Olivia, but he just stares straight ahead.

We drop Levi off at my truck, and he follows us the short-distance back to her house.

Olivia squeezed her eyes shut as we passed the scene of the accident, but it had already been cleaned up, and the vehicles towed away. I still didn't miss the opportunity to pull her close to me and wrap my arms around her.

Levi sat with the girls in the locked truck while Hayes and I checked the house. She has a full security system that we installed, but neither of us trusts that completely. I know that I wouldn't have been able to relax unless I physically checked out the entire house twice.

We gave them the all-clear, and Hayes hopped back into the driver seat while Olivia said her goodbyes to them. Before she could get out, I scooped her into my arms and carried her through the door. She sighed but wrapped her arms around my neck.

Small victories. Small, small victories.

I keep my hold on her, not even breaking a sweat while carrying her. She feels so small in my arms, no longer looking like the smiling, vivacious woman I first met. It feels like a lifetime ago when she was twirling that flower and giving me sass.

"I can walk." I ignore her request and carry her directly through her bedroom and into her bathroom.

"Shower, sleep, talk." I set her on the chair by her vanity and took a few steps into the walk-in shower to get the water turned on and warmed up for her. The memories of us doing this before, under entirely different circumstances, hit me at once, and I can't help the sad sigh that escapes.

I hear her groan, and when I turn around, I see her trying to bend over to get her boots unzipped.

"Let me help, please." I practically beg as I crouch down in front of her, grabbing her ankle. She sets her hand on my shoulder but doesn't stop me as I start to pull the zipper down off her over-the-knee boot.

I look up at her after I get the first one off, those honey browns staring at me with so much sadness.

"I appreciate you helping me." A sad smile plays on her lips. "I know Levi would have, but it probably would have scarred him for life."

"Hmph." I can barely dignify that with a response. I highly doubt seeing her naked would scar him. She's every man's wet dream. Then again, if he thinks of her like I think of Odessa, maybe it would. He's mentioned before that he considers her to be a sister, and that's how I think of Odessa.

I gently pick up her other foot, and she clears her throat before asking, "Is this... Is this going to get you in trouble?"

My brow furrows, and my gaze shoots up at her, confused by what she's asking. Her boot is unzipped, but I pause, waiting for her to finally look at me again. When she does, I ask, "Is what?"

I hear her swallow and then watch her tongue dart out to wet her lips. A nervous tell. I guarantee she's one step from sucking that bottom lip in and chewing on it.

"You helping me. I saw Heather today in your office. Levi mentioned they couldn't get a hold of you." There it is: the lip bite. I drop her still-booted foot and move so that I'm on my knees before her.

I cupped her chin with my right hand and used my thumb to pull her lip out. "No. Yes, Heather was here. I've been calling her for days, and she wouldn't answer. I even booked a ticket for tomorrow to tell her about us."

She bobs her head as she tries to blink away tears from her misty eyes. "Why did she fly here?"

"She's pregnant." I watch her inhale a sharp breath as her jaw drops and her eyes go comically wide.

I smirked at her. "Twins. Not mine."

"Holy shit! Lead with that next time!" She playfully shoves my shoulder, but winces as she does it.

I grab her waist to steady her, and she places her arms lightly around my shoulders.

Fuck, this feels good. Like home. Holding her, breathing the same air, and fixing what I broke.

"She wanted to tell me before I found out at the wedding. Well, Ledger, the father, pretty much insisted on it."

"He did? Do you know him?"

I let out a little chuckle. "Yep. I played football with his younger brother. I had a nice chat with him when I dropped her off at her hotel." Maybe "nice" is the wrong word. More like mildly awkward, but so damn relieving at the same time.

"Okay, and how do you feel about all that?"

"Relieved. So fucking relieved."

"You're not disappointed? That could've been you... Having a baby with her."

I finished taking her boot off. "Nope, do I want kids someday in the future? Sure. But the older we got, the more I realized she wasn't the one I wanted to have kids with." She doesn't know it yet, but I'm still praying that the future is with her.

A look I've never seen before crosses her face, but it's quickly gone.

"Can you help me get these clothes off?"

"I thought you'd never ask," I say with a wink and cocky smirk.

She exaggerates an eye roll but stands to let me help her. I unzip her skirt from the side and gently pull it down. Next are her ripped tights and tiny black underwear. I should probably close my eyes, but I'm a glutton for punishment. I stand to my full height, careful to hide the fact that I'm turned on, and help her get her arms out of the sleeves of her shirt. She turns, and I unsnap her bra, letting it unceremoniously fall to the ground.

I scan her full body, which is now beginning to darken with bruises and scratches. The anger I felt when I first saw her in her hospital bed is rearing its ugly head again. My jaw feels tight from clenching it, so I take a step back and close my eyes. She doesn't need to see me lose my shit right now, not after everything she's been through.

I take a seat in the chair she was just in, trying to calm my heart rate. I hate feeling like a goddamn mess of emotions. I'm turned on by the fact she's naked a few feet away from me, while also angry that someone hurt her.

I hear the water turn off so I grab her towel, careful to gingerly wrap her up in it. "Can you help me get my clothes back on now?"

I stick out my lip and frown. "Do I have to? I much prefer you naked."

She laughs—the first heartfelt laugh I've heard from her in days. "Yes. Levi said he'd be checking on me every few hours."

Definitely putting her in layers upon layers. I scurry into her walk-in closet, bigger than my bedroom, and find her pajama drawer. I pick out the least sexy thing I can find—oversized basketball shorts and one of my tees she stole.

"There." I take a step back, feeling more confident seeing her in my shirt.

"Whatever, help me into bed."

Chapter Thirty-Two

Olivia

I wake up in the morning feeling okay—a little sore, but okay. I took some painkillers in the middle of the night, and they seem to still be working. I'm not ready to open my eyes yet, though. I'm using Andrew as a large, hard body pillow. My head rests on his shirtless chest—definitely not how we went to sleep—but my traitorous body can't resist him.

His hand begins lightly drawing circles on my back, and I smile when he says, "Good morning, beautiful."

"Morning."

"How you feeling? Need more meds?"

I snuggle into him closer, not quite ready to give up this moment. "Nope, if I don't move, it doesn't hurt."

A light chuckle shakes his chest, making me smile even more. "Happy to stay right here for the rest of the day, but your phone has been ringing off the hook all morning."

"Shit." I guarantee half the town has heard about my accident, and I'm sure they'll be stopping by any second now.

I open my eyes and pout at him. "I don't want to deal with people today."

He kisses my forehead and says, "K, then we won't."

My eyebrows must hit my forehead. "Is that an option?"

"Olivia, you could have been killed in that accident. If you want to stay here for a week, I'll stay here with you. Levi and Hayes can deal with everyone else."

Wow, who knew having someone on your team could feel so good?

"Thanks. I should call the kids, though. Let them know I'm okay."

He nods. "I've been texting Ben. Letting him know I've got you."

"You have?" I suddenly feel a little choked up. He knows all the right things to suck me right back in.

"Yep, I also asked for his permission to take you on a date. I hope that's okay." That same stupid, sexy smirk is back. Then, when he tacks on a wink, I lose all hope of holding on to this grudge.

"A date?" I squeak out.

"Yep." His eyes are soft but pleading. "I've fucked up a lot. I didn't put you first until it was too late. Then I fought like hell to fix that mistake, only to find out that I almost lost you in a completely different way. The accident yesterday—when I saw your SUV smashed like that. It damn near killed me, too. I'm so fucking in love with you, Boots. I'll spend the rest of my life proving that to you and the kids."

Something about the sorrow on his face mixing with regret has my stomach twisting. I don't want to be mad at him anymore. I want us. I want this to work.

"I'm pregnant!" I blurt out, wincing right afterward. That was definitely not how I intended to tell him. "With your baby," I add softly.

His mouth opens and closes, shock clouding his features. "You're pregnant?"

It's impossible to tell if he's happy or sad while he lays there staring at my stomach with the widest eyes I've ever seen.

When he finally glances up to make eye contact, I nod. "Not twins. But it is *yours*."

He sits up and places his hand on my stomach, under his shirt. There's a twinkle in his eyes, but he still hasn't said anything. It's like he's staring at his hand with wonder and disbelief.

I fill the silence when I can't take it anymore, rambling it all out. "I found out last night. I couldn't remember my last period, and when they did the blood test, it was positive. They gave me an ultrasound. I'm about nine weeks. I'm sorry that I didn't tell you! But I couldn't let my happy news be tainted by everything yesterday."

His smile is slow, but eventually consumes his entire face. "Our happy news. I'm glad you waited. But it's our happy news," and then he's kissing me. His body hovers over mine, just enough to push me back into my pillows without any real pressure on me.

"I love you, too," I mumble back into our kiss.

He pulls back. "Say it again."

It's my turn to smirk at him. "I love you. I think I've loved you since that first Friday night movie night."

He starts to pepper light kisses all over my face, telling me that he loves me after each kiss.

His phone starts to ring on the nightstand, and he sighs, rolling off me to answer whoever is calling. "Luke, it's not even seven yet. What do you want?"

His jaw clenches and his eyes narrow while he listens. Finally, he says, "Fine. See you in fifteen."

He hangs up and looks at me. "Luke said he needs to talk to us. Assuming he needs to get your statement and fill us in on everything else."

I nod, ready to just get this over with. "Help me get dressed."

"I really wish you'd stop asking that." The smirk is there, but it doesn't quite reach his eyes.

Ten minutes later, my phone chimes with an alert that someone is pulling into the driveway. I opted for a long-sleeve henley tucked into my fleece joggers, my hair somewhat brushed, and minimal makeup. My face has a few bruises, mainly just under my left eye, but once I covered the stitches with a few of Ellies princess bandages, I felt better.

Andrew gets the door while I sit on the couch. When Luke walks in, I flinch at the sight of him. He looks like he's had a worse night than I have. "How ya doing, friend? Need a coffee? Beer?"

He lets out a half-hearted laugh. "I fucking wish. A coffee would be great, though." He runs his hand through his already-ruffled hair. I have a feeling he's been doing that all night, by the looks of it.

Andrew nods and grabs a mug for Luke, making him a coffee so that I don't have to get up.

"So, how'd the investigation go last night?"

Luke sighs and grumbles something like, "Which one?" while rubbing the stubble that he hasn't had time to shave this morning.

My eyebrows lifted, waiting for him to go on.

"Good news. We know who hit you last night. We had the entire team out running patrols. It took a few hours with the snow coming down, but we found the vehicle around 0100. Security footage from your office showed a Nissan Xterra with an off-road bumper following you shortly after you left. It was confirmed to still be following you by the Lansings' security cam once you passed their house."

"Holy shit. So you caught them?"

He lets out a puff of air and says, "Yep." He rolls his neck and shakes his head, clearly not ready to say the next part. "Bad news. The vehicle belongs to Jeff Walton." Isla's boyfriend.

My dramatic gasp has me wincing from pain. I knew that Jeff had a problem with me, but to try to murder me? That's insane.

"It gets worse. We only found the vehicle because Isla was in the middle of the road, beaten to hell. She told him about the car, where it was hidden, and why she looked as if she had gone through a war zone. Apparently, Jeff had gone completely off the rails and attacked her."

Andrew looks murderous. "Told *who*, where the car was hidden?"

"Everett."

"Fuck!" Andrew slams his palm down on the countertop.

"Yep." He takes a small sip of his coffee.

It seems like they're silently talking right now, and I'm the only one not understanding what's so wrong about Everett being the one to find Isla.

I glance between the two of them, trying to figure out what's going on. "Is Isla okay? What about Everett?"

"Isla's okay. She's at the hospital and Charlie is with her. Hayes picked up Everett from the station about an hour ago. He'll be on paid leave until the investigation is settled."

My head rears back, confused. "Investigation? For the hit-and-run?"

Luke buries his hands in his hair. "Standard protocol for an officer involved shooting."

"Officer involved shooting?!" I shriek.

He looks at me grimly. "Jeff's dead."

Epilogue

Olivia

"Feeling nervous?" Andrew asks while reaching over and setting his hand on my bouncing knee.

"More than I should be." I reply with a sigh. The pilot just announced that we will be landing in Raleigh, North Carolina, in forty-five minutes. Then we have an almost three-hour drive to Emerald Island, where I'll get to meet my biological dad officially, his wife, and my four half-sisters for the first time in person.

It had taken a while after the events that transpired between Everett, Isla, and Jeff, but Hayes eventually filled me in on everything that happened with the note on my SUV. My biological dad, Rich, hired a private investigator to search for me after my biological mother tried to get money out of him recently. He hadn't even known about me until she reached out to him and insisted he pay child support. Child support for a child she hadn't even raised. It turns out I was conceived during a summer romance, a few weeks before he left for medical school. Thankfully, he didn't give her a dime and instead hired someone to investigate her claims.

I was hesitant at first to reach out, but eventually, I did, and to my surprise, they're a great family. We've video-chatted, called, texted, and become friends on all social media platforms. It feels like I already know them, but that doesn't mean the nerves are any less. Especially being seven months pregnant and bringing along my kids. Thank God for Andrew. I probably wouldn't have gotten on the plane without him. He's been my rock for the last few months. Every problem we had before the accident is nonexistent now that we are officially together. He parades me around town and makes me feel like the most important person in the world, both inside and outside the bedroom.

"You'll like the island. It's small, but the beaches are nice. The kids aren't going to want to leave." Andrew says, bringing me out of my thoughts.

"I have no doubt about that. They'll probably try to convince me to buy a house out here. Actually, that might not be a bad idea now that Connie is moving to Three Sisters. We won't have her house to stay in, so we could find a vacation house out here. I still can't believe she is selling her house."

Andrew smirks, "Well, all her little birdies are finally in one nest. Except Odessa, that is. I have a feeling she'll be the next to move, though. Especially with all the new babies." Hayes and Charlie had a baby boy a few weeks ago, August Roger Carrington. The tiniest little bundle of joy came out with his mom's green eyes and his dad's dark hair.

After we got settled into our rental house, we made the quick drive to Rich and his wife Alice's house. Andrew and I both exchange impressed glances as we pull into the driveway. It's a beautiful three-story home, right on the beach. The lot itself is three times that of every other lot. I knew that Rich had done well for himself as an orthopedic surgeon, but I hadn't realized how well.

The introduction was chaotic, but it felt nice to see them all around each other. All the girls are surprisingly close and not very far apart in age. Rich met Alice a few months after he started medical school at Duke. They got married and then started having kids quickly after that. I'm only about two and a half years older than my half-sister, Mila. Gianna is eighteen months younger than her, and the twins Lucia and Chiara are eighteen months younger than that. Rich and Alice had it planned down to the month and day, it seemed, but they swore that wasn't the case.

Mila just started her first year of residency and intends to work in family medicine. She's the calmest of all four but also the most personable. The spitting image of our dad, with her dark hair and light-brown eyes. Actually, she looks the most like me. For the first time, I feel like I belong to a family

Gianna is in her final year of law school and looks like she's always ready for a fight. Her blonde hair is perfectly pulled back into a ballerina bun, and she has Alice's blue eyes but our dad's height.

Lucia and Chiara are the perfect blend of our dad and their mother, both stunningly beautiful. They're the only ones that I have trouble talking to—my own anxieties surface any time they talk about their careers. They've chosen the same paths as Levi and Dan did, one joining the police force while the other became a medic. The fact that they're identical twins doesn't help either. I wanted to scream at them that I've already read their story and know how it ends, but in all honesty, I haven't. They're two different people with two different lives. Dan and Levi's story is theirs and only theirs.

The entire family welcomed us into their folds, never once making us feel like outsiders. I couldn't help but wonder how different my life would have been had I known them from a young age—maybe even been raised with Rich as a father and

Alice as a stepmother. If it hadn't been for Lovey saving me, I may have even been sad about it. However, I can't deny that my life turned out to be more than I ever thought it could be.

I've embraced every heartbreak and broken dream, and like a flower, I've used the rain to grow. Turning surviving into thriving.

Also by TJ Deal

Already ready for more TJ Deal? Read on for a sneak peek of Book 3 in The Cascadia County Series—Behind the Larch.

Chapter One
Isla

I watch from the second-floor balcony of the Cascadia Property Management building as the sun dips behind the Cascade Mountains. I've been off work for almost an hour, but I haven't had it in me to go home yet. Not that it even feels like "home" to begin with. Jeff, my boyfriend, insisted we rent one of the nicest houses in Cascadia County, although it costs nearly my entire paycheck to cover it. He offered to pay for the utilities, loan me one of his cars, and pay for our membership at the golf course. At the time, it felt like a fair trade, but looking back, I see the mistake—he doesn't pay for anything; his parents do. Now, I live paycheck-to-paycheck and contemplate every day why I haven't had the courage to end things with Jeff.

So instead of going home and facing reality, I contemplate life. It certainly has a way of throwing unexpected curveballs directly at your face, doesn't it? One day, you're a brazen five-year-old telling off a bully for pushing you down. The next day, you're twenty-six and in a toxic relationship that you can't seem to escape. I can't help but wonder what the hell happened to that courageous little girl. How on earth did she lose every ounce of confidence she ever had? Was it the move to a new state? Was it the lack of friendships starting over? Was it the childhood cancer? Or was it simply the lack of parental support she's received throughout the years? Who the fuck knows? At this point, does it even matter? I'm still dating an asshole to please my parents, who don't even care how I'm treated.

The wind rips through the trees below me, sending the distinct smell of an impending Central Oregon winter storm wafting up to me. It smells like fresh pine and smoke from a nearby fireplace, a reminder of the harsh yet beautiful winter to come. The cold air stings my cheeks, but I snuggle down deeper into the Canada Goose down jacket that Jeff's mother, Christy, purchased for me. Normally, I donate all the "hush-money" gifts I receive, but this one is the exception. She left the wrapped box on my doorstep after the first argument Jeff and I had. Stupid me assumed it was an "I'm sorry" gift from him because he genuinely felt bad about yelling at me. It wasn't until months later, when several more gifts appeared, that I understood Jeff had nothing to do with the designer items. Christy was doing what she does best: buying forgiveness for her son. I fell for the whole charade. Since then, I haven't kept a single gift.

Two knocks sound from the door to my right, and I laugh when Everett opens the door, his signature cheesy grin already showing. "Do you mind if I join you?" he asks with his best Austin Powers impression.

A small smile forms before I nod and scoot over on the small loveseat, making room for him.

Everett may not work in my office or even in the adjacent suite for EFSC, but he's here more often than not. His best friends, Hayes and Drew, started the Elite Forces Security and Contracting business a few years ago and take up residence in the building now. Ev worked for them for a little while until he was offered a position with the Cascadia County Sheriff Department. Now, he's formally a sworn in deputy, but his main position is Rotary Wing Pilot.

"What brings you into the CPM/EFSC building today?" I ask, already feeling a little more at ease with his energy around me. He has an infectious lightness about him that makes me want to stick to him like a leech, sucking out all that positive energy.

"Wanted to see my favorite people and then get a workout in." Hayes created a state-of-the-art gym on the first floor of our building for himself and the guys on their team. I hadn't noticed the black joggers and running shoes when he walked out, but that's because I tend to avoid looking directly at him. He's the definition of sex appeal, and he doesn't have to try. His smile alone does things to me that it absolutely should not. He looks like a clean-cut Charlie Hunnam, and I'm not the only one that thinks so—he offhandedly mentioned that his call sign during his days in the Army was Teller, after Jax Teller from Sons of Anarchy.

"Is everyone still in there? It's been ten levels of awkward all day." My boss, Olivia and Everett's friend, Drew, ended their months' long fling last week despite obviously being in love. To say the turmoil in the building is nearly palpable would be an understatement. The entire office building is downright dreary, and it doesn't help that the suites are open to each other and only divided by large glass partitions.

"Drew, Delta, and Liam were in the gym, punishing each other with their workouts. Don't think they'll stop until I send their asses home. Drew's really going through it, trying to figure out how to get out of this promise thing with Heather before it's too late with Olivia."

With a heavy sigh, I nodded. "Olivia's in business mode.

She won't talk about anything else apart from properties and clients. On the work side, it's incredible how much we've gotten done in four days. However, on the personal side, it must be _really_ bad." It's a little reminiscent of a few years ago, when her husband, Dan, died. She became hyper-focused at work, not allowing herself to think of anything else.

"Is that why you're out here freezing your ass off? My little empath was avoiding the depressing energy inside." I can't prevent the chuckle that escapes, but I at least attempt to shove down the giddy feelings that always arise whenever he calls me "his" anything or shows me the slightest bit of attention. Everett is one big, complicated situation that I don't have the faintest idea what to make of. He's become my closest friend, yet no one knows about it. Everything we do is in secret— texting, phone calls, sitting on this balcony. He's done nothing more than treat me like he treats everyone else, yet the massive crush I've developed on him makes it difficult to see things clearly. Would things be different if I wasn't in a relationship? Does he only treat me this way because he feels bad for me? Is all of this one-sided, or could I actually be the girl who gets the perfect guy?

His shoulder nudges me, reminding me that he asked me a question that I needed to answer. "Sorry. No. I mean, yes, it was exhausting in there. But that's not why I'm out here. Jeff is having 'colleagues' over tonight. I wasn't ready to go play hostess to a bunch of drunk men who expected me to cater to their every need." I'd rather listen to an angry Jeff reprimanding me for working late than deal with his obnoxious friends.

"Isla—" He says my name with a hint of his own reprimand coming, but I cut him off before it could start.

"I know, Ev. I know..." I attempt to settle my head on his shoulder, but he places his arm around me before I can get comfortable. Once I feel the slight pull as his hand settles, I sink into his embrace, my head resting against him. "I know that I need to end things with him. It's going to be catastrophic, though. My parents aren't going to understand, and they will be upset." Our families are so intertwined that I know they will all choose his side. They always do. Jeff could scream at me in front of my parents, and it would somehow end up being my fault. It's happened before, and if I don't end it soon, it will surely happen again. They think he walks on water because of who his parents are and what they've done for our family.

"Let it be catastrophic then, La. You have so many people in your corner, ready to support you. If your parents can't do that when they know how he treats you, then they don't deserve a place in your life."

My head nods in agreement, but the words coming out don't match—a constant battle of logic and emotion. "It doesn't feel that simple. They're still my parents. Before we moved here, they were good parents—devoted and caring throughout all my treatments. They weren't these high-class people who only cared about money and what the Walton's thought."

When I was seven, I was diagnosed with ALL, or acute lymphoblastic leukemia. Everything was different before that; my dad had just finished law school, and we were barely scraping by financially. About a year after my initial diagnosis, my dad was offered a position by Jeff's dad, Cyrus, at his firm, in Three Sisters. When Cyrus found out we were struggling financially because of the treatments, he paid off all the medical debt. He didn't even tell my dad he did it, but one day we got a call that it was paid in full. Still, to this day, he hasn't fully admitted to being the one to pay it, but there isn't anyone else who knew we were having trouble and could have afforded to pay it. My parents still feel like they owe the Waltons and hold it over my head from time to time.

He stays quiet for a moment, lost in his thoughts. His hand

on my shoulder doesn't move, but I can see out of the corner of my eye that his thumb is tapping on his index finger in a slow, rhythmic pattern. His little anxious habit that he always has when he's feeling uneasy or unsure about something.

"Is it about the money still? I could write a check to cover the cost so that you don't feel indebted to them." The seriousness of his tone clenches my stomach, making me realize just how much my situation is weighing on him.

"With that massive Astor Trust fund that you refuse to touch?" I poke at him, trying to lighten his sudden, dark mood. He likes to throw his knowledge of my history in my face, but two can play at that game. Everett comes from a very prominent family in South Carolina. His trust fund is well beyond the millions, but he hasn't spent a dime. He had the courage at eighteen to do what I still can't do at twenty-six—cut off his parents, consequences be damned.

"For you? I'd personally hand it all to them." He pulls me in a little tighter, and my head involuntarily turns to catch a glimpse of his expression.

He's already looking at me, his eyes filled with concern and something else. My heart hopes it's admiration but knows it's probably only pity. Either way, I place my hand on his chest and feel the steady rhythm of his heartbeat beneath my palm.

"I don't want your money, but I appreciate the offer. Olivia and I had a massive talk a few weeks ago—about some things that Jeff has said." A small line between his eyebrows forms, but apart from that, he keeps his expression neutral. "She told me not to worry about anything and that she would have a condo in town available soon. Once I have the keys, next week, I'm going to end things with Jeff." No one, not even Everett, knew about what Jeff had been holding over my head for the last few years. He's been working for his dad in the mayor's office since he moved back to Oregon. Any time Olivia needs a permit or license approved, Jeff threatens to deny it. At the time, it felt easier to appease him so that Olivia didn't suffer from his sabotage. Now that she knows, it feels like I'm finally one step ahead of him.

"Good. La, you deserve the world. You're the best woman I know, and I know countless good ones." His head dips back, and he turns to look at me with those electric blue eyes piercing into mine. His tone becomes icy when he says, "Call me before you talk to him. I'm dead-serious, Isla. Guys like him... I don't trust that he'll willingly let you go."

I nodded as my eyes turned misty all of a sudden. He doesn't know that I've tried to leave Jeff before, and I ended up with a broken windshield and a lecture from my parents. If he, or any of our friends, found out, Jeff would have had his ass kicked more than once. Everett spent over a decade in the Army as a helicopter pilot, and Drew and Hayes are both former Navy SEALs. The guys they work with are all Special Forces as well. It's probably the only reason Jeff isn't as aggressive as he used to be, and why he hates that I work for Olivia and Charlie in a suit next to alpha males.

"I would rather not drag you into my mess. I'll be okay." I don't know how much control he has over the sheriff's department, but I'd hate for Everett to get caught up in Jeff's bullshit. It's safer if he stays out of it.

"It's not dragging if I'm jumping head first. I need to be there for you. To make sure you're safe. Please." He wraps me back up in his arms and I let myself sink into his embrace.

"Thanks, Ev." It's easy to forget about all of tomorrow's worries when someone like Everett is there to hold you together.

Without intending to, he weaved his way into my life and changed everything.

Without intending to, he helped me find the confidence that I lost all those years ago.

Without intending to, he made me fall in love with him.

TJ Deal

About the Author

TJ Deal is a Pacific Northwest-based aspiring author who often daydreams about writing stories in the incredible places she travels to around the world. Thanks to her husband's unwavering support and her lifelong obsession with reading, she has decided to follow her passion for writing. Her days are mostly spent drinking coffee, relishing in the daily grind of motherhood, and capitalizing on every free moment to work on her latest novel.